TRIANGLE
OF
TREASON

by

Bob Richards

Published by
Filament Publishing Ltd
16, Croydon Road, Beddington,Croydon,
Surrey CR0 4PA
+44(0)20 8688 2598
www.filamentpublishing.com

Printed in the UK by 4Edge.

What people are saying

"A fast-paced, intriguing thriller that turns the pages for the reader."

-JAMES MACMANUS, AUTHOR

"Bob Richards draws from his intimate knowledge and experience in Bermuda to craft a masterful debut thriller, drawing us into a World War II adventure that will satisfy."

- KFMG-FM "THE CULTURE BUZZ"

About the Author

Bob Richards, following a successful career in finance and public policy, became Finance Minister of Bermuda.

He grew up during the period of segregation and witnessed its demise, then participated in the incredible transformation of Bermuda into a strategic military and financial pivot in the middle of the Atlantic. All this gave him a unique, often confidential, insight into this important 'Rock' in the middle of the ocean.

He now pursues his lifelong interest in history which has so far led to three books embedded in military and geo-political events.

CONTENTS

...

PROLOGUE

HOOKS COULD WAIT NO LONGER, he was about a half mile from the sub and the traitor was fast approaching. He loaded the flare gun and fired three shots up in the air, angled towards the sub. Then he fired the remaining three. Lehman was on top of the conning tower looking at the double agent through his binoculars. He was very close and could see the agent's face in detail. He was waving frantically. Then he heard popping sounds and swung his head towards the noise. *Flares!!! Oh my god!!*

"ALAAAAARM!!! ALAAAAARM!!! ALAAAAARM!!!"

"Forget about the agent! Get the men below at once! This is an Alarm!" Lehman disappeared below. It took the two men on deck many extra precious seconds to drop their hooks and lines, scramble back up to the top of the conning tower, plunge down the hatch and secure it. Inside U-66 there was organized chaos. All crew that weren't required to conn the boat were rushing forward to the bow to make a quicker dive. Lehman barked, "All ahead flank, set bow-planes to maximum dive - 60 degrees down." The crewmen repeated his orders as they performed the task.

I

"Kapitan, what's wrong? What happened?" demanded the navigation officer.

"We've been discovered. Someone let off flares. Flood forward tanks! Right full rudder! Set course to 045 degrees! Rig the ship for impact!"

Hooks stopped *Jezebel*. He didn't want to get too close to what he knew was coming next. The Nazi agent heard them before he saw them. The flares caused everybody to panic. He was just about to climb aboard the sub when the flares appeared. To his absolute horror, the crew members who had been deployed on deck to assist his boarding, turned and looked at the captain on the conning tower. They then ran to the tower where the main hatch was. He could hear the captain yelling, "Alaaaaarm!"

"Hey! Come back! You can't leave!" It was obvious that the sub was about to dive. The Nazi agent threw his duffle bag on the sub's deck and leapt aboard. But the sub had gotten underway and the bow was sinking beneath the surface. Seawater streamed over the surface of the deck and swept him overboard. A plane appeared out of the moonlit sky and started to strafe the sub. He saw flashes from the machine guns. The ocean around him erupted as the rounds hit the water in a line that led directly to the sub. One of the bullets ricocheted off the steel hull of the sub and hit him in the shoulder. It burned like fire as he felt despair enclosing him. More planes! The night was alive with them. The sea convulsed around him as bombs fell from the sky. Then his world suddenly stopped.

I

THE CLUB—LONDON, APRIL 1929

Captain Rodney Horatio Grant RN Retired, was a managing partner at a firm of stockbrokers in the City of London. He was tall and trim, with dark neatly clipped hair greying around the temples. His regular features were punctuated by a thin Clark Gable type moustache. His eyes were dark and penetrating and sometimes mesmerizing to the ladies. He wore a perfectly fitting, wool worsted navy-blue suit with pale blue pinstripes. Underneath his jacket was an equally well fitted vest. His crisp white dress shirt featured a collar pin underneath his silk, bright paisley tie that was squeezed between the collar's wings. He had already checked his fedora with the coat-check girl when he came in.

As a retired naval officer from a very distinguished naval family, it was expected that he would use his position and connections to entice wealthy clients to the firm. Part of his job was to analyse and comment on a wide spectrum of investment opportunities for clients. Occasionally, these opportunities were overseas, traveling to Canada, the US and parts of Europe to appraise them for himself. On this particular evening, he was regaling some of his friends at his club about his experiences on one such trip. Among the listeners was a certain Mr Michael Allenby. Like Grant, Allenby was of aristocratic lineage having attended Eton and read Philosophy at Oxford. He was a true gentleman and didn't have to work. He therefore spent most of his time socializing at polite soirees, getting drunk at his club, or when he was in the mood, driving his Rolls down to the East End to do a bit of whoring.

Allenby listened intently. "Remember men we now have a most opportune moment to invest in Germany? This War has created serious poverty and has paved the way for investments that will cost us half nothing"

"Oh yes, poor buggers! But business is business, old boy," one of the members exclaimed.

"Yes indeed. There was a fine investment opportunity in a steel mill in the Ruhr Valley. I had a good look around and it was obvious to me that despite the economic situation, the operation was very efficient, and people were working extremely hard but getting paid in Reich Marks which are being devalued more and more every day."

"I can't imagine how awful that must be. Thank God our capital is in Pounds Sterling"

"For foreign investors like us this would make for a very compelling investment, especially if the steel could be sold to British customers and paid for in pounds."

"It's certainly a very good argument Grant"

"I took the train from the Ruhr to Frankfurt and spoke

to the company's bankers. After presenting my business card to the secretary, I was shown through and introduced to a man who spoke perfect English, 'How do you do, Captain Grant. I'm Saul Goldstein he said. I was dumbfounded, bowled over for duck! The man was a damn Jew! I had to fight to regain self-control!"

"Did Goldstein notice?"

"It appeared not, either that, or he just didn't care. They're very professional when it comes to business. In any case we began to discuss the matter at hand. Then I thanked Goldstein and took my leave. The investment seemed guilt edged but no way was I going to do anything to further enrich those Jewish bastards. I find it offensive that so many innocent Germans are suffering in such appalling conditions while the Jews are living high off the hog, it's an affront to natural justice!

"So, what did you do"?

"I submitted a negative report to my partners and the firm rejected the proposal".

Later, and after a few more rounds, Allenby took Grant aside and said, "Look, old boy, I understand your feelings about those damned Jews. Next time you pop over to Frankfurt, why don't you call on Hans Lindeman. He has a bank over there and knows all the right people."

The next time there was an investment opportunity in Germany, armed with a letter of introduction from Allenby, Grant called on Herr Lindeman. Lindeman was a big man in more ways than one. In addition to his pot belly that threatened to burst through the last two buttons of his shirt, he had a big voice and an even bigger personality. Grant was welcomed like a long-lost cousin. "You must come home for dinner," Lindeman insisted. The German banker's house was even more impressive than the bank and Frau Lindeman ordered the servants to prepare a splendid meal for their guest. After the meal, they retired to Lindeman's study for cigars and cognac.

Lindeman said, "There is a move afoot in Munich that has the potential to pull Germany out of this mess and rid us permanently of these parasitic Jews that are sucking our lifeblood."

"Really?"

"Yes, and I believe that now is an excellent time to invest, to get in on the ground floor."

"Sounds interesting. Anything to give those damn Jews their comeuppance."

This was the beginning of a close friendship and on one of his many subsequent visits to Germany Hans said, "Rodney, I want you to come to a private party with me there are some special people that you must meet."

After another superb dinner at the Lindeman's, they hopped in Hans' Mercedes Kompressor and drove to a grand estate in the countryside. It was guarded by men in strange brown uniforms who saluted Hans and allowed them in. The party was nothing unusual, wealthy Germans and their female consorts having a good time. They went through a doorway, down a hall and into what looked like a large study. At the back of the room was a group of men listening in rapt attention to another man speak. Grant's German was rudimentary, and he found it hard to follow what was being said but it was obvious this man had the others spellbound. The man was small in stature with a little "toothbrush" moustache and intense, piercing eyes. They saw Hans and his guest arrive and waved them over. Hans said, "This is Captain Grant, the Englishman I was telling you about." Then in English he said, "Rodney, I would like you to meet Herr Adolph Hitler, the Fuhrer of the National Socialist German Workers Party." Grant managed to say in German, "It's an honour to meet you sir." The Fuhrer extended his hand and smiled and after some pleasantries in German that Grant only partially understood, returned to whatever point he was making to the group. "He is a great man and will make Germany a world power again, you wait and see," Hans said leading the way back to the main party. This was the beginning of a new chapter in Grant's life.

2

CONTACTS IN GERMANY

ADOLPH HITLER WAS NOW ENJOYING a meteoric rise to power. His political party, originally concentrated in Munich, was now known to the outside world as the Nazi Party. Initially the Nazis were anti-everything—anti-big business, anti-bourgeois, anti-capitalist as well as anti-communist. But what caught Grant's attention was that the Nazi's were steadfastly, rabidly anti-Semitic. As they gained more popularity, they courted big business, but stayed resolutely racist, anti-Communist and anti-Semitic. By 1930, as a consequence to the cataclysmic unemployment following the Wall Street Crash of 1929, the Nazis, riding a wave of anger, were now gaining huge momentum in German politics. There were also many Nazi sympathizers in Britain, the US and elsewhere. They were particularly appealing to the conservative elements of British aristocratic society who viewed communism as the real threat to their privileged positions. Grant knew that his views on Nazis and Jews were not all that out of place within the social circles that he frequented, but he was careful to whom he candidly expressed them. He made many trips to Germany to meet members of this new movement and made donations to their cause. He was convinced that they were the only thing standing between the old order and being subsumed by a red tide of communism and Jews.

Grant had cleverly dodged the financial ravages of the Great Depression by investing in gold and property, and now decided it was time to enjoy his accumulated wealth. He didn't like what London society had become, and in any case, he hated the damp and dreary weather. He wanted something warmer, simpler, away from the complexities and tumult of Europe. He wanted somewhere in the British Empire but not in the Far East. He'd heard Bermuda was a nice place. He would give it a try. He wrote to his friend Hans Lindeman of his intentions to emigrate. Hans begged his friend to come to Frankfurt one last time. He did. By this time Lindeman had become hugely wealthy because anti-Jewish laws had enabled him to take over many Jewish banks for a token payment or even nothing, including that of Herr Goldstein. "The Fuhrer might ask you to do him a favour or two when the time comes." Although Grant didn't know what the favours might be or what, "when the time comes," meant but Grant was eager to be of whatever assistance he could be to the cause. "Whatever I can do Hans. Don't hesitate to contact me." Hans seemed pleased and bade him farewell.

3

THE JONES'

IT WAS JANUARY, A BEAUTIFUL COOL DAY in Bermuda. The sea had a gentle swell like the rhythmic breathing of a slumbering giant. The little cedar boat of Alan (Hooks) Jones rose and fell with each successive breath of the giant. However, he was less interested in the surface of the ocean than he was in the depths beneath him. He was hunting rockfish, a prize catch for a local fisherman: its flesh was light, tender and juicy. Such a catch could feed many mouths. Rockfish were predators of the reef, but this day the predator had become prey to Hooks Jones. He was in his favourite spot where he had previous success not only with rockfish but also with yellow tailed snappers and turbots. Hooks' lure was cleverly designed to appear to be one of those hapless small fish that rockfish preyed upon. Other than hook and line, Hooks also had a fish pot, a contraption of wire mesh and slender pieces of wood. Fish would wander into the device but would not have the intelligence to find their way back out and were trapped until the fisherman came back to haul the pot to the surface and empty its contents into his boat. You couldn't catch the big rockfish in a pot, so he tried to catch them by hand line. Having a fish pot, plus hand line fishing enabled Hooks to augment his meagre wage as a ferryboat pilot for the Bermuda Transportation Company.

Hooks lived near Somerset Bridge, "the world's smallest draw bridge," which connected Somerset Island to the main island. The bridge opened just enough to allow the mast of a sailboat to pass through. He kept his boat, *Jezebel*, moored in the protected bay next to the bridge. *Jezebel* was nothing more than a hand-made cedar launch with an old primitive engine in it. Hooks used all his innovative powers to keep that thing going. It was a hard way to spend his days off and dangerous too, particularly in bad weather, but he loved it because it gave him temporary independence from his bosses at the company. That was what he treasured the most. Out here he was his own boss, answerable to no one. Well, almost no one, there was his wife, Edith.

Like a large number of Caribbean residents had done, Hook's father had emigrated from St. Kitts, where there was little work, to Bermuda to work at the Royal Naval Dockyard. He had married a Bermuda girl whose family originated in Grand Turk and the marriage produced three boys. His two older brothers left school early to learn their trades at the Dockyard. Hooks was expected to follow his father and older brothers, but as he grew, he was drawn to the sea and took the opportunity to work as a deck hand on one of the ferries. Over the years he learned the skills of seamanship, to read the channels and knew the locations of all the unmarked reefs like the back of his hand. Edith Jones, Hooks' wife, worked in a small shop adjacent to the entrance of Wreck Hill, which itself was close to their Somerset Bridge cottage. Edith was not originally a Somerset girl, she hailed from the other end of the island, St David's. Her heritage was typical of folks from St David's: a mixture of Caribbean, Irish and Pequot Indian. Notwithstanding that distinctive combination, most Bermudians referred to St David's Islanders as "Mohawks."

Hooks had met Edith when he was working as a deck hand on the Bermuda Transportation Company's St. David's/St. Georges ferry, Daisy, a small ferry that shuttled from St. David's across the harbour to St. George's carrying passengers, construction materials and general cargo. St. David's women were renowned for their beauty, and Edith was no exception. While working in the east end, he'd courted Edith and they'd eventually married and moved to Somerset. However, his marriage to Edith was no foregone conclusion: first he'd had to gain the approval of Edith's father, Reverend Ronald (Rusty) O'Conner. Reverend Rusty, as he was called, was the pastor of a small chapel in St. David's and was very strict when it came to young men calling on any of his three daughters. The first time he'd appeared at the O'Conner residence to ask permission to see Edith he was subjected to an inquisition that lasted for over an hour. Hooks was careful to be extremely respectful to Rusty and Lizzy O'Conner at all times but still under no circumstances was he allowed to be alone with Edith. Most of the time they were only permitted to sit and talk to each other on the old cedar bench outside the front door, under the constant gaze of either one or both parents. Touching was strictly forbidden. Edith was most impressed by Hooks' persistence and admired his willingness to tolerate the continuous gauntlet laid down by the elder O'Conner's, a gauntlet that had discouraged several other potential suitors in the past. She and her two sisters cleverly covered for each other under the guise of sibling group outings, whereby, as soon as they were out of their parents' sight, Hooks would appear, and the two other sisters would go off and leave them alone. Eventually Hooks persistence wore Rev. Rusty down and he permitted the young man from Somerset Bridge to marry his daughter.

Their home was very modest. According to the community tradition in those days, the family, friends and neighbours, all pitched in to help Hooks build a home for his new bride. It greatly helped that the males in his family were all skilled Dockyard artisans, so building a modest Bermuda cottage was child's play for them. The house was located on Somerset Island in very close proximity to where the high railway trestle across the Somerset Bridge inlet made landfall. In fact, when the train passed by, the house shuddered as if the train were rumbling through their kitchen. This inconvenience was balanced by the convenience of having the Somerset Bridge railway stop a mere 200 yards down the track. For Hooks the location was even more convenient, as the Somerset Bridge ferry stop was a mere 500 yards in the opposite direction. There he would get picked up in the early morning by one of the small Bermuda

Transportation Company work-boats, either the Princeton or the Inspector and be conveyed, along with other ferry employees, to the overnight ferry berths to prepare the vessels for their daily ferry service. The couple (especially Edith) was very religious, so when children did come along, it was imperative that they receive good biblical names. Their two children were Rebecca (Becky), now 18, and Joshua (Josh), 10. Becky was clever with numbers and had finished school and was helping her mother in the shop, as well as working as a cashier at the little cinema in Somerset Village. Josh was still in school and it was important to Hooks for his son to have a better education than he'd had.

4

PILOT TRAINING

Hooks had become the regular pilot on the ferry Frances, but the long journey to obtaining that position, resulted in him being hugely overqualified. In his first job, while serving as a deckhand on the ferry Daisey, Hooks became friendly with a retired pilot named Sidney O'Connor, known to all St. David's Islanders as "Old Sidney." Their friendship was cemented by their passion for the sea. Even though she didn't approve of his behaviour, Old Sidney was, nevertheless, Edith's great uncle. When his shift on Daisey was over, Hooks used to find Old Sidney down at the dock fussing with some fishing paraphernalia, or just drinking rum. Old Sidney was a man of fair complexion with long, tangled grey hair underneath a filthy, worn, pilot's cap. His face was covered by an equally scruffy grey beard. His front teeth had all long disappeared and those that he did have were black with decay and often gave him great pain. On such occasions he would growl and curse loudly to anybody that would listen. His self-prescribed pain killer for this affliction was copious amounts of Black Seal rum. He was often seen sitting on the ferry dock muttering and laughing to himself. Neighbourhood children were afraid of him and most adults simply avoided him. It would have been easy to pass off Old Sidney as just another old rummy but Hooks liked to engage him in conversation as he knew that, in his day, Old Sidney was a master pilot. "Eh, Sidney what was piloting like in your day. You know, one day, I'm going to be a pilot?"

"Look here, bye," Old Sidney growled, "When I was a pilot none of we-byes worked for de Government or some big company. We all worked for ourselves! I had a crew of three and de first pilot boat to get to de ship, got de job. We had a skiff with two sails, and with all four of us rowing we were pretty fast. When we spotted a mast or sail off St. David's, we-byes would run down de hill to our boat and we'd be gone! We used to beat them other byes all de time!"

"So, how'd you get to know the reefs so well? I mean they didn't have any channel markers in those days did they."

"No, bye, there weren't any markers. You just had to use your eyes and your head and memorize every one of those damn reefs. When you go out there, it's not for fun, its serious business. Each one of those reefs has got a certain shape, size, location and depth, and as a pilot you have to memorize which one it is, where it is in relation to de next one and de island itself. You have to know it so good that you can see them laid out before you with your eyes closed. Look here, bye, that's when you know you're a real Bermuda pilot."

"So, Sidney, who taught you?"

"Henry Darrell, great grandson of old Jimmy Darrell, the master of all masters! They say that man had a mind like a steel trap."

"Could you teach me?"

Old Sidney laughed and said, "Sure bye, the best offer I've had all day. You got a boat?"

"Got a rowboat. Look, it's over here." They went over to the other side of the dock and Hooks' rowboat was pulled up on the shore.

"We're gonna need some sails to give us some power, other than your young back, 'cause I ain't doin' no rowin'. My old back is all messed up, so my rowin' days are done! Let's find a piece of cedar that we can make a mast from." And off they went through the bushes looking for a mast.

They went out as often as Hooks' working schedule and his courting of Edith would allow. Sometimes they would fish, sometimes not, but Old Sidney happily imparted his encyclopaedic knowledge of Bermuda's waters to young Hooks. The only compensation he required was the provision of 40 oz. of Black Seal Rum—strictly for medicinal purposes, of course.

"Look here, bye, you've got to be able to immerse yourself in de sea. I'm not talkin' about jumping overboard, I'm talking about your senses. You've got to be able to read de swells, smell de salt air, feel de wind, read de sky—both day and night. All these things make you a better pilot."

When Old Sidney judged that Hooks was proficient enough for daytime navigation, they started to go out at night. Hooks learned about the stars and how to use them as reference points, even though they had no sextant or traditional navigational tools. One evening before dusk Hooks and Old Sidney took their little boat out through the Narrows deep into the North Channel. Night fell, it was choppy and visibility was limited. Hooks said, "Sidney, what are we doing out here at night in this weather?"

"So you can show me what kind of pilot you are. What if this-here boat was a steamer with a 20 foot draft? Show me how you would get her into St. George's Harbour?"

Hooks concentrated and studied his surroundings. He could see land and he noted a few reference points. A fleeting smile crossed his face because he realized he knew exactly where he was. The little sail on their skiff was flapping about noisily. Hooks grasped the trimming rope, set the sail and they moved forward. In his mind's eye he could see the menacing reefs before him, and even though the sea was as opaque as graphite, he picked his way through them. Old Sidney watched their heading, course changes and progress very carefully, and took a satisfying swig from his rum bottle with each course change as if to celebrate the success of his student. Eventually they transited the Town Cut Channel into St. George's Harbour. Old Sidney raised his rum bottle, then, after draining it, declared with a toothless grin, "Hooks, my bye, congratulations, you're now good enough to be a Bermuda pilot!"

The steep learning curve that Hooks had scaled was scarcely noticed by the bosses at the Transportation Company. Hooks became one of the youngest men ever to obtain a pilot's license but he still had to work his way up just like everybody else—he was still a deck hand. When he moved back to Somerset, he worked on the old Somerset ferry, Corona. Corona, was originally a Hudson River steamboat, built in the 1800's. As a deck hand, he had to fulfil certain duties peculiar to Corona. She was a coal burner and two or three times per week before going into service, the crew including Hooks, would take her from her berth at Dock # 7 in Hamilton to Agar's Island, adjacent to Two Rock Passage, to fuel her for the next few days. Coal was stored in bunkers on Agar's island and young Hooks, along with the rest of the crew, would laboriously push wheelbarrows laden with coal from Agar's bunkers to supply Corona's bunkers with fuel for her daily duties. Of course, after this chore there was black coal dust everywhere and the crew would have to hose down the entire ferry, and clean themselves up too, before any passengers were allowed to board.

As a steamboat, Corona also required huge amounts of fresh water aboard to provide the steam for propulsion. About once a week Corona would have to negotiate the tricky channel to Hawkins Island where there was a large freshwater reservoir. Once there, Hooks learned the technique of transferring the 15-20 tons of fresh water from Hawkins Island to the old ferry so she could make steam. Despite these ancient special requirements, Corona was very popular with commuters and tourists alike, as she was fast, quiet, stable and had a marvellous steam whistle which, when it blew, told everyone for miles around that the Corona was nearby. The Frances and the other ferries were diesel boats and had neither of these requirements nor attractions. One day fate presented Hooks with an opportunity to distinguish himself: Corona's skipper, Mansfield Tucker, known locally as Manny, was a heavy drinker and after backing out of the Hamilton dock, he took Corona out for her regular run, which in those days, included a sweep from Cut Wharf in Dockyard and around Commissioner's Point to the public dock at Mangrove Bay. Manny had been on a heavy bender for a few days and asked Hooks to take the helm. Hooks agreed and Manny settled into a corner of the wheelhouse and passed out. In those days, it was quite common for ferry "Engine Drivers," to emerge from the overwhelming heat of the engine room once the ferry had left the dock and was cruising. After Corona had left Cut Wharf, engine driver Billy Stewart emerged from his hell hole below decks for some fresh air and a smoke. Corona was cruising at her normal speed of about 15 knots. It was a beautiful day and the caress of the warm, salty breeze allowed his mind to wander far and wide. He lost all track of time. Soon Corona was approaching the Mangrove Bay dock and Hooks rang down to the engine room to reduce speed. Nothing happened. Hooks rang down again—still nothing! Hooks stuck his head outside the wheelhouse and shouted down to another deck hand, "Hey, Noel! What the hell is wrong in the engine room? The engine's not answering. Where's Billy?"

"I dunno. Last time I saw him he was on deck taking a smoke."

"For Christ's sake, Noel! Go find him and get his ass down below!"

20

"OK, Hooks." And off he went.

Corona, full of commuters, continued on a collision course with the Mangrove Bay dock. Hooks rang down for the third time to cut the engine. This time the engine disengaged. He rang down for full reverse, but he knew it was too late, there was no way he would be able to stop the big ferry in time to prevent it from slamming into the dock. He spun the big spoked wheel to starboard and blew a long warning blast on Corona's steam whistle. Guided by Hooks, the steamboat, unable to stop, swept past the Mangrove Bay dock and slid up on the nearby sandy beach at Cambridge Beaches Resort. No one was hurt. Corona was re-floated the next day, miraculously undamaged. After a brief inquiry, the bosses at the Bermuda Transportation Company summarily fired both Manny Tucker and Billy Stewart and promoted Hooks Jones to skipper the ferryboat Frances. Frances was a wooden ferry distinguishable by the fact that she had two decks, a very wide beam with twin diesel engines whose exhausts were at the waterline at the stern. Therefore, if a passenger sat in the lower cabin with the windows open, he or she would run the risk of dying of asphyxiation from diesel fumes. Frances was also famously slow. But what Hooks liked about Frances was that passengers could easily come to the wheelhouse and interact with her skipper.

Over time Hooks' reputation grew and he became regarded as one of Bermuda's top ferry pilots: an expert at navigating, not just the areas the ferry served, but all the reefs that surrounded the island as well. He could take a boat through the reefs day or night: a very handy skill since the channel lights were not lit due to the war and also for night fishing which he enjoyed—provided Edith was in a mood not to make a fuss. Even though she was a St. David's Islander, people who prided themselves as seafarers, Edith had a fear that someday he would not return from night fishing. Hooks, on the other hand, didn't fear the sea, he respected it. Fishing helped provide food for the family during the difficulties of wartime rationing and selling his surplus catch to other locals was a way for him to supplement his rather modest income.

But the winds of change blew everywhere the war went, including the tiny island of Bermuda. The island was being, "Invaded by all these foreigners!" They were mostly servicemen: British, American and Canadian. Plus, there were all these women from abroad working at, "Lord knows what," at the Princess Hotel. They were actually censoring every piece of mail that traversed the Atlantic. The quiet, idyllic life in Bermuda was undergoing a major shift to, "Who knows what." It was being dragged, yet again, into another transatlantic conflict between great foreign powers, a conflict not of its own making. Many Bermudians were worried, or at the very least unsettled, about the whole matter. As for Hooks, he didn't mind the changes. So long as he could feed his family and be on the water, he was happy. Besides he didn't mind new people once in a while as it "spiced things up!"

5

GRANT ARRIVES

THE FOUR-INCH FORWARD GUN was constantly firing, the barrel almost glowing from the heat. The ship was heeled over to starboard from the zigzag course he was demanding of her at flank speed. They were trying to dodge incoming shells from enemy cruisers. Everyone on the bridge was holding on to something. Enemy shells could be heard screaming overhead. Then there was a howling sound that grew painfully loud, followed by a blinding explosion. The windows of the bridge shattered into a hurricane of deadly rain. The concussion knocked Grant flat on his back, his head spinning. He opened his eyes and strangely, everyone on the bridge was still standing motionless, their clothes torn to shreds. They slowly turned to look at him. He saw, through the acrid smoke, that their skin, flesh, muscles and sinews had been torn from their bodies. Their limbs had become skeletons clad in shreds, fluttering in the stinking breeze. Their faces were bare white skulls with grimacing teeth. Their eye sockets and gaping mouths were black holes from which serpents slithered forth. Beckoning to him, their mouths dripping with blood, they intoned—in unison, "Come, brother, come!" He shrunk from them in horror, fending them off with his hands. Then he saw his hands! They were covered in blood. "No, no!" he cried. Then he awakened with a start, his twisted bed sheets soaked with sweat.

Collecting himself from this recurring nightmare, he remembered he was on board the QTEV Queen of Bermuda and something was wrong. As he gathered his wits about him, he realized that it was the absence of the hypnotic throbbing of the ship's screws that had awakened him—they were dead-in-the-water. He quickly threw on some clothes and rushed out of his stateroom. He hurried down the long elegant wood panelled passageway, having to occasionally grip the highly polished brass railings as the ship gently wallowed without headway. His first impression of these passageways had been the unique scent of a mix of wood oil and brass polish, but he didn't notice that now, as he climbed the stairs to the observation deck. Morning had broken and there, off the port bow was the island of Bermuda. The little pilot boat with the big red and white flag had the name St Brendan emblazoned across her stern. As he looked down, he observed the Bermudian pilot, dressed in his whites, clambering up the Jacobs Ladder to take his place on the bridge to guide the Queen through the channel. The morning was overcast, and the calm sea had taken on a silvery grey tone. The sun was in evidence only around the edges of the thick, low, grey cloud cover. However, when looking straight down from where he was, Grant was struck by the incredible clarity and transparency of the water. The tranquillity of the sea disguised the swell which he could feel gently lifting and lowering the ship, even one the size of the Queen.

Shortly after the embarkation of the pilot, the ship got underway once again, carefully gliding past the dark sentinels silently guarding the section of the channel called, The Narrows. In about 40 minutes they approached the Royal Navy Dockyard. He could see the famous floating dockyard with a vessel captive in its u-shaped belly. The Queen turned to port, past the jagged shoals called Stag Rocks. Grant was awestruck by the beauty, colour and serenity of the Great Sound. Two local tugboats from the Dockyard joined them: one named Justice and the other Bermudian. They were dirty steam engine tugs, streaming long tails of black soot from their tall yellow and black funnels. Justice took a position ahead and Bermudian a position astern.

After they passed buoy # 40, the procession turned to port again. Looking above he could see the crew had strung a line of flags that stretched from the tall foremast to the mast near the stern, giving the Queen a very gay, festive appearance. Looking ahead, he perceived that they were headed for a small gap between two tiny islands, a gap that didn't look wide enough for the Queen to fit through. As they glided nearer, "Two Rock Passage," his apprehension about their ability to fit wasn't very much assuaged.

But nevertheless, the dirty little Justice was leading them through. Just as the bow of the Queen was approaching the passage, he heard a loud hiss from above, followed by an even louder melodious three-part chord from the Queen's steam whistles. Huge white plumes of steam soared from the first two of her three red and black funnels. This long blast was an announcement to all that the Queen of Bermuda had entered Hamilton Harbour. Grant was enthralled.

As the graceful vessel glided towards her berth, she dropped her port anchor off a place called Albuoy's Point. There was a loud clattering noise that could be heard and felt throughout the ship, as the large steel links in the anchor chain ran through the anchor hole. The Queen immediately started to turn to port. The dirty little tugs, Justice and Bermudian, got to work, both of them pushing from the ship's port side to turn the ship around, then nudge her gently toward Number One Shed, her designated berth in Hamilton. The Queen was a vessel fitted with four turbo-electric motors (hence QTEV) specifically designed to facilitate the tight manoeuvring required by Hamilton Harbour. A dirty little grey boat with the name Princeton displayed along her wheelhouse appeared. Grant doubted if the mandarins of that august university would have been pleased with its name being associated with that grubby little vessel. Notwithstanding that mismatch, Princeton collected the Queen's docking lines and conveyed them to gangs of men who secured the heavy ropes to on shore bollards.

The Queen dominated the Hamilton skyline, dwarfing all the shops and people along the main street, unimaginatively called Front Street. Grant moved over to the starboard side of the ship and noticed a little crowd had gathered alongside, others gawking as they went by. It was obvious that, even though this ship called on the Island every week, the arrival of the Queen was a significant event in the life of the inhabitants of Bermuda.

6

IMPRESSIONS OF BERMUDA

IT WAS LOVE AT FIRST SIGHT. The island was beautiful and peaceful. Grant inhaled the moist salty Bermuda air, a mariner's delight. After storing his belongings at the Belmont Manor Hotel, he immediately paid his respects to the British Governor, Lt. Gen. Reginald Halyard, KCB, CMG, DSO who warmly welcomed him to the island.

"Uh, Grant, Grant! Any relation to Admiral Sir Robert Grant by any chance?"

"Why yes, Your Excellency, he was my grandfather."

"Jolly good! First class man he was, and one of the best minds in the Navy! While this Bermuda posting was supposed to be a reward by my superiors for being a good and faithful servant, it's turning out to be quite a bit trickier than anticipated."

"Oh, how's that? Your Excellency."

"Well, old boy, with all the rising tension in Europe, and if diplomacy with Herr Hitler turns out badly, Bermuda may turn out to be important, from a military standpoint."

"Oh, yes, I see."

"By the way, let me introduce you to our Commissioner of Police, Peter Radcliff. Peter, this is Captain Rodney Grant."

"How do you do, Captain. If there's anything I can do for you on the island, please don't hesitate to contact me."

Commissioner Peter Radcliff was originally from London's East End, having grown up close to Upton Park, home to his beloved West Ham United "Hammers." Young Peter had a prominent, sharp nose with close-set, beady eyes. So much so that the boys used to call him "Ratcliff" in school, or simply "The Rat." He joined the Metropolitan Police straight out of school and spent several years as a constable on the beat, your typical London "Bobby." But Radcliff was ambitious and was always on the hunt for an opportunity for advancement, even though his hunt had come up empty after years of searching. One day he noticed a small advertisement in the paper for constables in the island of Bermuda. He had to dust off his schoolboy map to see where Bermuda was, and was shocked to learn how small it was. Notwithstanding these misgivings, he applied for and succeeded in getting the job.

Coming from the rough precincts of East London, the job of a policeman in sleepy little Bermuda was a breeze. There was little to no serious crime and policing consisted principally of directing traffic, breaking up drunk and disorderly patrons at bars, the odd domestic dispute and things of that nature. His police vehicle was the standard edition black police Humber pedal bicycle. However, unlike

London, opportunities in Bermuda abounded, particularly if you knew the right people. Radcliff made it his business to ingratiate himself to such people, including senior officers in the government apparatus like H.E., The Governor, and the Colonial Secretary and of course, members of the wealthy local gentry. By playing his cards right, Radcliff rapidly moved up the ranks from constable to sergeant, to inspector and eventually to commissioner when that position became vacant. He enjoyed all the celebrity, privilege and deference accorded to an officer of that rank in local society. People still called him Ratcliff, or merely "The Rat," but only behind his back. No one would dare say that to his face.

Grant instantly picked up the Commissioner's Cockney accent. "Thank you very much for the offer Commissioner. I'm looking for a house, at the moment, but I have someone working on it for me. How nice of you to offer." Grant also made himself known to the officer in charge of the Royal Navy facilities on the island including the Dockyard, Commodore Ellington Greaves. His title was the Commander-in-Chief, North America and West Indies Station. Greaves rolled out the red carpet for Grant. He knew of Grant's deep Navy lineage and assumed that he was still connected in the upper echelons at the Admiralty.

"Captain, welcome to His Majesty's "Gibraltar of the West!" You are among friends and colleagues here." Greaves exclaimed, making a grandiose gesture.

"Commodore, I am most grateful for your welcome."

"I say, why don't you come for dinner up here at the Commissioners' House? We have an excellent chef here."

"You're most kind, sir".

"Let me introduce you to my ADC, Lieutenant Nigel Brodie. The Lieutenant and I served together at Jutland, on the HMS Black Prince."

"Oh, God, that must have been awful."

"But Brodie, here, saved my life!"

"Incredible!"

"I say, Brodie, arrange a launch to take the Captain back to Belmont, if you please."

"Aye sir."

Built like a British bulldog, Brodie was short and squat, and equally as tough. He was no patrician like Grant, instead he came from the mean streets of Glasgow. He spoke with a strong Glaswegian accent that even some of his fellow Royal Navy counterparts had difficulty deciphering. Having always longed to go to sea, Brodie joined the Navy straight out of school as an able seaman, and had seen action during the Great War. He excelled in his duties and as the war provided enhanced opportunity for promotion, he soon moved up the ladder to Petty Officer. He was principal helmsman on the cruiser HMS Black Prince, in Admiral Jelloco's Grand Fleet in the Battle of Jutland. HMS Black Prince took an incoming German battleship shell just aft of her main forward gun turret. The blast not only hurled the entire turret high into the air, it also ignited the magazine below and blew the entire forward section of the ship to pieces. Those men on the bridge, including Brodie, were themselves thrown into the cold North Sea. Brodie's ears were ringing so loudly he could hardly hear a thing. He was able to grab onto a piece

31

of flotsam, the chilly North Sea stabbing at his body with a million small blades. HMS Black Prince was sinking fast, bow first, before his eyes.

As the ringing in his ears subsided, he heard a desperate cry, "Help! Help!" A sailor was caught in some pieces of steel that were weighing him down. Brodie leapt over to help his floundering shipmate, he dove down into the dark sea cut the man loose and dragged him to his piece of flotsam. It was only after the sailor started to thank him profusely that Brodie realized that the sailor he had rescued was Captain Ellington Greaves, his very own skipper. Greaves was eternally grateful to Brodie for saving his life and every subsequent ship he commanded featured Brodie as part of his crew. Moreover, Greaves took an interest in Brodie's naval career, encouraging him to study for and take the exams required for further promotion. It was not common for a man from the mean streets of Glasgow to be an officer, but with Greaves' encouragement Brodie was allowed to take the exams which he subsequently passed. Therefore, as CINC of Royal Navy operations in Bermuda, Commodore Greaves' most trusted assistant was Lieutenant Brodie. These introductions enabled Grant to quickly become plugged into the formal and informal British social scene on the island.

Grant found Bermudian society to be very curious indeed. As small as the island was, there were five distinct groups of people. First, there were British expatriates, including naval, other military officers and members of the colonial civil government apparatus. Second, you had local whites, who totally controlled the local political system and the economy.

He had heard they were collectively referred to as, "The 40 Thieves." Third, there were other foreign military personnel, mostly Canadian and American. Then you had the Azorean Portuguese who were mostly employed in agriculture, and lastly, at the bottom of the pyramid, the blacks, who had no political nor economic power but performed all the tasks that were necessary to keep the place running. While Grant found it curious, it seemed like it manifested the natural order of things. Of course, Grant naturally and easily fitted into the top group. However, because the island was so small, you couldn't really help having encounters with the members of the other groups, whether you liked it or not. One such place was on the ferry. If you wanted to get into Hamilton from, say, Belmont in Warwick, you either had to take a long bumpy carriage ride along the narrow winding roads, walk a considerable distance to a Bermuda Railway stop, then enjoy or endure, depending on your liking, the train ride, or you could hop onto the ferry and you could be in Hamilton in 15 minutes. Overt racial segregation was something new to Grant, such outward displays of social or racial schisms not being the norm in Britain, the British being a culture that prided itself on subtlety rather than brazen crassness. In Bermuda the arrangement was more like, "Jim Crow" in the Southern United States, or as he understood Apartheid to be in South Africa. He noticed, however, that such separations were really not practicable on the ferry. Thus everybody, whites, blacks, British, and Americans all rode the ferry together.

As a nautical man, he adored the little ferryboats that

provided essential transportation around the western parts of the island. He was also impressed with the boat handling skills of the local pilots. On his first ferry trip, Grant wandered up to the wheelhouse of the Belmont ferry, Frances. The vessel's master, a local black man greeted him, "Morning mate! Lovely morning, init?"

"Yes indeed. Lovely morning."

"I'm Hooks Jones."

"That's an unusual name, isn't it?"

"Everybody calls me that. It's 'cause I love fishin'. Truth is, I love anything to do with the sea."

"Me too. By the way, my name is Rodney Grant, Royal Navy, retired."

"Well, Mr Grant, it is Mister, init?"

"Captain actually."

"Well Capt'n, you'll love Bermuda. You connected with the dockyard in any way?"

"No, I've just moved here, getting to know the lay of the land, you know."

"Right. Hope you enjoy it here."

"I'm sure I will."

Although Frances was an aging vessel, in need of some paint and attention to rust, Grant noticed that her pilot, Hooks Jones, was the embodiment of fastidious attention to detail. He was attired in his navy-blue uniform whose trousers were perfectly pressed. The Bermuda sun shone from each of the six perfectly polished brass buttons on his double-breasted blazer. A black tie was knotted around the collar of his crisp white shirt. His black shoes were highly polished, and his pilot's cap was perfectly cocked to one side, topping off the appearance of a man who was proud of his profession and one who took his responsibilities seriously. The wheelhouse was Spartan, but the brass fittings—the wheel, the small binnacle and the engine signalling devices— were also as highly polished as the buttons on his blazer. In fact, the air in the wheelhouse was suffused with the scent of brass polish, the same scent he remembered on board the Queen of Bermuda. The pilot's dark brown skin showed creases around his eyes from years on the sea and in the sun. His broad smile lit up his face and infected everything around him with warmth. However, Grant noticed he directed his crew with stern authority, an authority that was clearly, deeply respected. Grant liked that. Grant was struck by the open, welcoming nature, with that irresistible smile, that Hooks showed to a newcomer from England. As a regular passenger on the Frances, Grant grew to enjoy his conversations with the local ferryboat pilot.

Hooks always had a story to tell, although it took Grant a while to decipher Hooks' thick Bermudian accent. On board HMS Solent and at the Admiralty, Grant had experienced the many different variations of the English language that are found in the British Isles, ranging from the King's English, which of course he spoke, to East London Cockney, to the Scottish brogue and everything in between. Men from all parts of Britain served in the Senior Service. However, his experience of dialect or accents in the further reaches of the British Empire was non-existent so it was, at first, a challenge to understand local Bermudians. Under normal circumstances he wouldn't have even cared to understand it but as the island was so small, he found it a necessity. Even the wealthy oligarchs spoke a version of the local dialect, and as would be expected, the working classes spoke entirely in this manner.

Despite their differences in social and financial statuses and divergent racial backgrounds, it was the love of the sea and all things nautical that the two men had in common. Hooks' open nature eventually wore down Grant's reserved persona, and he began to regale the local pilot with his own stories about his days in the Royal Navy. Hooks had become Grant's first "friend" in Bermuda. Of course, this friendship was strictly limited in its scope. It was unthinkable that he would invite his "friend" Hooks to have a drink with him at his club or a local bar. Such venues would have refused to serve Hooks in any case. It would have also been inconceivable for him to invite Hooks to dinner at home. So, their friendship was constrained to that little marine world that centred round the ferry service, a place where local segregation was just not practical. Sometimes when looking out over the islands of the Great Sound, Grant reflected on the irony of his friendship with Hooks Jones, a working class, black, colonial, versus himself, a white, wealthy, patrician, who if he wanted to be, could actually behave like he was Hooks' "Colonial Master." The thing was, Grant found the actual Colonial Masters here, except for H.E. General Halyard, to be totally pretentious. Those who were actually born in Britain were usually from a lower or middle station in the home country. They were "putting-on" to the

36

locals to have come from something loftier than was the reality. The actual local whites, virtually all of whom were of British extraction, were in some ways, ridiculously pretentious in their efforts to attach to themselves attributes they associated with upper class Britishness.

The most absurd example was their own "Hunt Club." The local elite had organized a totally fake fox hunt, complete with horses, bright red tunics, bugles and hounds. And off they would go, arrogantly "fox hunting." The only problem was, there were no foxes in Bermuda, so the whole ostentatious ritual was an exercise in pretension of being British landed gentry. And while they certainly were wealthy and possessed valuable land holdings in Bermuda, in England they would still be considered mere "Colonials." Grant was a self-confessed snob—of the highest order—but at least his black pilot friend was authentic—the genuine article, not trying to impress anybody or to be anybody that he wasn't. Grant could respect that.

As if to unwittingly underscore the asymmetry of their social relationship, one day Hooks invited Grant to go fishing with him on the weekend. Early one Saturday morning, well before the break of dawn, Grant hopped onto *Jezebel* at Belmont dock and the clattertrap boat clattered and puttered across the Great Sound, around Commissioner's Point and out into the blackness. Somehow, Hooks seemed to know exactly where he was. Grant was completely disoriented. After a while Grant noticed a change in the sea, even though it was very calm. The swell became deeper and *Jezebel* started to rise and fall over the undulated ocean. Hooks said, "We're going through De Gate. De real name is Eastern Blue Cut, but we-byes just call it De Gate. It's a gap through de north-western reefs into de deep. We should be able to catch some good fish out here." And indeed, the fishing was good.

After they returned Grant took his share of the fish home for Mavis, his housekeeper and cook, to prepare the evening meal. He also gave her a few fillets to take home to her family. Mavis Simmons was a middle aged, quite portly, local, coloured Bermudian woman. With large doe-like eyes, chubby cheeks, a quick smile and a great sense of humour, Mavis was well liked in the Warwick community although her curiosity in other people's business sometimes got her in trouble. She was married to Arnold, known to everyone as Arny, and they had five children. Arny was a stone cutter by trade and worked in the quarry close to Cobbs Hill Road in Warwick. It was back breaking work that paid a pittance; thus, it was imperative that Mavis worked to make ends meet and too often they didn't. They and their five children lived crammed into a humble cottage near the quarry. Fortunately, her eldest son, Jimmy, known to everyone as Doc, was working as an apprentice at the Royal Naval Dockyard and was able to help with the family expenses. Mavis walked to Grant's house every day, but on Sundays she would come to make Grant's breakfast, wash the dishes and leave early to attend church service at the tiny Cobbs Hill Methodist Church, a church that was built under moonlight by slaves in the 1800's. Mavis had worked as a housekeeper and cook for what seemed like her entire life. The only breaks she ever had, had been to have her five children, if you could call those breaks. Over the years she had worked for a few of the prominent families of the island, all in the Paget and Warwick areas because it was close to home. She had worked for the well-known Smith family in Paget for many years prior to her employment with Captain Grant. She was well known for her superb desserts: cakes of all types, including artfully created icings, pastries, pies and puddings. The daily walks to work didn't seem to compensate for the generous and frequent tasting, sampling and taking home of leftovers of these delightful and carefully crafted culinary creations.

Her employment with the Smiths ended when the matriarch, Mrs. Bonny Smith, passed away at the ripe old age of 97. It was fortuitous that Captain Grant passed the word around at the Yacht Club that he was looking for help at home at around the same time as she was finishing up at the Smiths. Mavis had had a hard life, but she had a pleasant disposition and always got along with her employers despite their idiosyncrasies. Grant didn't pay her much, but she often was able to take-home excess or left-over food for her family. The fact was, he was not at all demanding, compared to some of the other white families she had worked for, particularly seeing that he was single and had no children for her to clean up after. Moreover, Captain Grant's old naval habits of orderliness made her job much easier than it could have been. The only thing her boss was a stickler for was his privacy. He swore her to confidentiality before he gave her the position of housekeeper and cook. His military air and authoritarian mannerisms were a bit frightening but her need for the job overcame that. She thought it was a bit unusual, but knew these English had their peculiarities. In the final analysis, Mavis was grateful for the job.

Immediately after giving Mavis the fish to cook, Grant began to study the map of the Island. In particular, he studied the bathymetric contours showing the various reefs, channels and depths. He searched for the Eastern Blue Cut and found it. There was a Western Blue Cut too. As a retired Royal Navy officer, he considered himself an expert navigator and he was confident that with a compass and a few reference points upon which to take bearings, he too would be able to navigate these treacherous waters. Of course, Hooks appeared to be able to do this without a compass and in the dark, but one had to start somewhere. The "somewhere" was that he had to get his own boat. For somebody of his background, it was easy for him to become a member of the Royal Bermuda Yacht Club, a place where polite society regularly met. He put the word out that he was looking to buy a small boat to run around in and it wasn't long before he found one to his liking. It was more like a navy launch than a conventional pleasure craft, with one diesel engine, a small cabin, about 40 feet long and shallow draft—top speed 12 knots. He thought about naming her "Solent," after his former command, HMS Solent, but rejected that idea as an insult to that once fine vessel. Instead, he named her Scapa, after the home port of the Royal Navy, Scapa Flow, up in Scotland. He had two moorings for Scapa. The convenient mooring close to Belmont was not safe in foul weather, so he kept a second mooring close to the Yacht

Club for convenience to Hamilton and for safety in the event of hostile elements.

He set about the task of finding his way around Bermuda waters. With his compass, his chart and a few prominent land objects to get his bearings, he diligently marked out the various courses through the channels and the reefs.

Pretty soon, Grant was feeling confident about his ability to navigate the inshore and offshore waters of Bermuda during the day, but night-time was something else entirely. On most nights, once your eyes became accommodated to the dark, you could see objects using starlight, or if you were lucky, moonlight. So, he started out, step by step, learning how to navigate around Bermuda waters at night. Generally speaking, unlike the ferries, he didn't go out in foul weather. After several months he started to feel comfortable with night navigation and occasionally went out at night to fish.

7

SWORDFISH

ON PATROL OVER THE WESTERN ATLANTIC, hunting enemy U-boats; Lieutenant Harley Harvey, call sign, "Swordfish," his buddies called him SF, guided his patrol airplane over its designated patrol, "Area B," his slice of the Atlantic Ocean for which he, as skipper, and his crew of one other, were responsible. The sea was empty, the sun glistened on the ocean like an endless, dark blue carpet strewn with billions of flashing diamonds. Even in fine weather like this, it would be hard to spot a small object like a surfaced submarine and virtually impossible to spot a periscope. But that was the job: to find a pinprick in a sparkling carpet, to detect the virtually undetectable. Harley thought it was something like fishing— hours of boredom punctuated by moments of excitement and exhilaration. He liked fishing, so he was not dissatisfied with this job.

Since he was a boy, growing up in Gloucester, Massachusetts, he had always wanted to fly. But he was from Gloucester, and everything in Gloucester was connected to the sea, particularly harvesting the bounties of the seas of the North East Atlantic. His father, Jack Harvey, was a swordfish boat skipper, like his father before him, and his two older brothers, now working with their dad as crew, who would one day have their own boats. But Harley was different, he was kind of bookish, particularly good at math and science. He had dreams of becoming a navy pilot, a "Naval Aviator," as they were known. He wanted to fly fighter planes off aircraft carriers. Jack thought that such crazy dreams were utterly unrealistic and that he should, like his two older brothers, follow in the family tradition of rugged intrepid Gloucester fishermen, battling the hostile elements to provide their families with a livelihood. However, his mother, Marion, quietly encouraged him to pursue his dreams. In her mind, America was at peace, so it wasn't as though the Navy was going to be fighting anybody, after all, they had already endured the "War to End All Wars."

Harley studied hard, and in 1935 his grades were good enough to gain admittance into the US Naval Academy in Annapolis. However, in order to be admitted into the US Naval Academy one had to have the written recommendation of a member of the US Congress. The Harvey's, a family of Gloucester sword fishermen, did not know any such lofty personages. He therefore enrolled at the Massachusetts Marine Academy (MMA) in Buzzards Bay, hoping that, he would, one day, be flying fighters off carriers.

Halfway through his four-year stint at MMA, Navy recruiters appeared at his school looking for students who wanted to train to be US naval aviators. Apparently, the US government, in casting its eye on the rise of Nazism and Fascism in Europe and in Japan, decided that, even though America was a neutral country, merely for the sake of prudence, it was time for major increases in the number of planes available to the army and the navy. But where would they get the pilots? There was no way they could achieve their expansion goals by using only those young men at Annapolis and West Point. They were going to have to mine the human resources in Colleges and Universities.

Harley jumped at the chance and signed up. After basic training, the Navy divided potential pilots up into two distinct groups: those who would be flying fighter and attack planes off aircraft carriers and those who would be flying naval patrol aircraft. When the two lists were posted, Harley discovered, to his horror and dismay, that his name was on the patrol list, not the carrier fighter list. He immediately complained to his superiors about it, and asked for reasons why, but was flatly told, "That's the way it is." Depressed, he returned home on a brief leave to tell his family how disappointed he was. But, much to his surprise, they would hear none of his negativity. They were all thrilled that their son/brother was going to be a naval aviator, the first ever in their family's history. Their pride and joy overcame his disappointment. He returned to Pensacola, where they trained naval pilots, feeling much better about himself.

Naval patrol planes were seaplanes, so in addition to learning all the technical details and skills of being a regular pilot he had to learn the additional skills of landing and taking off on water. His first aircraft was the Vought OS2U

"Kingfisher." The Kingfisher was a single engine, two-seat airplane—rugged, easy to fly, but slow. Behind the pilot was seated the radio operator/rear gunner. The Kingfisher featured a main floatation pontoon that ran down its central line, plus two smaller stabilizing floats under each wing. It carried two machine guns, one forward and one aft, and could carry four 100 pound bombs, two under each wing, or two 325 pound depth charges. The Kingfisher was also used as a trainer for flying-boat pilots, so this is why it was Harley's first plane.

When Harley learned the capabilities of his airplane he said to himself, "Well this is more like it. This is a real combat aircraft." However, pilots called them, "Ninety knot wonders", because they climbed, cruised and landed at 90 knots. They were small planes with a wingspan of just under 36 feet with a single 450 horsepower, Pratt and Whitney, air-cooled, radial engine. It had a range of 805 miles with a ceiling of 13,000 feet. While the Kingfisher was classified as a scout/reconnaissance aircraft, it was armed as an attack plane. What it definitely lacked, however, was the speed and manoeuvrability of an actual fighter plane.

Harley quickly became a proficient pilot of the Kingfisher. In addition to the challenges of navigating over open ocean, he learned the techniques of carrying out accurate bombing runs using the bombs under the plane's wings or dropping depth charges against theoretical enemy U-boats. He also perfected the technique of strafing ground targets using the Kingfisher's on-board machine guns. Special techniques to be learned included launching from a ship's catapult and being recovered while the ship was still under way.

Harley Harvey, after achieving a proficiency level acceptable to the US Navy, received his naval aviator wings and a commission of Second Lieutenant. Back in the barracks his buddies unanimously decided that Harley's call sign should be "Swordfish," due to his family's sword fishing background. He had assumed he would be posted to a cruiser or battleship somewhere in the Pacific, like Pearl Harbour or perhaps Subic Bay in the Philippines but fate had different plans for Swordfish.

8

BELMONT MANOR HOTEL GOLF COURSE

RODNEY GRANT GAZED OUT from his balcony at the splendid vista afforded him by the choice location of his residence. Located a mere 200 yards west of the Belmont Manor Hotel, in the middle of the hotel's golf course, his home, cleverly named "Belmoral", provided him with the best of all worlds: utmost privacy, but with a perfect view of Hinson's Island, Darrell's Island, the Great Sound, the Little Sound, Morgan's Island, the Royal Naval Dockyard, and even Hamilton. His location was also convenient—just a short walk or even shorter bicycle ride to the Belmont Ferry Dock where he could board a ferry to Hamilton or the Darrell's Island seaplane port or the Dockyard.

His only inconvenience was the occasional errant golf ball hit by players on the nearby links. For Grant this was a small price to pay for this prize location. Besides, he too played golf, and he knew how easy it was for those wretched golf balls to seem to have minds of their own. "Belmoral" had been modified to Grant's own specifications and had many features of an English country estate, the kind in which Grant was born and raised. It was however, outwardly, of the traditional Bermudian architecture, but featured the interior refinements that he appreciated. While he had daily domestic help in the house there were no servants' quarters as he did not want staff staying either in the house or next door. They came and went each day. Grant enjoyed his solitude.

On "Belmoral's" northward facing, covered balcony, Grant adjusted the focus of his powerful, brass telescope which was mounted on a large wooden tripod. He could bring any ship, airplane or boat up so close you felt that you could touch it. The telescope allowed him to engage in one of his favourite pastimes—ship and plane spotting. One day, after his usual early morning routine, Grant hopped on the ferry to Hamilton. The closest thing in Bermuda to a "London Members Club" was the Royal Bermuda Yacht Club, just next door to the Hamilton Ferry Terminal. The Club featured hallways with pictures of Commodores dating back to the dim distant past, plus pictures of various sloops, ketches, yawls and schooners that had at some point featured in Newport/Bermuda yacht races. The bar had various models of different sailing vessels, including those of the famed Bermuda Sloops which were, once upon a time, the fastest sailing ships afloat. This was where the upper echelons of Bermudian society frequented, and Grant felt fully at home here.

Sitting at one of the tables with a few club members was Bobby Soames, Commodore of the Yacht Club. He was a huge sailing enthusiast and owner of a Bermuda fitted dinghy, a local sailboat with a huge sail relative to her small size and draught, making it barely seaworthy. Members raced these top-heavy vessels in Bermuda inland waters with the winner often being the only boat that hadn't been swamped before the finish line. Soames, himself from a vaguely aristocratic lineage in England, had regularly sailed the biennial Newport Bermuda yacht race. Thus, he was drawn to Grant and liked to hear stories from a genuine British mariner.

"Um, Grant, how'd a man like yourself end up here anyway?"

Relaxing with a cigar, Grant felt in an expansive mood and surveyed the men at the table, all eager to hear from this patrician English gentleman.

"It's strange how fate steers your course through life and how I ended up here," ruminated Grant. "The fact is, war has been a primary guiding factor in my life. Twenty odd years ago, in England, 'The War to End All Wars' dragged on much longer than anyone had ever anticipated, and young men were dying by the millions, on both sides.

There arose a critical shortage of men to carry out normal everyday jobs: like working in factories, driving buses, trains and ambulances, etc. Incredibly, many of these jobs were being performed by women!"

"They should stay where they belong—at home!" One of the men interjected.

"Quite! The war radically altered the traditional, proper order of society. The established deference's and privileges accorded to members of polite society were rapidly dissolving, and this notion of egalitarianism was spreading unchecked, like the black plague that had once engulfed Europe."

Chuckles all round.

"The working classes had discovered that, over there on the Western Front, when riddled with machine gun bullets, arrogant, infallible aristocrat officers, like me, bled the same red and died the same death as lowly coal miners. Those lucky enough to return home were overturning the old traditional social structures and talking dreadful things like unionism, socialism and communism. Women were even demanding the right to be Members of Parliament, how ridiculous was that! The Great War turned the whole world upside down. Proper became irrelevant, good became evil and safe became dangerous."

"Upside down, that's right! Let's get right side up again, we need another round here," Bobby declared with a grin. "Hey, Derrick!" he turned around to the black bartender, Derrick. "Another round for this table."

"Coming right up, Commodore!" In a few short minutes the bartender had replenished all their drinks. Then Grant resumed his story.

"You know, I spent some time at the Admiralty, and it had one positive effect on me, it taught me about money and business. My grandfather, the late Admiral Sir Robert Grant, was kind enough to leave me a few quid after he joined that Grand Fleet in the sky, and after the Armistice, I retired from the Navy, at the ripe old age of 36, and bought my way into a management position in a firm of stockbrokers in the City of London."

"Stockbrokers! And all this time we-byes thought you were just a retired sea dog!" Bobby exclaimed.

"You're right. I am that too! But I'm telling you, the timing was perfect. The celebration of peace and the ebullient business climate were infusing waves of wealth throughout the City. Stock markets were strong, and business was good. On the other hand, the harsh reparations that the Allies were extracting from the defeated Germans were further crushing the German people.

In my business, I encountered a significant number of Jewish owned stockbroking firms and merchant banks in the City. Some of them old and venerable, like the Rothschild's, and others were more recent upstarts. I have to say, gentlemen, I grew to detest these firms and the people that owned them. I found the aggressive ones to be outright money-grubbers: crude and conniving; while the sophisticated and more refined Jews were slithery, obsequious and untrustworthy. The Jews' penetration of polite society in Britain is a travesty and a threat to good British Christian values."

"Quite right Captain. We don't encourage them here either," Bobby said.

"That's right!" Another member chimed in. "Here we've got it all arranged that anybody with one of those Jewish-type names, like Goldberg or 'whatever-stein' are not allowed to stay at any of our finer hotels. Inquiries from would-be customers of that persuasion are always met with, 'We are fully booked,' at our hotels. Naturally, the same applies to any rich coloured's who might try to get in as well."

A mere ten feet away, behind the bar, Derrick, the bartender, stood, outwardly impassive, but seething inside. I must be bleddy invisible! Or so damn unimportant that I may as well be.

Grant laughed, "You chaps here have got it just right, then. But I'm telling you, in those days there was plenty of business and money to go around, in spite of the Jews. It was 'The Roaring Twenties,' the dawn of a new age, an age of excess and fun. Remember the Charleston?"

Chuckles and nods all round.

"Bye, I never could do that dance, but the women loved it," Bobby mumbled.

"Gents, limitless supplies of cheap credit meant prudence and risk were banished forever. As stockbrokers, our firm's profits swelled to levels unimaginable five years earlier. Those were great times, both socially and financially. Despite all that, I always found ostentatious living very vulgar, you know, the sort of thing the bourgeois, nouveaux riche do."

Grunts of approval.

"While I didn't like the Jews, they did get one thing right. They were great collectors of gold and other precious metals. It was vital to have one's assets in something tangible like gold and silver coins and bullion. I kept mine distributed among the vaults of four separate banks in the City. I asked myself, 'What if that hyperinflation in Germany happened to Sterling? What then?' Without a stable currency my savings and investments in stocks could have been wiped out.

So, I redoubled my purchases of gold and silver—for a rainy day.

The rain came sooner than I thought. In September 1929 the London market crashed, then, about a month later in New York, a disaster that reduced the roaring twenties to a whimper. Many of the members of my profession were instantly ruined and jumped out of tall buildings. On the other hand, with my holdings of precious metals and my country estate, I was not seriously affected. In fact, I used the opportunity to buy out the other partners of my firm, for a song. Despite that, it was the worst investment I've ever made.

Germany was hit the hardest. Its currency became worthless, its government was insolvent, and its people were starving. There were riots in German cities."

"Bad for business here too. We still haven't fully recovered."

"The Great Depression was especially bad for the stockbrokerage business and I decided I'd had enough. There was no point in soldiering on with the business. I shut it down and set sail on the proud British Cunarder, RMS Berengaria, for New York."

"RMS Berengaria. Never heard of her, which one is she?"

"Ironically, the Berengaria's original name was the SS Imperator, a German liner built in Hamburg. She was seized by the British after the Great War, as part of war reparations."

"Oh… I didn't know that."

"After spending a few months in New York, I reconfirmed to myself that I could never live there. I craved for something more British, less frenetic and more maritime. I seriously considered Canada, Halifax perhaps, but decided the long cold winters would be intolerable. So, gentlemen, in September 1937, I boarded the British luxury liner, QTEV Queen of Bermuda, and set sail for the island of Bermuda. And here I am."

Bobby gushed, "That's a great story. An officer and a financial wizard. Fantastic!"

"I'll drink to that!" Grant laughed. So did everybody else.

"Derrick, another round for this table!"

9

CHRISTINE

CHRISTINE LIVERPOOL LOOKED OUT of the window of the Pan Am flying boat Yankee Clipper. The plane's cabin was luxuriously appointed, and the service was professional and attentive, but none of these amenities could compensate for the constant and dreadful roar of the Boeing 314's four powerful engines. Also, the ride was occasionally very bumpy, and it terrified her when suddenly the aircraft fell as a result of some invisible force. Each time that happened she thought she was going to die. The fact was, she hated flying, but there was no other way to reach her destination to start her assignment on time. The flight route was Southampton, Marseille, Lisbon, Azores, and Bermuda. Her assignment was to be one of the mail censors for the Imperial Censorship Department in Bermuda. All mail from the US to Britain and back was to be routed through Bermuda, where it was opened and read to identify any illegal passing of state secrets, espionage of any kind or secret movement of jewels or securities. It was well known that there were numerous Nazi sympathizers in the US and Britain, and it was vital that any written material that went through the mail containing information that would damage the war effort or money to support enemy elements be intercepted, and those involved be identified and arrested.

When war was declared in 1939 both Christine's father and two brothers enlisted, her dad in the army, her brothers in the RAF. She had studied languages at university and very much wanted to do her part in the war effort too and she volunteered for service. But, after a series of evaluations, it was determined that her ability to read German and French qualified her for this posting. So, she gritted her teeth with every downdraft that the lumbering Yankee Clipper penetrated in order to do her duty for King and Country. Upon arrival she was informed that she would be one of over 1,500 staff working at the Princess Hotel, just outside Hamilton. She was billeted close by at the Bermudiana Hotel. The work was highly repetitive and boring. The Pam Am Clippers called on Bermuda three to four times a week requiring the censors to process about 30,000 pounds of mail weekly. At first, she felt awkward, reading through other people's personal and private messages. She was invading the privacy of thousands of people, on both sides of the Atlantic, but she convinced herself that the war effort took precedence over individuals' rights and privileges.

There were many other women like herself: unmarried and engaged in the censorship effort. To balance the boredom, and to boost morale, efforts were made by Captain Humphry Cotton-Michell, head of the Imperial

Censorship Department, to arrange social activities for them. There were many dances and parties laid on for the staff with the on-island British gentry, as well as some local colonials - all within the overriding strictures of the local segregation laws, of course. The only evidence of blacks at these functions was the people providing the service and the music. On one such soiree, she was in the company of the Commissioner of Police, Mr Peter Radcliff, who was trying mightily to impress her of his importance in local British and Bermudian polite society, and that he, the Commissioner of Police, was one of the key links between the two. After all, British Governors were replaced every three years, but he was the permanent liaison between the Crown and the Colony. She found him to be a bit of a bore in terms of personality and rat like in appearance. Notwithstanding those dubious qualities, she appreciated the fact that he would do anything to please her and amused herself at having the Police Commissioner at her beck and call. She saw her roommate, Mary, talking to two gentlemen: one a young navy officer and the other a more mature gentleman in civilian clothes. Her friend was waving her over. Christine assumed that her friend wanted her to take over the older gentleman, so she could be alone with the young officer. And she was right. But she had to get rid of Radcliff. So, she said, "Peter, do you have a Marlboro?" Knowing full well he smoked Players.

"Well Christine, I only have Players."

"Could you get me a pack please, I really need a smoke."

"Of course, my dear, I'll find some." And he beetled off

on the errand.

She then came over to help out her roommate. She noticed that the older gentleman was tall, trim, with a Saville Row, exquisitely tailored, wool worsted suit. He was greying at the temples with a salt and pepper, neatly clipped moustache. He had an erect, somewhat aristocratic bearing, but not overbearingly so.

Hmm, this may be interesting. She thought.

The gentleman introduced himself, "Good evening, my name is Rodney Grant."

"How do you do, Mr Grant. I'm Christine, Christine Liverpool."

"From Liverpool, are you?" Grant said playfully, "But I'll wager everybody asks you that."

"Yes, that's true, actually I'm from Sussex." She picked up his rather posh British accent. "And you, sir, what are you doing in this remote outpost called Bermuda?"

"Oh, I live here. Retired Royal Navy, you know. Wonderful place to escape the world and its turmoil."

"Well, I'm glad you can. Unfortunately, I've been posted here to read other people's mail. I'd rather be driving an ambulance in London or working in a munitions factory."

Grant was impressed and somewhat surprised by her patriotic enthusiasm. He shuddered to think of this obviously genteel young woman working in a munitions' factory or something similar. This was, of course, part of the new world paradigm that he found most objectionable. Nevertheless, it was pleasant to be in the company of a lady of some breeding, and besides, she was quite beautiful as well.

"May I interest you in a libation, Christine?"

"Love one, thank you. I'll have some of that local rum. What's it called?"

"Black Seal."

"Yes, that's right, Black Seal, neat please."

My, my! - no shrinking violet! Grant thought.

Off he went. He quickly returned with the drinks and they spent the rest of the evening wrapped in deep conversation. Radcliff eventually returned only to discover the lady in conversation with another man. He approached them saying, "Here you are my dear." He proffered her the pack of Marlboros.

"Oh, pardon my manners, Rodney Grant this is Commissioner Peter Radcliff."

"Oh yes, we've already met. Nice to see you again Commissioner."

"Likewise, Captain."

Grant then returned his attention to Christine and she to him, as if Radcliff weren't even there. After a minute or so he realized that he had been dismissed and retreated from the pair.

When the party was over for the evening, and they were parting ways, Christine said, "It was very nice to meet you Captain."

"The pleasure was all mine, Christine."

"You can call me Rodney. I hope I can see you again sometime soon."

"I would like that. Goodnight."

"Goodnight."

Christine returned to her room at the Bermudiana and was greeted by Mary.

"How was it?"

"That guy I took off your hands, retired Royal Navy—quite high brow. Good company but we talked all night and, other than that he's a retired Navy captain, he told me very little about himself. An interesting, but mysterious man. And why isn't he helping with the war effort? He's retired but he's not too old to be helpful in some way! Actually, he looks pretty good to me. My Dad's in the Army and he's much older than him."

"Sounds to me that you did most of the talking, as usual." Her roommate said with a twinkle in her eye.

"I guess so, but it's still strange."

"Hmmm. I'm turning in. Goodnight."

"Goodnight."

10

SHIPPING OUT

WAR HAD ALREADY BEEN RAGING in Europe since 1939. It was in the early spring of 1941 when, now, Second Lieutenant Harley Harvey, call sign, "Swordfish," received his deployment orders. When they came Harley was crushed. He was to report to a new scouting squadron operating out of the island of Bermuda. "What was in Bermuda?" "Nothing!" was the universal response. "It's an atoll in the middle of nowhere." "The US doesn't even have a base there," someone said. "We're going to be operating alongside the British," one of his buddies added. That didn't set too well with Harley either. Even though he was from Gloucester, Mass., a part of "New" England, named after a place in Old England, he wasn't too enamoured with the British, with their snobby accents, stiff upper lips, and all that "Pip-pip, tally-ho and jolly good show," stuff. Really! They cannot be serious, can they? And their preoccupation with tea! Didn't we get rid of tea at the Boston Tea Party centuries ago? He did, grudgingly, have to give the Brits some credit. The air battle that took place over England last summer, what Churchill called, "The Battle of Britain," was the conversation on every airman's lips. Harley followed events in Europe very closely from the newspapers and the Newsreels that preceded every movie in theatres. By the end of June 1940, Hitler had defeated Allied forces in France with only Great Britain standing in the way of his total domination of Europe. The Fuhrer's half-hearted offers for peaceful coexistence with Britain were met with the Prime Minister's, "We shall fight them on the beaches ... we shall never surrender!" speech in Parliament.

As a precursor to invasion, the Luftwaffe, had orders to annihilate the Royal Air Force to enable the easy crossing of the English Channel by German invasion forces. Harley saw, from Newsreels, that during the summer of 1940, wave after wave of Luftwaffe bombers and fighters crossed the English Channel from their bases in France with the objective of smashing, initially, English airfields and subsequently English cities and factories. But the RAF doggedly hung on, despite being heavily outnumbered. He'd even studied the numbers in the newspapers. At the outset the RAF had 754 single-seat fighters, primarily Spitfires, (his favourite) and Hurricanes, and 149 two-seat fighters of various types, while the Luftwaffe boasted 934 single-seat fighters— primarily Messerschmitt ME109's, 289 two-seat fighters, 1,482 medium bombers primarily Heinkel 111's, 327 dive-bombers - consisting of Junkers JU 87's, also known as Stukas.

It was clear to Harley that the best fighter plane in the

skies was the RAF's Spitfire. He voraciously read all the specs on Spitfires he could find. The Spitfire was more manoeuvrable, had a faster level speed at 336 mph, and a faster climb rate than the ME109's. He would give his right hand to fly one of those. Instead he was flying the Kingfisher, top speed 165 mph. In some of his more sombre moments, Harley took note that on the flip side of that heroism and the presumed exhilaration of aerial combat, was raw carnage. He had recently gone to a movie and the Newsreel before the show had reported that at the end of that epic battle, the British had lost 1,964 men and 1,744 planes while the Germans had lost 4,245 men and 1,977 planes. While German aircraft losses were not that much greater than the British, the Germans had not achieved their strategic objective, which was to clear the skies over England, as a prerequisite to invasion. The Gerries had given up that objective, exploding the aura of Nazi invincibility they had acquired, thus marking a major turning point in the war. Of course, those casualties didn't include the thousands of people on the ground who had perished from the bombing. He thought, "War is a hellish thing," and even though it was still, "over there," a knot in his stomach told him it was coming his way.

It was with mixed emotions that he contemplated working with the British. But what was he going to do in Bermuda when he wasn't flying? It wasn't like Pearl Harbour with all those bars, hotels, nurses and "Hawaiian Hospitality" houses; or over there in Subic Bay with all the Philippine versions of the exact same thing. According to his buddies,

Bermuda was a barren outpost with no kind of social outlet to balance the rigours of flying. Harley had definitely drawn the short straw—again!

In April 1941, members of squadron VS32 shipped out of Norfolk onboard the navy patrol support ship USS George E. Badger. The squadron leader Lieutenant Commander Bradley A. Davidson, call sign, "BAD," gathered his men together during the outward-bound voyage. BAD was an experienced naval officer and pilot. He was relatively casual, for the Navy that is, with a good sense of humour. Of course, you would expect that for someone with the callsign of BAD. But you could tell that he was not going to tolerate any nonsense from men under his command. Many of the men, pilots, radio/gunners, mechanics and support personnel, were from different bases and didn't know each other, so BAD went around the room and had each man introduce himself and his function.

BAD addressed his squadron. "Gentlemen, I think for men to do their jobs well they should know why their job is important. Do any of you know why you're being posted to this rock in the middle of the Atlantic?" He looked around the room at a lot of blank faces. "Gentlemen, the global political situation is getting more dangerous by the day. Hitler has already rolled into the Ruhr Valley, Austria and Czechoslovakia unopposed. The Wehrmacht has crushed Belgium, the Netherlands, Norway and France." He unfurled a large map showing Europe, the Atlantic Ocean and the Americas.

"Our superiors at CINCLANT and in Washington, are

looking at the map and asking, 'What if Great Britain were to fall to the Nazis?' Then they would control her empire, including Trinidad, here," pointing to that island on the map with a long pointed stick, "The southern gateway to the Venezuela oilfields and the Panama Canal, the Bahamas, here, strategically controlling the Florida Strait which is the northern gateway to the US oil terminals in Louisiana, and worst of all, Bermuda, here," he slapped the map hard with the stick, "Which guards the accesses to New York, New Jersey, Philadelphia and the Chesapeake Bay, and therefore Baltimore and Washington DC itself."

CINCLANT was one of the myriad of acronyms used by the US Navy: CINC stood for Commander-in-Chief, and LANT stood for Atlantic. Therefore, you had CINCLANT for the Atlantic fleet and CINCPAC for the Pacific fleet.

"Do any of you know that Bermuda was the launch-pad for the British attack that burned down the White House and blockade of Baltimore in the War of 1812? Did you know that it was Bermuda that was the escape valve for the Confederate blockade runners to help prop up the Confederate economy that the North was trying to strangle? To have the Nazis in control of Bermuda would be like having a dagger at our throats. In spite of the British success in the Battle of Britain, our folks in DC don't rate Great Britain's chances of holding out very high."

He certainly had their attention now.

"Gentlemen, I know that many of you are not happy with this assignment, being posted to Bermuda, that is. Some of you would prefer to have been posted to a battleship, or a cruiser, to fly these large toy planes Uncle Sam has provided us. You may think that Bermuda is a backwater, a place with no action over the ocean and none on land either, for that matter." A few of the men chuckled. BAD continued, "I can't tell you about the action onshore Bermuda, but I can promise you action offshore—over the Atlantic. America is not at war, at least not yet, but CINCLANT has advised our commanding officer that the waters surrounding Bermuda are infested with German U-boats."

BAD continued, "Our President is providing our British friends with tons and tons of supplies so that they can hold out against the Nazi stranglehold. Hitler is trying to starve Britain out by cutting these supply lines, and he's winning! The supplies are not getting through because the supply ships are being sunk by the dozen by U-boats. Last year almost 1,000 Allied ships were sunk in the North Atlantic. This year's looking even worse. Our job, along with our bigger brothers, the PBY's, is to provide anti-submarine recon for our British friends, as well as search and rescue for torpedo survivors and downed airmen. We, the Kingfishers, will do the shorter-range patrols, with the PBY's doing the long-range jobs. So, check your kit so that when we arrive, we can get settled and airborne as quickly as possible. By the way, we will be sharing facilities with the Brits, initially, because our base is still being constructed, so, try to get along."

11

DAWN IN BERMUDA

USS GEORGE E. BADGER WAS AN OLD World War I destroyer. She showed her vintage by having four funnels and decks flush with the outside hull. This meant it could be dangerous for the crew to be on deck, particularly in foul weather. Despite her age, with a top speed of 35 knots, the Navy felt she was still useful. However, speed was not a requirement for the seaplane tender duties she was now performing. Even though the US was a neutral power at that time, the ship was under strict war time protocols. At night she was completely blacked out. She also maintained strict radio silence during the entire voyage, and she sailed a zigzag course to protect against submarine attack. She was sailing alone, not in a convoy, and had limited submarine detection capabilities, and therefore was highly vulnerable to U-boat attack. Nobody thought the mere fact that Badger was flying the Stars & Stripes would dissuade some eager U-boat skipper from attacking. Everybody's nerves were on edge because of the hidden threat below.

It was with great relief that in the predawn greyness of the third day Harley could clearly see a low-lying smudge on the horizon. They had raised Bermuda. The weather was placid, and the air was warm. In anticipation of the appearance of the golden orb, the sky and the ocean melted into an amalgam of multiple shades and layers of reddish blues, purples, violets and mauves that defied description. As the sun approached the horizon from below, its rays chased the violets away from it, although they lingered in areas further away from where the sun was actually rising. The sky became lighter as the cool mauves and violets were melted by the hot orange rays from below. As the orb broke the surface, a reflected orange-yellow-red tongue lit the ocean between the sun and the ship.

Harley had seen many a dawn in Gloucester Massachusetts, but never anything like this. As Badger approached the island the steady, hypnotic rhythm of the screws began to slow. The sun was 30 degrees in the sky now and he looked down to the water. To his astonishment, the ocean was changing right in front of his eyes. The deep, impenetrable, marine blue that they noticed when they had entered the Gulf Stream was giving way to something else. Its impenetrability was giving way to a translucence. He could see shafts of light piercing the water, going down to infinity. The closer they got to the island the more the ocean changed. The deep blue had given way to an aqua marine. The translucence was increasing until it was almost transparent. He looked around and he saw darker sections, menacing and ominous. Those must be coral reefs, he thought. He'd read about the many ships that had approached Bermuda only to perish upon an encounter with one of these coral reefs. The rhythm of the screws was slowing to barely idling speed now. He then spied a little boat approaching them with a large red and white flag on its staff—a pilot boat. A local man, resplendent in his white uniform, nimbly stepped off the wallowing pilot boat onto the Badger's Jacob's ladder. The pilot's brown skin was further burnished by years of sun and salt. He climbed up the ladder and after a few brief pleasantries with the officer in charge, he proceeded to the bridge to instruct Badger's skipper how to negotiate these dark submarine sentinels guarding the entrance to this strange small island.

They entered the channel near the oldest settlement in the island, the town of St. George. There were coral reefs everywhere. At one point, in a section of the channel aptly called, "The Narrows," Badger seemed to barely slide between the jaws of a group of sinister looking coral heads, as they rounded the point off the ancient fortification known as Fort St. Catherine, and headed west parallel to the coast. Bermuda was not what Harley had expected. He had read about coral islands when he was in college and he expected to see someplace mountainous and volcanic, surrounded by a ring of coral reefs. This island was hilly but not mountainous. The hills were heavily wooded. The coastline was very irregular, giving way to several marvellous natural harbours. And the water, well, it had to be seen to be believed. The colour and clarity were not like anything he had ever seen before. Having successfully navigated the

Narrows, Badger cruised easily through the rest of the channel, although he did occasionally see some dark shadows silently passing by the ship's hull in relatively close proximity. As they approached the Royal Naval Dockyard, they turned to port and the channel narrowed again. Here, jagged rocks could be seen penetrating the surface but under the expert guidance of the local pilot, the ship glided safely past these hazards. They soon turned to starboard and entered into what was called the Great Sound. They dropped anchor in a section of the Great Sound called Grassy Bay.

Harley could immediately see that the Great Sound was very well protected from wind and wave from all points of the compass except the north and north east. As the prevailing winds were from the Southwest, it was ideally suited for seaplane operations. The island was shaped like a giant fishhook with the Royal Naval Dockyard at the hook's tip and the Great Sound nestled in its curve. The land bordering the Sound was not at all heavily populated; the sprinkling of white roofed houses forming a clear contrast to the dark green woodlands that dominated the hilly landscape. On top of the highest hill stood a tall, white lighthouse. From his vantage point on Badger's deck in Grassy Bay, looking east, behind what looked like a cluster of tiny islands, he could see the city of Hamilton, Bermuda's capital. He would have to explore it during his down time. In his mind's eye he envisioned the glide paths he would have to take to land his Kingfisher in the Great Sound. It would be relatively easy for his little plane during either day or night flying, but he could foresee it could be challenging for the larger PBY's. They were going to have to skim over some of those hills to the east of the Great Sound to make their water landings.

An announcement over Badger's p.a. system jolted Harley out of his reverie. It was time to get to work. The planes in VS32 squadron had been transported and disassembled. Mechanics had to reassemble them, fuel them, put them through a series of tests, then winch them overboard for the pilots to conduct further taxiing tests, then finally flight tests. The mechanics got to work with a deafening cacophony of noise from the pneumatic wrenches, cranes and other machinery required to reassemble the aircraft.

It was not until around 5:00pm, after taxiing around the Great Sound and testing his radio communications gear, did Swordfish receive the green light to take off. From a position at the eastern perimeter of the Great Sound, close to that cluster of islands he had seen, he gunned the Pratt & Whitney engine. The plane lurched forward on a westerly vector with a loud roar. Gathering speed quite quickly, it was soon at its 90 knot take off speed. He eased back the stick and the Kingfisher was airborne. The purpose of this flight was to further test the aircraft, to make sure it had successfully endured the disassembly, packing and reassembly process and was completely and reliably airworthy.

He took the plane west over Somerset Island, continued off the coast and was immediately shocked by what he saw. Those dark, menacing shapes beneath the surface he had seen, just that morning, were transformed into irregularly shaped, glistening, living amoeba like creatures set in an almost totally transparent pale aqua sea. The motion of the ocean altered the refraction of the light through the water, causing these creatures to appear to be slightly swaying this way and that. From the air he could see straight to the ocean floor, the transparency was so complete. Many of the amoeba like reefs had coral sand in their interiors, dramatizing the contrast with their outer shells. There were several small sailboats at anchor in one of the little harbours in Somerset Island, and they appeared to be suspended above the sandy bottom by some invisible force, their shadows clearly visible on the sand below. His navigator/gunner was also in awe of the sight and exclaimed, "SF, what kind of place is this?"

Harley took a wide right-hand turn that took him around the Dockyard, then east to the city of Hamilton. After a turn around the city, a quite small and unimpressive town alongside a very good and safe harbour, he lined the Kingfisher up for his first landing in the Great Sound. Reducing the airspeed to 90 knots, he approached over what clearly was a commercial/military flying boat terminal on a flat island. He could see a commercial flying boat there as well as a PBY, what the Brits called "Catalinas", as well as a few ramps to drag them out of the water. He approached on the same vector that he took off with and gently touched down. The test flight was a success—his Kingfisher was operational.

12

STARTING OUT

THE SQUADRON'S BASE HAD NOT been built yet, so they were sharing facilities with the Brits. They were billeted in a local hotel called the Belmont Manor Hotel, which was on a hill very near the coast. The hotel's posh name was all that was posh about it. However, it was very convenient because there was a dock below it for the men to be ferried directly to Darrell's Island where their aircraft were going to be located. Darrell's Island was that flat island with the patrol plane facilities Harley had seen on his first Bermuda flight. There were many RAF personnel all around, because Bermuda was a major launching station for brand new PBY's—Catalinas—which had been built for the RAF and were being ferried over to Britain. Pilots were not only required to ferry these aircraft over to Europe, but also Bermuda was a training centre for RAF pilots to get checked out on the Catalinas before their long flight over the Atlantic.

The next morning Harley and his rear gunner/radioman were among a group at Belmont ferry dock waiting for the ferry to Darrell's Island. As the ferry approached, he noticed that it appeared to be a floating antique: painted white, a double decker, made completely of wood and with old truck tires strapped on her flanks, acting as fenders. The chains securing the tires were rusting from the sea and salt, bleeding reddish brown rust stains down her flanks. As it moved closer, he heard strange bells ringing onboard and he wondered what they were. As a Gloucester, Mass. fisherman's son, he was interested in anything having to do with boats. The name printed on her side was Frances. The ferry came along side with the ease of being handled by a skilled pilot. They all stepped onboard.

Out of curiosity Harley climbed the stairs and approached the rounded wheelhouse up forward. Standing inside the wheelhouse he found the master of this small, fat vessel, a dark-skinned local man, his skin creased from many years exposure to sun, sea and salt.

Harley greeted him, "Good morning Skipper, nice morning."

The pilot grinned, "Mornin' mate. Another Bermudaful day. You one of those Yankee fliers just come in?"

"Yeah, just got in yesterday. I fly one of those small single engine seaplanes out there on the island."

"Ya, I saw 'em flying around here yesterday afternoon. Looks pretty dangerous if you ask me. I'll stick to boats."

"I love boats too."

"Ain't nothing like a boat."

Harley was having some challenges with the strong Bermudian dialect. He concentrated hard.

"What were those bells I heard when you were docking?"

"Oh, that! This boat works on bell signals to the engine room. You see these three brass rings?" The skipper pointed to three simple devices in the wheelhouse. Each was a brass ring that you could put your finger through to pull up. Each was attached to a small rectangular sleeve bolted to the bulkhead of the wheelhouse, one on the left, another on the right, and a third was bolted to the support for the steering wheel in the centre. At the bottom end of each ring there was a cable attached that disappeared through the deck. "There is no direct control of the engines from up here on this boat, so I give bell signals to the guy in the engine room to operate the engines. Look here, I'll show you." He walked past Harley and peered over the port side. "Let go!" He yelled. The deck hand manning the line at the aft access point let go his line. "Herman, hold those turns on the forward post." The forward deck hand, Herman, held the line around the forward post, very close to where the hull of Frances narrowed toward her bow.

The pilot reached over with his right hand and pulled up once on the brass ring on the starboard bulkhead of the wheelhouse. All over the ferry you could hear the bell ring, "Thrrrring," in the engine room. The starboard engine engaged slowly ahead, but because the forward post was secured, instead of moving forward, the Frances turned her nose into the dock and her stern swung away. When the ferry had swung enough, the skipper gave two quick pulls on the starboard brass ring -- "Thrrrring– thrrrring," -- the starboard engine disengaged. Herman then let go of his forward line. The ferry was now diagonal to the Belmont dock. The pilot reversed the starboard engine, again with a "Thrrrring– thrrrring," and he also reversed the port engine. The port bell sounded completely different from the starboard, it rang like, "Chick– Chick". The Frances backed away from the dock. After a few seconds the pilot gave a single pull on each engine ring - "Thrrrring, Chick." Both engines were disengaged. During this whole process he had not touched the helm. Momentarily, he gave a single pull on the port and starboard brass rings and the ferry moved forward under the power of both engines. He then pulled the brass ring in the middle, it made a tinkling sound and the Frances quickly accelerated to its cruising speed, a stately 9 knots. The pilot turned the wheel and headed for Darrell's Island, Bermuda's only airport.

He said to Harley, "So, you see how it works?"

"Yeah, cool. I saw the ferry running last night. How do you guys navigate?"

"Well, all we ferry pilots need to know how to navigate at night. Night navigation around here ain't easy cause many of the small islands in the Harbour and Great Sound are uninhabited and have no lights at all. There's lots of unmarked shoals and reefs too—you just have to know they're there. In any case, with the wartime blackout, a pilot has to have every island, rock and reef in his head and know how far they are from his boat, at all times. There's no book to learn this from, mate, only years of experience. I'll tell you, it's real tricky on dark nights or when the weather and visibility are bad."

"Yeah. Amazing! By the way, my name's Harley Harvey." And he stuck out his hand.

"I'm Alan Jones, but most people call me Hooks." He shook it.

"Hooks? Why's that?"

"Cause I'm crazy 'bout fishing. You like to fish?"

"Yeah, love it. My dad is a swordfish boat captain in Gloucester, Mass., so fishin's in my blood, I guess."

"Maybe you'd like to see how we-byes fish in Bermuda. You can come out with me when you have some time off."

"Yeah, that would be cool."

They were approaching Darrell's Island, so they parted ways, each to his respective duty: Harley to his Kingfisher and Hooks to the Frances.

13

THE MOVIES

VS32 WAS GETTING INTO A ROUTINE NOW. Kingfishers, the VS patrols, were performing the near shore patrols from the Island while the VP patrols, the Catalinas, were patrolling further afield. All aircraft were performing so called "Neutrality Patrolling" which was decreed by President Roosevelt once hostilities broke out in Europe. The Neutrality Patrol was the mission given to the US Navy to patrol the Atlantic up to a longitude of 65 degrees to identify and report on any and all military vessels in the area. Of course, Bermuda was just on the perimeter of that area and therefore a natural place from which to conduct Neutrality, or any other type of patrolling. In the short time they were stationed on-island, radio operators had detected several transmissions from German U-Boats in Bermuda waters but when an aircraft had been dispatched to the purported location, they found only an empty ocean.

One day while they had some down time, Harley and his navigator/gunner James Yates (call sign Jay) decided to take in the Humphrey Bogart movie, "The Maltese Falcon," which was showing at the theatre in Somerset. Starting out from their digs at the Belmont, they had to take two ferries—the Frances from Belmont to Hamilton, then the Corona from Hamilton to Watford Bridge in Somerset. At the Hamilton terminal Harley said so long to his friend Hooks Jones, Frances' skipper, and the two men boarded the Corona. He remembered how he had thought Frances was an antique, but Corona made the Frances seem new. After talking to one of the crew, he discovered that she was an old 19th century coal burning steamboat,—incredible! He didn't know any of those still existed. She had the same bell messaging system to the engine room that the Frances had, except she had a single screw. After a high-pitched moaning blast from her steam whistle, she backed out from her berth in Hamilton and got underway. Despite her age, Corona was quiet, fast and comfortable, and they made good time to their destination, Watford Bridge.

After a brief walk to Somerset village, they spied the little cinema and approached the box office. The cashier looked at the two GI's and said, "Good evening gentlemen, how many tickets?" Then she smiled. Harley was stunned by that smile. Her smile lit up the whole room. She was a local "coloured" girl with her hair pulled back in a simple bushy ponytail. Her hazel eyes were multi-coloured liquid pools that instantly hypnotized Harley. Her perfectly unblemished skin was the colour of Skippy Peanut Butter. Her full lips only magnified the allure of that smile. He just stared, unable to speak. "Sir?" she said. His tongue, his lips and his mouth refused to move—they were frozen by that smile and those eyes.

"SF, what the hell is the matter with you, man! Here, I'll get it." Jay took out some money and paid the cashier. "Please excuse my friend, miss, he's a little retarded. Come on man!"

They went inside and sat down. Jay took out a pack of Lucky Strikes and they both lit up. "You see that girl—kinda cute, huh?"

"Huh—what? Oh yeah, she's cute alright," Harley said trying to act nonchalant. He took a long drag on the smoke and exhaled slowly. He'd never had that kind of reaction to a woman before, particularly to a coloured girl. There were a number of coloured people in Gloucester, all in the fishing business. A lot of the guys were hands on sword fishing boats, but not as captains, of course. They eked out a living off the ocean like everybody else in Gloucester. He'd seen them with their families, but he had not seen anything like that before. This island of Bermuda, in the middle of nowhere was full of surprises. They didn't have to wait long before the show started. They caught up with what was going on in the world with the obligatory newsreels, both British and American—albeit in the circumstance of Bermuda, one or perhaps two weeks delayed.

14

ORDERS

CAPTAIN GRANT WAS GRATEFUL he was not involved in this war because it was obvious to him that, this time, Britain was not going to prevail against the Germans, as they had done 20 odd years before, when he was with the Senior Service. This time, he thought, Britain was finished, even with American intervention. He was convinced that British society had become so corrupted by egalitarianism and mongrelism that they didn't have a chance against the highly disciplined, pure-bred German forces. He gave Britain a one in five chance of surviving past the end of the year. He was happy to be on the side-lines of this fight. Besides, he was too old to be of any use to anybody. His warrior days were over.

Grant was living in happy, peaceful, idle bliss in Bermuda. His routine was, as would be for a military man, totally predictable. Up at 6:00am, make himself a cup of coffee, put on his walking shoes and cap and head out for his morning walk. He would walk around the golf course, then out onto the street, along Ord Road, turn left and climb Cobbs Hill all the way to Harbour Road. There he would pop into the little snack bar next to Darrell's Wharf and pick up the daily Royal Gazette. He then would continue west and return to his residence on Belmont golf course and read the morning paper. After that he would partake of a proper English breakfast of scrambled eggs, sausage and toast prepared by his housekeeper and cook, Mavis. He would then head to the bathroom for his daily ablutions. Mavis would have a shirt, tie and hat, appropriate for someone of his station, already laid out for him. But before he headed for the ferry, he would go out on the balcony and check what ships were at the Dockyard and anything else of nautical or aviational interest.

When the Frances arrived, he would board her and head straight for the wheelhouse to exchange pleasantries with his friend, pilot Hooks Jones. Their conversations were always about boats, planes, fishing or the sea. There was plenty of time for such discussions as the Frances was dreadfully slow. Upon arrival in Hamilton, Grant would walk along Front Street, climb the slight hill on Parliament Street and check his mailbox at the General Post Office at the corner of Reid and Parliament Streets. He would then stroll west and find himself at the Royal Bermuda Yacht Club. There he would read his mail and have conversations with any of the other local gentry that might be there.

On this particular day he had a letter from a Mr Freddy Wentz of New York. His name was actually Friedrich, but he went by the name Freddy. Grant had met Wentz during his brief stay in that city. The letter was quite brief and to the point,

"Will be passing through Bermuda en-route to Nassau. Will be staying at the Princess. Let's have a drink on Monday October 15th at three o'clock. Best regards, Freddy Wentz."

Nothing else? Grant was puzzled and curious. No pleasantries nor information of what this was about. He didn't know Wentz all that well, having only met him a couple of times in New York. He was an acquaintance of his friend Lindeman from Frankfurt and they had had a few rounds at a bar.

On the appointed Monday afternoon Grant entered the Princess Hotel and headed for the bar. He spied Wentz seated at a nearby table sipping a pilsner. He saw Grant and waved him over. Freddy Wentz was a New Yorker and a man of indeterminate means. Grant remembered there was something rather malevolent about him. On the outside he was friendly enough, but there was always a subcutaneous "bully-boy" persona that was straining to be unleashed from the affable outward persona. The sense was magnified by Wentz's considerable size, highly toned muscles and overall superb level of fitness. He moved like a cat - a very big cat. Anyone who was around when that alter ego was unleashed was going to be in a world of trouble.

The two men shook hands and Grant ordered a pilsner for himself. When it arrived Wentz said, "Hey man, is there somewhere we can talk more privately?"

Grant said, "Well, I don't know, maybe we should talk outside by the Harbour."

They sat down by the waterside. Wentz casually did a 360-degree scan before he sat down. No one was around. "So",

Wentz said, "How are you enjoying retirement in paradise?"

"Jolly good. How was your passage down here?"

"Yeah, smooth as silk, man." Wentz replied in his New York accent. "I've got something for you."

Grant dug a pack of Craven A's out of his inner pocket and offered one to Wentz. He took it, whereupon Grant produced his Zippo lighter with his ship's emblem on it, and they both lit up.

Wentz reached in his jacket pocket and fished out a sealed envelope with the name "Rodney Grant" handwritten on the front. Grant opened it—it was from Hans Lindeman!

"My dear Rodney;

I hope this letter finds you well. Its contents are of a very sensitive nature and must be handled with the utmost discretion. In fact, you must completely destroy it after having read its contents."

Grant couldn't believe what he was reading.

"You will recall the last occasion you were here in Germany, I said we will contact you when needed. Well, the time has come. We need your help in the effort to restore the proper order in the world, a world which, you would doubtless agree, has gone horribly wrong.

Wentz is a delivery boy and has no idea what is in this letter. We know that mail traversing the Atlantic is being intercepted and censored by the British in Bermuda that is why I have had to use Wentz. You will never see him again.

Rodney, fortuitously, you are perfectly placed to render assistance to the Fuhrer, right there in Bermuda. You are in a good position to report to us the movement of British and American naval vessels as well as merchant shipping in and out of Bermuda. As you, no doubt, know the Kriegsmarine are quite active in your area, so intelligence on ship and aircraft movements from Bermuda is crucial to their continued success.

There are two packages that will be essential to your activities, one is contained in a steamer trunk that Wentz has brought with him. He will leave it with you and instructions are contained therein. There will be a second package that will be delivered to you by a Mrs Molly Smith of New York. She is an innocent, who is visiting her sister in the island. She thinks she is bringing you a typewriter that you have bought at Sears Roebuck in the States. She arrives next week by flying-boat, and will contact you directly.

Rodney, you will be making an important contribution to the return to the old-world order of structure, strength, honour and discipline.

Yours faithfully,
Hans

He was aware that Wentz was intently observing him and his reaction to the letter, which told him that Wentz knew more about this matter than Hans had indicated. In a flash of insight, he realized that his visible reaction at this moment might have consequences for him at the hands of Mr. Wentz. He therefore kept his cool, like a good ship's captain, reached into his pocket again, grasped the Zippo and set the letter alight. When it couldn't be held any longer, he dropped the remnant overboard.

He met Wentz's gaze head-on and demanded, "What is the procedure on the transfer of your package?"

"That's up to you Cap'n."

"I'll have somebody pick it up tomorrow at noon." After which Grant turned on his heels, and without any further word, left the hotel.

In another section of the Princess Hotel, Christine Liverpool looked at her watch, it was three o'clock. "Max, it's time for my break," she said to her supervisor. Spying on the spies— trying to identify secret messages cloaked in ordinary correspondence was a boring business. "I'm going for a smoke." She exited the main operations room, which she called the dungeon. Dad would be appalled at my smoking, but all the modern women were smoking these days. What's more, over here we can get American cigarettes which are much better than English smokes. She ambled out to a small third storey balcony facing the harbour, lit up a Marlboro, inhaled deeply, and then blew out the smoke with great satisfaction. Below she noticed two men walking to the dock in conversation. Hey, I know that walk, that's Captain Grant. Don't know the other bloke. Even though Grant was tall, this man was much taller and broader. She saw the man reach in his jacket pocket and give Grant a letter which he immediately opened and read. Then she saw Grant take out his lighter and burn the letter, allowing the remnant to fall into the harbour. That's strange! Why would anybody do that? What could be so secret that a letter had to be destroyed immediately after it was read? Perhaps the mysterious Captain Grant was engaged in the war effort after all, just under cover. She smirked to herself.

The two men below her, apparently having finished their business left the area. Her break was over, she butted her cigarette in the ashtray and returned to the dungeon, never giving the incident another thought.

15

STATION ACTIVATED

As a retired Royal Navy captain, Grant was completely beyond reproach—nothing he could do would raise suspicion. After his meeting with Wentz, he made arrangements with one of the contractors that moved goods off the docks when ships arrived. The man had a horse drawn cart and agreed to pick up a steamer trunk at the Princess and take it to his house on Belmont golf course. He paid the man in advance. That evening Grant opened the trunk and found a complex piece of electronic equipment in a number of constituent parts. As indicated in Hans' letter, hidden in the inside liner of the trunk, there were detailed instructions as to how to assemble the device. Grant presumed it to be a radio transmitter. While he was familiar with the rudiments of radio transmission at sea, it had been up to the Signalman's Mate of the ship to be conversant with the guts of the device which he was, not only responsible for operating, but also maintaining and repairing. However, the instructions were quite detailed and, if closely followed, the device could be rendered operable. But this was no ordinary radio transmitter. This was to be a clandestine radio transmitter, so it was essential that the device be kept a total secret along with its antenna and the transmissions themselves.

The first problem was where to place the antenna so that it could be effective as well as invisible. Grant hunted around the house looking for a suitable place. He was in the kitchen - nothing suitable there. On leaving the kitchen he stopped dead in his tracks. He was in the buttery, a room, just off the kitchen which had a very high ceiling, designed to keep perishables cooler than in the rest of the house. From the outside it looked like a step-pyramid with a little ball at the top. Putting the antenna in the buttery ceiling would be perfect. All he would have to do was to hide the cables. He would have to do all this by himself—no one else could be involved.

The other issue was sending messages that would not be decipherable if intercepted. In the trunk with the radio was a code book. The instructions made it clear that the code book was only half of the encryption process. The other half of the puzzle was to be brought to him by Mrs Molly Smith—the "typewriter." It was clear to Grant that this was no mere typewriter, but a very sophisticated encryption device called an "Enigma Machine." His instructions stated that all transmissions had to be coded according to the code book then further encrypted with the Enigma Machine before they were transmitted over the air. Moreover, all communications were to be kept as brief as possible to deter any eavesdroppers from triangulating on his position. While the instructions didn't say, Grant assumed that his new device, due to its small size and low power output, didn't have a reliable range of more than 50 miles, so the recipients of his intelligence must be U-boats in the area.

On the afternoon before he started the assembly process from his study, he approached Mavis, "I say, Mavis, I'm having some construction here starting tomorrow and it seems pointless for you to come and clean because the construction will just mess everything up again. So why don't you take the rest of the week off until we're done here. Don't worry, it won't have any effect on your weekly pay packet."

"Thank you very much Cap'n. You're very kind. What about your meals?"

"Oh, I'll manage. There's always the Club you know."

"Hmmm."

He had observed the methods of some of the local tradesmen with respect to Bermudian construction techniques and was certain he could manage to do a halfway decent job. It took him several days to assemble and install the radio and antenna concealed in the buttery.

The radio was hidden in a nearby locked cupboard. He hid the key underneath the desk in his study, secured with a piece of Scotch Tape. With the antenna hidden in the ceiling and the wiring covered over with lime-based mortar, Grant was satisfied that this action was sufficient to obscure his activities.

A few days later he picked up a local letter from Mrs Smith of Devonshire, informing him that she had his typewriter, and would he come and collect it. The next day Grant hired a horse and buggy and paid Mrs Smith a call. "Oh, Captain Grant, what a pleasure to meet you. Please come in. Won't you stay for some tea?"

"Why, Madam, you are most kind. I would love a cup."

After tea he collected his package, bid Mrs Smith, "Good afternoon," and returned to the Hamilton ferry terminal, alighted the Frances, climbed the hill to "Belmoral" and anxiously opened it.

He hadn't felt this way since he was a boy wanting to see what "Father Christmas" had brought him. It did indeed look like a typewriter, but it was far more complicated than any mere typewriter. It had internal tumbler cylinders and a plug board and came in a wooden box. Hidden in the lining of the top of the wooden box was a further set of detailed instructions of how to set the machine up and how to use it.

Grant spent many evenings poring over this device, studying all its aspects and details. He had to wait until Mavis finished work each day to commence his studying. This is a work of sheer genius, he thought. No one will ever be able to decode any messages encrypted by it.

He was now fully set up to provide useful intelligence to the Kreigsmarine U-boats within a 50-mile radius about aircraft and ship movements in and out of Bermuda. He was about to be activated as a German spy. He was about to betray his country.

Grant sat alone in the dark in "Belmoral's" study. The last section of his detailed instructions set a date and time of his initial, test transmission: December 15th, 1941, 01:30 hours. At 01:20 he switched the radio on, waited for it to warm up, and checked the transmission frequency, the power dial and a few other details. Everything was working, as far as he could tell. It was now or never. This was the point of no return, no turning back now!

The Enigma Machine was the wonder of the age. Operating it was simplicity itself. You simply typed in a letter, say, "A", and the machine would encrypt that letter into another letter, say, "Q", by lighting the "Q" up on an array of lights configured to look like the physical keyboard. The operator would simply write down "Q" and input the next letter of the message he wanted to send. The device would output 17,000 different combinations before it repeated itself. The Enigma Machines of the sender and receiver had to be set up identically for the encryption to work. The encrypted message would then be sent out in simple Morse code.

He stared at the luminous dial on his watch as the sweep second hand slowly approached the time for the first transmission. It took forever, but the moment finally arrived. He put his finger on the telegraph key and tapped out a brief encrypted test message in Morse code—to who knows whom. He waited and waited and waited. Five minutes passed, ten minutes, then fifteen minutes. He checked his equipment. He was beginning to doubt if the signal had actually been broadcast. Perhaps there was a loose wire, or maybe the cement plaster that surrounded the antenna was blocking his transmission or perhaps he made a mistake encrypting the message with the Enigma Machine, or maybe he had set up the device incorrectly. All these things were racing through his mind when he heard it through his earphones—a series of dots and dashes.

He scribbled down what he had heard on a piece of scrap paper. It was very brief, then silence. He turned to his Enigma Machine, checked the settings and typed the message he had received into the device. Each entered letter was displayed decrypted on the lit keyboard array. The decrypted reply was in German, of course, but it read, "MESSAGE RECEIVED. YOUR STATION IS ACTIVATED."

Captain Rodney Grant, RN (retired), had been activated as a German spy.

He had a predetermined schedule, every week, but not the same day or the same time, to provide an intel report to nearby U-Boats about British and American naval vessels and aircraft as well as merchant ship movements from Bermuda.

16

PEARL HARBOUR

FROM 1940, VS32 HAD BEEN conducting "Neutrality Patrols" from Bermuda. However, the base for these Neutrality patrol planes was not commissioned until April 7, 1941. A Carrier Division consisting of USS Ranger, Wasp, and Yorktown began using the base the following day. However, Yorktown was dispatched to the Pacific theatre soon after and was later involved with the historic naval battles with the Japanese Empire at Coral Sea and later in the battle of Midway where she met her end. For the members of VS32 these developments did not have a major impact on their duties or operations. The attack by Japanese carrier-based aircraft on Pearl Harbour, Hawaii, while shocking to the world, and America in particular, was merely the final stage of continuing escalation for the men of squadron VS32.

BAD called a special briefing of VS32 and announced, "Gentlemen, on September 11th President Roosevelt declared that Axis ships entering the neutrality zone do so, 'at their own risk,' and has ordered the Navy to attack any vessel threatening ships under American escort. This means that you have orders to release your depth charges or bombs on any U-Boat you sight, because, as you know, Bermuda is in the Neutrality Zone. Any U-Boat in the zone is there precisely for that reason—to attack ships under American escort. This is as real as it gets, gentlemen."

So, when war was declared by Hitler on the United States, in December 1941, directly after Pearl Harbour, VS32 had already been in a defacto state of war with German U-Boats for almost 3 months. But, the Japanese unprovoked, sneak attack on US forces at Pearl Harbour filled America with a collective, moral outrage and thirst for revenge. Before Pearl, VS32's pilots were doing their duty to assist a close ally. After Pearl, it was THEIR WAR, and they too were filled with that terrible resolve to destroy their enemy. However, their enemy was very stealthy and hard to find in the vastness of the Atlantic.

17

THE ARGENTINE

THE BERMUDA KINGFISHERS—VS32s—were now flying regular patrols covering a circle of 125 miles radius from the island. While there were the occasional night patrols, most VS32 patrols commenced before dawn, on the presumption that enemy U-boats having surfaced during the night to recharge their batteries, might still be afloat at the break of dawn and be visible and vulnerable. Harley and Jay methodically went through their land based pre-flight checks before boarding the launch that ferried them to their aircraft. It was moored nearby, fuelled and ready to go. The weather was inclement. There was a stiff northeast breeze which meant that it blew straight into the open mouth of the Great Sound. With no land to protect them, conditions were quite choppy. After completing their on-board pre-flight checks, Harley fired up the big radial engine, the seaman on the launch let go the mooring line and they taxied out around the eastern tip of the base into the Great Sound. They received clearance to launch. The Kingfisher was bucking wildly in the choppy waters and when Harley turned her into the wind, sheets of salt spray were thrown clear over the cockpit. He gunned the engine which responded with a great roar. The air wash from the propeller merely hurled the spray with increased ferocity over the cockpit whose canopy was partially open. The crew were getting soaked. As the aircraft accelerated the bucking turned into hammering. Harley's forward visibility was virtually zero as a continuous stream of spray totally enveloped them. But power was slowly overcoming nature, and while the hammering didn't stop, the speed became sufficient for the main pontoon, which ran along the central line of the aircraft, to rise enough to get on a plane. She was throwing much less water and spray now and the Kingfisher started to accelerate rapidly. Harley could now see ahead, and the way forward was clear. He checked his airspeed gauge, it passed forty knots, fifty, and sixty. The hammering of the waves was decreasing as the plane began to skim the surface. Sixty-five, seventy, eighty, eighty-five knots; at ninety knots Harley eased the stick back and the hammering disappeared—they were free from the tormenting grip of the sea—airborne.

It was still dark as they rose into the early morning sky. Harley put his heading at 045 degrees, his designated vector for this patrol. The island, in war time black-out mode, was barely distinguishable from the blackness of the ocean. Jay was busy checking the various flight information dials and the onboard communications equipment. This always had to be done after the saltwater bath everything took on take-off. After a few minutes, dawn started to break. Harley remembered the first Bermuda dawn he had witnessed from the deck of the USS Badger and how amazing it was, and even though he had experienced it many times since then, he never grew tired of it. The ocean was strewn with whitecaps and, as their patrol altitude was just 500 feet, their aircraft was also being buffeted around considerably. However, as veteran fliers, they weren't bothered by this in the slightest. They applied themselves to their mission which was to search for U-boats. They were coming up empty, as usual. In fact, notwithstanding the many torpedoing of British, American and other neutral flag ships by U-boats, they had never seen one. It was a very big ocean. When they were about 100 miles out Jay shouted, "Hey, SF, look over there—starboard beam. Looks like a flare!"

They could see the smoke trail of a flare.

"Yeah, looks like it. Let's check it out!"

Harley rolled the Kingfisher to the right towards the smoke. They strained their eyes, and through a pair of binoculars they could clearly see a lifeboat crammed with about two dozen people, waving madly at them. Harley overflew them and waggled his wings in acknowledgment.

"Hey, Jay, radio this into Bermuda, then drop a slow burning smoke float marker and let's see if we can find someone to pick these guys up."

The Kingfisher was too small to pick up survivors; the best they could do was to find somebody who could. He decided to fly a wide arc, using the lifeboat as a centre to see if there was any friendly shipping in the area. After about 20 minutes they spotted a merchantman. Upon close inspection they could see the vessel was flying a flag with two broad baby-blue, horizontal stripes on a white background—the Argentinian flag. Argentina was a neutral country, but it was well documented that that country had leanings toward Germany. It was well known that Argentina and Uruguay gave safe harbour to German surface raiders and their supply ships during the First World War and also during this current conflict. In fact, the infamous pocket battleship the Admiral Graf-Spee, had taken refuge in Montevideo, Uruguay during the Battle of the River Platte, the river Platte estuary serving both Montevideo and Buenos Aires, Argentina.

"Jay, signal them with the Aldis lamp to pick those guys up."

"Roger that."

Jay un-stowed the signal lamp and, while they circled the Argentine merchantman, flashed the signal in Morse code. The ship continued on its original course.

"Keep trying, Jay!"

Jay signalled the ship numerous times, with no response.

"I'll try using manoeuvres", Harley said. These were internationally recognized aerial manoeuvres that were used when there were no comms. Still nothing. The ship continued on its original course.

"You think these guys are dumb or they're playing dumb because they don't like us?"

"I think they're playing dumb!" Harley said. "Let's let them know we're serious, it's time for a shot 'cross the bow."

The Kingfisher carried two machine guns, one facing

forward controlled by the pilot and another swivelled gun facing aft controlled by the rear gunner. Harley pulled the stick left and rolled the plane to port and into a shallow dive pointing forward of the bow of the Argentine merchantman. He then fingered his forward mounted .30 calibre Browning machine gun. He let go a long burst with the weapon. A line of spray erupted across the path of the vessel.

Harley then repeated the aerial signal manoeuvre and started to fly towards where they had left the stranded sailors. This time the Argentine merchantman turned toward, and they escorted the vessel to the rescue point. They circled overhead as the sailors were rescued, as long as their fuel supply allowed, then headed back to Bermuda. They landed with just 10 minutes of fuel left in their tanks.

The next day the reluctant Argentine called into Bermuda and dropped off 24 Dutch sailors whose ship had been torpedoed by a U-boat. They had been drifting in the Atlantic for 8 days. For the first time Swordfish and Jay felt that they had really made a difference, if not to the entire war effort, at least to those stranded 24 Dutch sailors. The day after the rescue they encountered some of those sailors in a bar in Hamilton, and they were very pleased to accept as many free rounds of drinks as they could hold from their new best friends from Holland.

18

ON BOARD FRANCES

ONE DAY, GRANT BOARDED FRANCES and was heading forward to the wheelhouse to exchange pleasantries with his Bermudian friend when he noticed Hooks talking to a GI, in uniform. Hooks said, "Captain, let me introduce you to my American friend, Lieutenant Harley Harvey. Harley, this is Captain Grant." The two men shook hands.

"How do you do."

"What service are you in Captain?" asked Harley, as Grant was not in uniform.

"Royal Navy, retired. What about you?"

"Oh, I'm a Navy pilot. I fly Kingfishers. What did you do in the Navy before you retired?"

"Well, I had a desk job just before I retired but before that I was the commander of HMS Solent, a destroyer."

"Fantastic! Did you see any action on her?"

"Yes indeed, I was her skipper at Jutland."

"Jutland! Wow—unbelievable!"

"What's Jutland?" Hooks queried.

"What's Jutland? It's only the biggest naval battle in history! Between the British Navy and the German Navy during World War I.

"Who won?"

"Well, it depends how you look at it," Grant said.

"Really?" Harley said in surprise. "How's that?"

"You have to look at it through my eyes. I come from a long line of naval officers, my grandfather and great grandfather were Admirals and my father a Commodore. So, it was natural that I follow the family tradition with a career in the Royal Navy. So, I have Royal Navy in my blood. As a youngster I moved up the ladder quickly. I was a midshipman on a battlecruiser, a sub-lieutenant on a heavy cruiser, a second lieutenant on a light cruiser, and a first lieutenant on a destroyer. I was promoted to Lieutenant Commander on the destroyer HMS Solent, my first command. HMS Solent was part of Admiral Sir John Jellicoe's Grand Fleet—the most powerful naval fleet in the world."

Harley and Hooks were spellbound. The slow fat ferry Frances gave him plenty of time to finish his story. "While ashore I spent most of my time with my father and grandfather, the Admiral. These idyllic interludes were often punctuated by animated, sometimes heated, discussions with the senior Grants about naval tactics and ship capabilities. One of the topics most discussed was the capabilities of the fleet's battlecruisers. The Admiral was of the opinion that battlecruisers were useless, if not, downright dangerous, because, while they had tremendous firepower and speed, they lacked the protective armour-plating of a conventional battleship. The light armour enabled battlecruisers to be faster than conventional battleships.

My father, the Commodore, argued that extra speed was equivalent to extra armour, because the speed made the battlecruiser more manoeuvrable and harder for the enemy to hit. In Admiral Jellicoe's Grand Fleet there were many battlecruisers, most of them assigned to the squadron commanded by Admiral Sir David Beatty. HMS Solent, my ship, was part of that squadron. Beatty's squadron was hailed as swift, and hard hitting—the tip of the spear. As a youngster, I agreed with my father. Speed was everything! I thought that my aging grandfather was a prisoner of old thinking: you know, behind the times. HMS Solent could do 35 knots and Beatty's whole squadron, moving together, could attack at 30 knots, much faster than the older battleships which could barely make 20 knots.

Well, gentlemen, this argument was emphatically settled at the Battle of Jutland. The Royal Navy lost over 3,000 sailors due to battlecruisers exploding when hit by enemy shells. The battlecruiser experiment was a tragic failure. The Admiral was right after all!"

"Wow!" Said Harley.

"While the capital ships had received all the headlines in the Battle of Jutland, it was the destroyers that engaged in daring and dangerous high-speed tactical runs in attempts to fire our most deadly weapon, torpedoes, at the enemy. The Royal Navy lost 8 destroyers in that melee. But HMS Solent was not one of them, although she received serious damage to her superstructure. She was struck by a shell from a

German cruiser. One hell of a mess! We were zig-zagging at full speed to dodge enemy fire; trying to get within torpedo range. Each time we swung the helm hard over, Solent would heel over so much that we thought she was in danger of capsizing, but we kept on charging forward. Everybody on the bridge was holding on to something for dear life. But I had to keep this reckless tactic up because German cruisers were firing at us. We could hear their shells howling overhead or falling short and exploding close-by, unleashing huge geysers of sea water. As we zigzagged closer and closer the cruiser firing became more accurate and our luck eventually ran out. One 8-inch shell flew clean through one of our funnels without exploding but was so powerful that the funnel was nonetheless completely torn away. A few moments later we heard a loud howling of an incoming shell. It struck the gun turret forward off the bridge. The ensuing explosion blew the turret right off the deck and partially demolished the bridge as well. All the men in the turret and those below feeding it with ammunition were instantly killed. There was a black smoking hole where the turret had been. Several of the officers in the bridge were killed as well, as was the helmsman. The rest, including myself were temporarily deaf and bleeding from shrapnel.

"Could you still steer the ship?" Harley asked.

"There was black smoke everywhere, both from the direct hit as well as from engine smoke from the nearby funnel that had been damaged by the unexploded shell. I could hardly breathe. The helm was gone but the voice pipe to the engine room was still functional. Through the voice pipe I shouted orders to the engine room and the auxiliary steering compartment located in the bowels of the ship. That was the only way to control her. Solent was in bad shape and we had to withdraw to save the ship and her crew. We were lucky though, because despite the direct hit, the forward magazine had not ignited. If it had, I would not be here talking to you today."

"That was a close call, bye" said Hooks.

Grant nodded. "I have to say, though, I certainly was impressed by the accuracy of the German gunnery, the brilliance of Admiral Sheer's tactics and the disciplined precision with which the German fleet carried out its orders. Our fleet's tactics and poor communications between ships resulted in disastrous losses in both ships and men. The world's largest, most powerful fleet performed poorly on that day and I thought it was a stain on the reputation of the once proud and indomitable Royal Navy."

"I thought you guys won the Battle of Jutland!"

"Well, from the British standpoint, the strategic objective of the battle, was to either destroy or keep the German High Seas Fleet bottled up in the Baltic, preventing them from being a factor in the global conflict. From that perspective we won, because, after Jutland, the German High Seas Fleet never ventured out again."

"Is there another way of looking at it?"

"Yes, the Royal Navy's Grand Fleet lost many more ships and many more men than did the Germans. But of course, the Grand Fleet was much larger than the German fleet to begin with, so it could have afforded to have greater losses, but because of that size advantage, we should have destroyed them outright. But we didn't, we took a hell of a beating. Their tactics were brilliant. Ours weren't. That's why I say it depends on how you look at it."

"Ya, I can see that. So, what happened to your ship, Cap'n? What was she named again?"

"HMS Solent. Yes, we were badly damaged, but we got her home OK. I received a commendation for my role in the Battle of Jutland, for bringing the crippled Solent safely back to port, and was soon promoted to the rank of Captain. However, I was consigned to a desk at the Admiralty in London thereafter and never commanded one of His Majesty's ships again."

"So, Hooks, were talking to a genuine war hero here!"

"Let's not overdo it mates," Grant said with false modesty. "That was a time long past. The days of big battle wagons, blasting away at each other, are gone. Today, it's about aircraft, their carriers and submarines. Lieutenant, you blokes are the tip of the spear now."

"Sure doesn't feel like it to me. We've hardly come across anything out there except ocean."

"The Gerries are a lot stronger this time around, on land, air and sea. Instead of the High Seas Fleet that you could see or detect with Radar, they have wolf packs of U-boats roaming the Atlantic that are totally invisible. Good luck with that Lieutenant."

"Oh, you can call me Harley."

"Ok, Harley." You can call me Captain, Grant thought to himself.

Frances was approaching the Hamilton terminal. The two naval officers watched, with admiration, as Hooks skilfully and effortlessly slotted the fat ungainly ferry alongside between two other boats. The men bade each other farewell; Grant headed for the Yacht Club and Harley for a Queen Street bar frequented by other GIs.

19

ACTION ON PATROL

THE ASSIGNED PATROL THIS PARTICULAR morning required Swordfish and Jay to proceed 60 miles on a vector of 300 degrees, approximately North West of Bermuda. The weather was somewhat blustery but nothing unusual. About 45 miles out, Jay said to Swordfish over the intercom, "Hey, SF! What's that over there?"

"Where?"

"2 o'clock, off our starboard!"

He pointed toward the grey smudge on the horizon.

"Oh yeah! I donno. Let's check it out."

He banked the plane right and headed for the unknown object. As they drew closer it was clearly a large ship, in grey camouflage paint.

"Relax, Jay, it's not a warship, but man, that baby is huge!"

They were getting quite close now. It was a large passenger ship with three funnels, headed east.

Then Jay blurted out, "Hey, that's the Queen! The Queen Mary!"

They flew right over the big ship. She was sailing alone.

"How you know that?"

"You kiddin? Man, you don't know nutt'n. That's the RMS Queen Mary, largest and fastest passenger ship in the world. With her wartime grey paint job, they call her the Grey Ghost. The Brits requisitioned her for the war, stripped her of all her luxurious fittings and packed her with thousands of bunks for transporting troops. She's so fast she sails alone without naval escort."

"If I were a soldier, I wouldn't feel so good about that!"

"If you knew the facts you would think differently."

They banked left to make another pass over the Queen. "She cruises at over 30 knots. Your average German torpedo's speed is 30 knots. So, if a U-boat fires at it he would have to have a perfect firing position to have the torpedo come even near that ship. To obtain such a position the sub would have to get well in front of her, but that won't be easy because the sub is much slower than the Queen. Plus, she zigzags every few minutes. Speed is her main defense. Also, she's faster than most naval convoy vessels who would only slow her down. That's why she sails alone." They made a third pass over Queen Mary as she steamed at breakneck speed over the choppy Atlantic, spray streaming off her blade-like bow. Swordfish waggled his wings then proceeded on their prescribed course.

"She's got the bone in her teeth."

"What? What the hell does that mean?

"You see that bow wave? See how it's climbing up the bow due to her high speed? The Brits call that, 'having the bone in her teeth.'"

"How do you know so much about that ship?"

"I'm a real ship aficionado, man, and that ship is one of the world's greatest ships."

"Man, you can't even spell aficionado!"

They both laughed out loud.

After resuming their prescribed patrol for about 30 minutes, their radio came alive. Jay occupied himself with the message being received in Morse code.

"What's going on, Jay?"

"There's been a sinking in our general area. We are to see if we can make contact with any survivors. We are to proceed on vector 352 degrees.

"Roger that." Swordfish adjusted his course accordingly. They scoured the ocean, Swordfish with his naked eyes, Jay with the binoculars. After searching for a while, suddenly Jay exclaimed, "Look! An oil slick!" In spite of the dark blue of the Gulf Stream, you could see the dark sheen on the water. They followed the oil slick. "SF, I see lifeboats! 10 o'clock!" Harley looked left and saw four lifeboats, full of survivors.

"Hey, SF, there's another ship nearby! Looks like she's a corvette but she's dead in the water. She's very low at the bow, looks like she's been hit too!"

"That means that Gerry might still be nearby! Look for it! He could still be on the surface!"

Jay swung his binoculars through all points of the compass. Suddenly he stopped and went back a few degrees. "Got it! SF, 5 o'clock! Let's get him!"

"I can't believe he's still on the surface! Must be admiring his handiwork or something."

"Or sticking around to see if that corvette needs another fish to finish it off."

Harley gunned the throttle to the max, yanked the stick hard over to the right and gave it as much rudder as it could take. Underneath each wing he had bombs that he was itching to release.

"He's seen us! He's seen us! He's crash-diving! Hurry up SF! Faster! Faster!"

"Man, this thing can't go any faster!" They vectored in on the sub. Its decks were awash. The little Kingfisher swooped down on the U-boat and released all four of its bombs which exploded issuing tall geysers of water on either side of the sub. But it slipped away into the depths, apparently undamaged.

"Damn!! He got away," Jay confirmed.

"We're going back to the survivors to give them some reassurance. Get your Aldis Lamp ready."

"Roger that."

Harley swung his plane back towards the survivors. The Corvette's bow was completely submerged now with her props and rudders high above the surface. She was on her way down. Lifeboats could be seen close to her as well. He circled around the corvette, as Jay flashed messages to them. Then they went to the other lifeboats, about a mile away, where the first sinking had occurred and flashed a message to them as well. Then Jay radioed the base to give them his best estimate of their position so that they could vector any friendly ships in the area to pick them up. Soon they received confirmation that there was a British destroyer in the area and that it was headed to pick up the survivors. Jay flashed that information to the two survivor groups and then they headed for home.

"I wish we had had a few more seconds with that sub on the surface. We would have had a better shot at him."

"I bet you one thing, though."

"What's that?"

"He won't be hanging around on the surface to admire his handiwork the next time he makes a kill."

"Damn right! Slippery little bastard, that Gerry. I won't miss the next time, I swear!"

When they returned to base they were met by their C.O., BAD. They saluted smartly. He returned the salute and said, "Good job men, you saved some lives today. The steamer that was sunk was the SS City of Manchester, on her way here to resupply the Island. She was escorted by the USCG Hamilton. All their crews are safe.

"Wish we could have gotten that sub, sir," Harley said.

"Don't be down upon yourself, Swordfish. Most of your colleagues haven't even seen a U-boat yet. Better luck next time."

The next day the survivors were dropped off at the Royal Navy Dockyard. Many of the crew were Bermudians, making a dangerous living at sea.

20

THE FREIGHTER AND THE CORVETTE

A SHARP, HISSING WHISPER from his hydro phone operator got Lehman's attention, "Kapitan, faint contact bearing 090 degrees."

"Number One, come right to bearing 090. All ahead two thirds. Battle Stations! Flood all tubes and open bow caps on tubes one, two, three and four for submerged firing."

"Aye Kapitan," then he repeated the series of orders.

Members of the crew who were not previously at their posts rushed around to man their battle stations.

After several minutes, the hydrophone operator whispered, "Contact getting stronger. Sounds like two ships, sir. Contact moving to 092."

"Number One, keep our bow on them."

"Aye, Kapitan, coming to course 092."

"Number One, come to periscope depth, all ahead one third."

"Aye Kapitan, periscope depth, all ahead one third."

Lehman jerked his thumb to the yeoman to raise the periscope, which he did. He then scanned the horizon 360 degrees. "I see them. Contact consists of one freighter protected by one corvette. We'll take the freighter and if the escort comes our way, we'll take her too, she's not fast enough to cause us much concern - about 17 knots. Number One, take the course bearings and set the attack plan." "Aye, Kapitan." Lehman yielded the periscope to the first lieutenant who went about his task in an efficient manner. Lehman usually would have done all this himself, but he wanted to train his officers in real combat situations. Most of them were, wet-behind-the-ears, fresh from the entanglements of their mothers' apron strings, and were totally dependant on his judgement and experience, not only for the success of their mission, but for their lives as well. This would be an excellent training opportunity. However, he kept a close eye on proceedings.

In order to torpedo a ship, a submarine commander had to solve a series of trigonometric calculations where the important inputs were estimates of the distance, speed and bearing of the enemy, as well as the angle the target was traveling relative to the sub. There were various analogue calculators on board that made these computations, but success depended on the accuracy of the estimates. The contact's speed was hard to measure. The faster the ship the harder it was to hit. Freighters were slow and lumbering, making them easy targets. Escorts were speedy and highly manoeuvrable and therefore difficult to hit. Lehman was comfortable with this corvette which he knew could only manage 17 knots.

After about one minute, the first lieutenant reported, "Kapitan, the boat is ready for firing."

"Very well, fire one!"

"One fired sir."

"Fire two!"

"Two fired, sir"

"Reload tubes one and two at once!"

"Aye, sir. Reload tubes one and two! Torpedoes tracking normally, sir."

"Very well."

Lehman and the other officers in the conning tower checked their watches. After many seconds, the time for the torpedo to hit the target arrived. A distant explosion was clearly audible. Then, after a few more seconds, another one. A murmur of satisfaction rippled through the crew. Lehman ordered, "Up scope!" He peered through the eyepiece. "Freighter has had her entire bow section blown off. She's going down. The corvette is doubling back at full speed, but from its course it doesn't seem to know exactly where we are. Come to course 185. Number one, let's put two in her as she comes across us."

The first lieutenant took over at the periscope, set the attack bearings and range on the corvette which was crossing from left to right in front of them. It was dropping ineffectual depth charges which could be heard on board as dull thuds.

"Kapitan, ready for firing, sir."

"Very well, Fire three!"

"Three fired, sir"

"Fire four!"

"Four's away sir."

They checked their watches. The time for the first torpedo to reach its target passed in silence. Some of the crew were muttering. Several seconds passed then there was the sound of an explosion. There was a cheer among the crew. Lehman checked the periscope, then ordered, "Surface!" U-66 surfaced and when the officers came out on the conning tower, they beheld the fruits of their endeavours. The freighter had already sunk but there were several lifeboats with survivors aboard. The corvette, on the other hand, had received a glancing blow: enough contact for the torpedo to explode, but her bow somehow didn't suffer the full effects of the blast. She was still underway, but her bow was on fire and starting to fall lower in the water.

"Prepare aft torpedo tube! In case that corvette manages to control the flooding," Lehman ordered.

"Aye, sir, preparing aft torpedo tube for firing."

Several minutes passed.

"Look, sir! She's dead in the water now! They're probably stopping in an effort to contain the flooding to keep her afloat."

After several more minutes the corvette's bow was getting lower and lower in the water and her rudders and screws were becoming visible. Lifeboats were being rigged out, as sailors abandoned ship.

"She's going sir."

Just then, they heard another sound. The sound of an aircraft!

116

"Enemy aircraft at 10 o'clock!"

"Alaaaaaaarm! Alaaaaaarm!" Screamed Lehman. "All ahead flank! Dive, Dive!"

All the men out on the tower jumped down the hatch which was secured by Lehman, the last one down. Many of the crew raced to the forward torpedo room, their added weight helping the sub to dive faster.

"Patrol aircraft overhead. Right full rudder, rig ship for collision! Secure all hatches and induction vents! Flood forward tanks! Switch to electric motors! All ahead flank! Bow planes to maximum down angle. Flood all tanks!" The aircraft was a Kingfisher. It had seen the U-boat and was vectoring in for a bombing run. Seconds seemed like hours as U-66 slipped beneath the waves. The enemy aircraft dropped four bombs on them. None were direct hits but exploded very close by as they hit the water. The deafening sound inside the sub made their ears ring, but the steel pressure tube held firm and was undamaged.

"Verdammt! Verdammt! Where the hell did that goddammed plane come from?" Lehman roared. "Did anyone see any other aircraft?" Lehman asked the lookouts that were on station.

"No Kapitan. We saw no other planes."

Lehman collected himself. "Very well, set your depth at 100 metres and speed at all ahead one third. Rig ship for silent running, just in case there are any other planes around. That one up there is out of ammo. Left standard rudder to course 360."

"I think that will be all for today, gentlemen. Number

One, you see the corvette's extra speed, even though it was only 17 knots, made her more difficult to hit. Imagine how difficult it is to hit a destroyer making 35 knots! Anyway, you got her. Good shooting! I'll be in my quarters."

The first lieutenant grinned and said, "Thank you sir." Then he repeated the captain's orders. U-66 disappeared into the deep.

21

AVIATORS' SHORE LEAVE

THE DREAD OF BERMUDA being a boring outpost was almost completely true. The GI's found island society to be rather prim and proper. There seemed to be few exciting nightclubs or rowdy bars where the guys could let off steam after the rigours of their duties. Hamilton, or "Town" as the locals called it, was relatively clean, safe and organized. But things were slow, partially because U-boat activity surrounding the island was having a restricting effect on shipping, particularly leisure passenger business. Since 1939 the US Neutrality Act barred American citizens from traveling in British-flagged or other warring countries ships. Therefore, ships like QTEV Queen and Monarch of Bermuda and the Canadian liners could carry no passengers to the Island from the States. Of course, there were plenty of sailors, aviators and marines around, but it was clear that the officials were too up-tight to openly provide the usual onshore pleasures available to the military that were to be found in Subic Bay or Honolulu.

Moreover, the US Army and Navy had agreed to abide by

the local Jim Crow laws. Therefore, there was a list of "Approved Establishments" that GI's were allowed to frequent and a list of "Forbidden Establishments" that were, well, prohibited. The approved list consisted of white owned establishments, while the forbidden ones were black owned. Of course, sailors weren't known to be always obedient when on shore leave.

One evening at chow, Jay said to SF, "I heard that there's a place in Town where there's some action."

"Really! Where'd you hear that?"

"One of the guys from VP Squadron told me about this place called The Grenadian Hotel. They've got booze and broads!"

"Deal me in," Harley said.

"Apparently, it's not on the approved list."

"Who gives a rat's ass about that?" Harley retorted.

"Roger that!"

Harley was not all that experienced as it pertained to intimate relations with members of the opposite sex. However, neither was he a virgin. There had been girls at high school and in Buzzards Bay, where his college was located, that assisted in his learning curve. His first encounter had been in the backseat of his friend's Chevy. He had fumbled around, and it was over almost before it had started. However, there was a girl named Harriet in Buzzards Bay who had taken a liking to him. While she was younger than him, she was considerably more experienced. She knew exactly what she wanted and how she wanted it, and Harley was eager to learn to be of service. And, as with all matters that interested him, Harley was a diligent student. He was sad to say goodbye to Harriet when he left to join flight school but, in his heart, he knew she would soon find another guy to take his place.

After the next patrol was over, he and Jay went looking for the Grenadian Hotel. After getting lost a few times, they turned east on Reid Street until they crossed Court Street and soon encountered the Grenadian. It had a somewhat ornate exterior and certainly didn't look run down. They climbed the stairs and entered the bar. The place was quite lively. There was a piano player, who also doubled as a singer, belting out the tunes popular Stateside. Most of the clientele were servicemen and all of the staff, male and female, were black. A large black man with a big, bushy moustache approached them with a smile and greeted them, "Welcome gents. I am always grateful to have US servicemen at my establishment. My name is Dick Grenadian, but most people just call me "Papa Dick." He beckoned them to the bar. They stepped up and ordered two drinks. Despite being a British territory, their US Dollars were gratefully accepted.

With a drink in his hand, Harley surveyed the place. As usual, the air was thick with cigarette smoke. In addition to the bar and the piano, there were several tables where servicemen, both British and American, were socializing with, what obviously were, local girls who were attractively, but properly, attired. He noticed one of the girls at a table got up, took a sailor by the hand and went through the door and up another flight of stairs. He glanced at Jay who gave him a knowing smirk. They ordered another round of drinks. After a few such rounds they took one of the tables. Two local girls appeared, seemingly, out of nowhere, and joined them. They were very friendly. By this time the two men were "feeling no pain." They ordered another round for themselves and the girls. The girl who was close to Jay was heavily made up and asked him for a light. He obliged and she gave him a broad smile. Her dress was cut low in the front, displaying her two best assets which, when she laughed, threatened to jump right out of that bodice. Jay couldn't take his eyes off them. Then she leaned in, put her hand between his legs and began caressing him. "Let's go upstairs flyboy." Jay was coherent enough to stagger up the stairs with her.

The other girl, the one with Harley, was no less sexy looking and was leaning close to him to give him a more intimate vantage point. Harley, for his part, started to hallucinate, and instead of seeing the girl in front of him he saw a vision of that brilliant smile and those liquid pool hazel eyes that had recently beguiled him. He tried to speak but the cat got his tongue—again... just before he passed out. Several hours later he awoke with massive pounding in his head and prodding in his arm. He fought the strong urge to throw up. Through the fog he recognized that it was Jay saying, "Come on man, we've got to get back to base. You been passed out here for hours!" Jay dragged his skipper to the door of the Grenadian Hotel, and they staggered out into the street toward the morning ferry.

22

SOMERSET BRIDGE

THE US NAVAL OPERATING BASE (USNOB) was now operational, so when the men were off duty, they got into town by catching the ferry at the nearby Somerset Bridge dock. On one such occasion Harley and Jay boarded the old Corona and noticed their friend Hooks in the wheelhouse. They clambered up to the wheelhouse which featured a steering wheel whose diameter was the height of an average man. In fact, there was a platform in the wheelhouse that the pilot had to stand on to see over it. After the usual pleasantries, Hooks said the next day was his day off and he was going fishing and invited the two fliers to come along. Jay, being a city boy declined, but Harley jumped at the opportunity, he wanted, in some vicarious way, to return to his own fishy roots.

"When and where?" Harley queried.

"Somerset Bridge dock - 5:30."

"You got it. Somerset Bridge at 05:30."

Early the next morning, before the break of dawn, Harley

rose and proceeded to the base gate. He persuaded the corporal there to give him a lift in the jeep to Somerset Bridge, which, in any case, wasn't very far. Hooks was already there in his home-made, cedar boat with an uncovered, beat-up looking engine amidships. There was no helm, just a tiller. The name painted on the transom was *Jezebel*. The boat was crude but sturdy. The craft was littered with a collection of different types of fishing lines, ropes, gaffs, hooks, nets and other fishing paraphernalia. Hooks waved him over.

"Mornin' mate, good day for fishing."

"You bet." Harley hopped on board.

Hooks pressed a button and the engine coughed and belched a cloud of black soot out of *Jezebel's* aft quarters, then started. There ensued a very loud clattering noise as it idled.

"Let go those lines and push off, mate," Hooks ordered, and Harley, recognizing that he was indeed the "mate" on this vessel, duly complied. Hooks moved the gear lever forward then gave her some throttle and the clattering noise grew even louder as they got underway—under Somerset Bridge and past the little adjacent anchorage, and the peninsular known as "Wreck Hill." They rounded Wreck Hill and headed out towards the reefs.

"Hooks, where'd you get this engine?"

"Oh, I got it from an old truck that the Royal Navy had thrown away because its axle broke. Me and my brothers took it off and put it in *Jezebel*. Had to make some changes to the cooling system but she runs pretty good. But I've got to be careful not to push her too hard because gas is scarce, and parts are even scarcer."

"Gas! What do you mean?"

"Well, you know, rationing, because of the war. Lots of stuff is hard to get these days."

"Man, we got plenty of gas on base, more than we need. I can bring you a Gerry-can from time to time for *Jezebel*."

"Thanks a lot. If we had gas we could go "out banks" and fish for some real big ones."

"Out-banks! What's that?"

"You Yankee byes don't know nutt'n' 'bout Bermuda, do you. You know Bermuda is on top of a mountain underneath the ocean - right?" Harley nodded. "Well, it's not the only mountain out here. There's two others sou'west of here. One about 14 miles out and the other 11 miles further. We call them the banks. Lot of real big fish out there. Cause of the gas it takes to get out there, we're sticking close to the reefs today." Harley nodded again; he had become quite used to the local accent by now.

Dawn was breaking, and Harley recalled the first time he had witnessed dawn in Bermuda waters. Nature's daily show still amazed and enchanted him. After an hour or so, Hooks cut the engine and they dropped anchor. There were coral reefs all around but directly beneath them the ocean was incredibly clear, with shafts of sunlight piercing the water, seemingly down to infinity. The men got to work with the gear, intent on harvesting at least some of nature's bounty. By 4 o'clock they had had a successful day. They restarted the clattering *Jezebel*, weighed anchor and headed for home. She was laden with a goodly number of rockfish, hinds and snappers. They had caught plenty of other types of fish, but they didn't have much commercial value, and Hooks either cut them up for bait or threw them back. Hooks had ice-chests onboard and the fish he wanted to sell were stored in them. Harley, as the mate, was assigned to gutting and scaling duties as they returned to Somerset Bridge. This so much reminded him of home, he was happy as a clam.

As they entered Ely's Harbour and were making their way towards the northern side of Somerset Bridge, Hooks said to Harley, "See those rocks?" Harley nodded. They're called Cathedral Rocks, cause they look kinda like a pipe organ of a cathedral."

"Oh yeah!"

There was a group of people ashore awaiting them— Hooks' customers. They all were very interested in his catch and he was able to sell it all, except for the ones he was taking home. After cleaning the boat and the equipment they moored *Jezebel* in the little harbour nearby, and took a punt back to Somerset island. Harley thanked Hooks for taking him fishing and was turning to make his way back to base when he heard,

"Where you goin' bye? Don't you want some of this-here fish?" Harley was surprised, he didn't want to impose, but Hooks was insistent. "Come over to de house, and we can have some fresh fish. Edith's a great cook!"

"Hooks, look, I don't want to impose. I mean, your wife's not expecting company so she might not be too happy for me to just show up unexpected. I don't want to cause any trouble."

"Don't worry 'bout that, bye. Edith's used to this-here, she'll be OK."

So, they took the relatively short walk over to Hooks' home. It was a small Bermuda stone cottage with white roof, of course, white walls and blue push-out blinds. Harley had never been to a local person's home before, so he felt honoured but was also curious. "So, Hooks, what's with the white roofs on Bermudian houses?"

"The white is lime and it helps purify the rainwater. See those gutters around the edges? They channel the water to that pipe. See it?

Harley nodded.

"That pipe takes the water over to that tank, see over there with the round top, there, next to the house?"

"Yeah, I see it."

"That's how we catch and store fresh water. It's pumped through the house by an electric pump."

"Oh."

"See that old-fashioned, galvanized, cube-type tank on a flat section of the roof close to the kitchen?" Me and Edith keep that old thing because electricity in the Somerset end of the island is still kinda unreliable and we use it as a backup. You can hand pump water from that outside tank over there up to the cube on the roof. Then you let gravity do the rest. This was how all Bermuda homes were before we had electricity. Got some other old stuff too. That chimney for the kitchen used to be for the old-fashioned wood burning type stove, but Edith managed to get a gas stove to replace it, so the kitchen chimney is still there doing nutt'n'."

127

Edith met them at the door.

"Edie, This-here's Lieutenant Harvey. We got a good catch today."

"Welcome to our home Lieutenant, Hooks has told us a lot about you." She welcomed them in with such ease and informality that it was clear that this was by no means the first time that her husband had brought home strangers to dinner unannounced. It turned out Hooks was right; Edith was indeed a great cook. Josh came to the table, still in his school uniform which was a bit grimy from the usual daily boyhood activities.

"Josh, have you washed your hands?"

"Yes, Mummy."

"Lieutenant, our daughter is still at work, but she'll be home later." Harley and his hosts enjoyed the dinner of fresh rockfish, mashed potatoes, carrots and mustard greens.

"You know, Harley, everything on the table is locally produced or caught. In fact, the potatoes, carrots and mustard greens are all from my own garden."

"Everything is delicious, Edith. I am so grateful to you for sharing your dinner with me."

He was overwhelmed at the generosity and hospitality of this local coloured Bermuda family.

He wondered if the roles were reversed, if his own family in Gloucester would have been so generous and welcoming to a foreign visitor of another race. He concluded sadly, probably not. As Edith was collecting the dishes, they heard footsteps on the outside steps, the rickety screen door opened and Edith smiled and declared, "Harley, this is our daughter Rebecca; Becky, this is Lieutenant Harvey from the NOB. He's a pilot." Harley turned and there in front of him was that dazzling smile and those liquid-pool, hazel eyes that had mesmerized him a while back, the same ones he couldn't get out of his mind. Again, the cat got his tongue.

She immediately did a double take and said with a quizzical smile, "I ... I remember you, you're the Maltese Falcon, I mean, you're the guy at the Maltese Falcon."

Harley was now totally embarrassed that she had remembered his foolish behaviour from their previous encounter and was sure he was now blushing. But sensing his distress, she quickly said to her parents, "The lieutenant came to see the Maltese Falcon at the theatre when I was in the box office. Nice to meet you lieutenant." She stepped forward and extended her hand and he awkwardly shook it. The sensation of that tender touch was something beyond description, sending Harley's mind into a temporary suspended animation. Realizing he was holding it too long he grudgingly let go. After what seemed to him like an eternity, he finally was able to speak, "Hi, please call me Harley."

And so it began. They chatted a while about the movies, Humphrey Bogart and whatever. For Harley, it seemed like time stood still. He was captivated by that smile and those liquid-pool hazel eyes. The rest of the world, the Navy, the war, even his beloved Kingfisher, were consigned to a parallel universe, a universe he had no desire to return to. Then they heard an aircraft pass overhead—on final approach, and it jolted Harley out of his reverie, back to the real universe. He realized it was time to go. He profusely thanked his hosts and took his leave. He walked all the way back to his barracks in the dark, illuminated only by the radiance of the smile of a girl named Becky. He kept saying to himself, "I can't believe that girl is Hooks' daughter! I've got to see her again!"

Later on, that evening Hooks remarked to his wife, "You know, I really like that bye Harley, real down to earth fella. He don't have no airs and graces like some of them other officers. And really knows 'bout fishin'. Man, he cleaned and gut those fish in a flash today. He can come fishin' with me anytime."

"Hmmm," Edith said thoughtfully. That American bye is totally, as the British sailors would say, "gobsmacked" by Becky, and there seems to be a chemistry between them, even though they just met. Rebecca doesn't seem to be fully aware of how much power her great beauty gives her over men. But of course, that only makes her even more attractive to them.

Edith let her mind wander. On the one hand, lookin' at the whole thing was amusing and delightful, on the other hand, it could be a big problem. This is a white American man! Bermuda is segregated, and from what I've heard, the States ain't much better. Interracial relationships are off-limits. It's not that interracial relationships between men and women don't happen on the island. Far from it. They very often do, but they are seldom, if ever, HONOURABLE relationships. They're mostly done under cover, on the side, on the sly, or under the implied threat of financial harm if you don't cooperate, or, strictly for money, like at the Grenadian Hotel.

Traditionally, Bermudian society has been separated by race. But it really ain't that simple: black versus white. And while there's overt racial segregation in most aspects of society, like restaurants, movie theatres, bars, clubs, hotels, employment and housing, there's a kinda class overlay on top of that. Like the Portuguese. In any other part of the world these people would be seen as white, as Portugal is, after all, part of Europe. But, in Bermuda they're treated almost as if they were black and they suffer many of the same indignities foisted on us coloureds. Even among the whites, military personnel, particularly those who are not commissioned officers, are also looked down upon by the Forty Thieves.

But Bermuda's so small, it's impossible to prevent an overlapping of these various groups. On the ferry service, for instance, there's no segregation, it's just physically impossible. Another area is sex. The most common location for interracial sex is in white homes. Many black women work in white homes as cooks, maids, nannies, even midwives. This was where the, "implied threat of financial harm if you don't cooperate," comes in. So, it's not that unusual for hanky-panky to take place between the white male members of a household and the domestic help. That's why we have so many biracial children (some acknowledged and others not). It also accounts for the wide variety of skin colour and facial features among coloured Bermudians. I hear Bermuda is a lot like the "Jim Crow" Southern States where, 'One drop of black blood made you black, no matter what you looked like.'

Edith was afraid for Becky. What if this American was

131

only interested in sowing his wild oats! What if he gets posted to some far-off place and abruptly leaves? What if he leaves my daughter in a lurch? All these thoughts swirled around in her mind.

Hooks noticed his wife's far off look and said, "What's the matter with you?"

"Oh, nutt'n'." She knew this was something that she could not talk to her husband about. He would tell her she was imagining things. Perhaps she was, but she was still worried.

23

THE CEDAR BENCH

THE DAY AFTER HARLEY HAD SHARED the catch of the day at their table, Edith was waiting for her daughter to come home from work. She was sitting down on an outside Bermuda cedar bench that had turned silver from weathering. Next to her was the family bible. Hooks was out tending to his jealous mistress, Jezebel, and Josh was doing his homework.

"Hi Mummy," Becky said brightly.

"Rebecca, we need to talk."

Becky knew that when her mother called her "Rebecca" she was in trouble. "What? What's wrong? What have I done now?"

"Come child, you're not in trouble, sit down, let's talk."

"You know, Mum, I'm not a child anymore."

"Yes, dear, I know, and that is exactly what I want to talk to you about. You're a young woman now and you have to find your way in a world that's full of dangers, especially for beautiful girls like you.

133

There are men out there that are attracted to you but have no other interest in you than to defile your body!"

"Oh, Mummy please!"

"It's true, Rebecca! I'm your mother and I'm worried about you." She reached over and picked up the bible and flicked through it until she found the passages she had book-marked. "Here, 1st Corinthians 3:16-17 says,

'Do you not know that you are God's temple and that God's Spirit dwells in you? If anyone destroys God's temple, God will destroy him. For God's temple is holy, and you are that temple.'"

She flicked to the next marked passage. "And Hebrews 13:4 says, 'Let marriage be held in honour among all, and let the marriage bed be undefiled, for God will judge the sexually immoral and adulterous.'"

"Undefiled! You know what that means?"

"Yes Mummy, but you know I don't let any of the guys I know interfere with me. You've raised me well. I've been a good girl and I've still not found the man I would want to marry."

"What about Lieutenant Harvey? I saw the two of you together last night. I saw how he reacted when you walked through the door. He's totally smitten by you, totally speechless; and you know it, don't you?"

Becky looked in her mother's eyes, then at the floor, a smile crept across her face, "Yeah, all right, he is. Well, what's wrong with that?" She said, defiantly.

"Rebecca, you're my only daughter, I can tell that you like him. My darling, this man is a white American! You're a black

Bermudian woman! There is no future for you with this man! Do you really think that, one day, he is going to come to that box office, dressed in his white navy uniform, and sweep you off your feet and carry you off back to the States—to Gloucester Massachusetts, to be his wife? Is that what you think? If you do, you've been watching too many of those Hollywood movies at the theatre. Do you really think his parents will be as welcoming to you, a coloured girl from the islands, as we were to him? Hmm?"

"Mummy, you always see the dark side of things! Who said anything about marriage or anything like that? I wasn't thinking about anything like that. He likes me, and I like that. That's all."

"Becky, that's never all. When these GI's are off duty, and stationed abroad to places like Bermuda, they've only got two things on their minds, women and booze, in that order. In Harley's case, when it comes to you, seeing that he's already quite taken with you, forget the booze, it's not just about women, it's about a particular woman -- you."

"Oh Mummy!"

"A lot of these white men just want to use us and throw us away when they're done."

"He's not like that!" Becky protested. Her eyes were starting to well up.

But Edith pressed on. "He's not uh, how do you know that? You hardly know him. I know of a few white men who've married black women they loved, a precious few. But what happened to them? They were totally shunned by their own white people. I know, there are a couple of 'em in St

David's. The whites in Town look at 'em like they're dirt!

My grandfather, your great granddaddy, was white—Irish. He hardly ever went into Town after he and Nana got married, it hurt him so much. He just stayed in St. David's or St. George's. So, I know what I'm talking about."

She couldn't stop now. "And what if your knight in shining armour is transferred to another base overseas? Is he going to take you with him, eh? He can't! Do you know that GI's are officially forbidden from fraternizing with coloured girls in Bermuda? Did you know that? They're not even allowed to go into bars or restaurants that are open to coloureds. They do it anyway, of course, but officially they're not supposed to.

And what about the Clap?" Becky wasn't exactly sure what the Clap was, but knew it was some kind of unspeakable disease. "You know sailors go to whorehouses, like the Grenadian Hotel, to satisfy their needs. Those girls carry all kinds of diseases and the men catch it. You want to catch that?"

Tears were rolling down both Becky's cheeks. "Mummy, why do you have to be so mean?"

"My darling, the real world is mean, not me. I'm your mother and it's up to me to force you to face up to the real world. You need to stay away from Harley before you get yourself into trouble."

Becky, sobbing loudly now, jumped up and ran inside. Josh came out to Edith, who was still on the bench. "What's wrong with Becky?"

"She'll be alright. You finished your homework?" He

nodded. "Then get to bed."

Edith felt sorry for her daughter, but she was relieved to have unburdened herself from these nagging concerns. However, there was still a lingering worry about Rebecca and the man from Gloucester, Mass. She was young once, and remembered how she used to fool her mother, or so she thought.

24

FIRST DATE

HARLEY COULDN'T STOP THINKING about Becky. He had to see her again. Since moving to NOB it was easy to get into Somerset Village—just catch the train from the White Hill train-stop and get off at the end of the line. It was a short walk to the theatre from there. On his next time off, he made his way to the little White Hill railway platform. He didn't tell his buddies where he was going, neither did he invite any of them to come along. This was a solo mission.

When Harley first arrived in Bermuda, he was curious about this train, so he and Jay rode it from end to end. The Bermuda Railway ran almost the entire length of the island, from St George all the way to Somerset. It consisted of a noisy, smoky, diesel engine pulling no more than three cars, one of which was for baggage, cargo and passengers' pedal bikes. He had also observed that, as private cars were not permitted on the island, there was no background noise from traffic. The absence of urban-type background noise allowed the ear to detect nature's sounds, sounds that would be drowned out by the blaring industrial creations of man. If he were anywhere near the south shore, he could hear the sound of the surf, Atlantic rollers hissing through the coral reef-line then pounding themselves to bits on pink sandy beaches. If not, the silence was only interrupted by the sounds of songbirds flitting through the trees, sparrows, cardinals and bluebirds, or wood doves cooing, or the chirping of longtails. Occasionally, he heard the squawking of sea gulls or crows. While exploring marshy areas he heard the call of egrets or the quacking of ducks, or on the rocky coasts, the croaking sound of the great blue heron or of storks. In certain other areas, usually those heavily wooded with cedars, the eerie sounds of thousands of tiny cicadas made the hairs on the back of Harley's neck stand up. Bermudians called them "singers."

When walking anywhere in the evening, the air was alive with the sounds of tree frogs, those diminutive amphibian creatures with oversized mating calls. On rare occasions, if you listened carefully, you could hear the beating of wings of the night hunters: owls preying on rodents. But the entire wonder of the sounds of silence and the sounds of nature would be obliterated by the sound of the Bermuda Railway. You could hear it miles away, roaring, rumbling, rattling and blaring as it approached. This evening, as he waited for the train, among the tree frogs and crickets, Harley was scarcely aware of any of these aural delights, his mind was on something else, or more accurately, someone else. He boarded the train. It had a first-class car, where whites and certain privileged blacks sat, and a second-class car where everybody else sat. Harley boarded the first-class car. The conductor sounded the horn, the engine roared, the beast shuddered and rattled and the short ride across the high trestle over the Somerset Bridge Inlet, past Hooks' house, along Somerset Island, around Fort Scaur, to the end of the line, began. The noisy little train afforded views of the Great Sound that were spectacular. It also passed through man made little narrow canyons that cut through the rolling hills. These canyons were so narrow that there was room for little else, as the train transited them. There one could notice the very essence of what Bermuda was made of: layer upon layer of sedimentary limestone, built up over the eons. But Harley didn't see any of this. His mind was on something else—someone else.

A short walk took him to the theatre and there she was in the box office. Her face lit up when she saw Harley. He looks so dashing in his uniform.

"Hi, Becky. It's good to see you. What's showing?"

"Casablanca, starring Humphrey Bogart and Ingrid Bergman. It's very good."

"Do you ever get to actually see these shows?"

"Sometimes. The box office usually closes about half an hour after the show starts. Most of the time I just go home, but sometimes I stay and see the show."

"You seeing the show tonight?

"No, I'm going home."

"OK, see you later."

"Bye Harley."

He went into the little theatre and checked his watch. The

minutes dragged by ever so slowly. On the screen, the newsreels were describing the horrors taking place in Europe and in the Pacific. It was slow torture. After 25 minutes he got up and went outside to the box office. To his dismay, the box office was closed down. My God, I've missed her! He thought.

As he was turning to go, he heard from behind him, "Harley, what are you doing out here?" He swivelled around and there she was. Like the first time he had seen her, her dark brown hair was drawn straight back into a simple bushy ponytail. But with a face like hers she didn't need any additional beautification by way of a fancy hairstyle. It was really the first time he had had a chance to look her over without the eagle eye of Edith watching him. She was dressed modestly, revealing no cleavage and with her hemline below the knee, but with the dress cinched at the waist with a belt, he could still tell she had all the womanly curves in all the right proportions. He also noticed the way she naturally moved—with the grace of a ballet dancer. The damnedest thing was, unlike most beautiful women, she didn't appear to be aware of her great beauty: there was no outward display of vanity, or flare for the dramatic, or coquettishness, as with many pretty girls he had encountered.

"I thought you were gone!" he managed to say.

"No, I just went to lock up the cash for the night. But what are you doing out here? The movie is just starting."

"Oh, I was bored. Anyway, I'm more interested in what's out here."

This time it was Becky who was embarrassed. She smiled

and looked away.

"How do you get home?"

"I walk. The train takes too long to come."

"Can I walk with you?"

"Are you sure, are you sure you want to walk with me?"

"I'm sure, if it's OK with you. I'll be an officer and a gentleman if that's what you're concerned about."

"No, it's not that. It's just that ... well..., sure, why not."

"Let's take the tracks," she said. She knew there would not be many people there this time of night.

"OK, sure."

They set out along the railway trail. The evening was still and quiet, with only the choir of hundreds of tree frogs filling the air with their intermittent peeps, beeps and cheeps. The air was suffused with the intoxicating fragrance of jasmine and night blooming cereus that were nestled in the overgrowth alongside the tracks. She felt so comfortable with him, as though they had been friends, or perhaps even lovers, from a former life. Then she remembered what her mother had told her about this man, and in fact, all GI's. They just want to use you and throw you away when they're done. Becky mentally shunted these admonitions aside, telling herself she had everything under control. She told him all about herself: her childhood, her family, her ambitions and dreams for the future. Her most fervent hope was to get off the island of Bermuda and see the world. She had never left the island and felt trapped. "I've got to get off this rock!" she told him. She had that indestructible optimism of youth and was confident that she could make it in the States or wherever she lived, as she was very good at figures and was prepared to work hard. The world she thought she knew was through the lens of a theatre projector; the movies and the newsreels looked so romantic, so grand, so exciting, albeit, so dangerous. She wanted to experience it, not just see it on the silver screen. To her, United States naval aviator, Lieutenant Harley Harvey, call-sign Swordfish, was the embodiment of that world.

For his part, Harley regaled Becky with all the aviation and sea faring stories he knew, and could make up, at short notice. It was incredible that they could be such instantaneous soul mates. They finally reached the Jones' residence, and as they said their good-nights their eyes met— his grey and hers hazel, and there was this overpowering gravity between them. They couldn't resist it if they tried— and they didn't try very hard. Harley took her hand in his. It was so soft and supple. As the gravity pulled them slowly closer and closer together, he gently stroked her cheek with the outside of his index finger. She was so beautiful. Becky shuddered as she felt his breath upon her face and closed her eyes. Their lips touched, lightly at first, then with more passion. Harley's tongue probed forward in search of hers and was eagerly accepted. Harley's loins went to red alert and Becky was melting inside. Then Edith's voice boomed in Becky's head and she pulled away, and ran off to the cottage, her heart pounding.

Harley started to frequent the movies very often, never taking his buddies with him. He had a constant aching desire for her. He would steal out after half an hour and walk Becky home. But they had to keep their relationship a secret. No one could know. They both agreed that Bermudian society, British society, and US military practice, would not approve. Harley didn't want to get in trouble with his C.O. and Becky didn't want to get in trouble with her mother. She rationalized it this way, I don't like disobeying or deceiving Mummy, but I have to see him. I just have to! Besides, Harley is a gentleman and I have everything under control.

One day after one of these clandestine dates, Harley took out his writing paper and pen. He had not always kept his promise to write his mother every day while deployed. In fact, it had been some time since his last letter, but this particular morning he felt moved to write home.

January 10, 1942

Dear Mom,

How are Dad, Hank and Harry? Things have been really busy here lately. We spotted a German U-boat on the surface, a while ago and dropped bombs on it, but it got away. It had sunk two allied ships and we were able to help the survivors get rescued. While I was angry at not getting the sub, I felt we actually made a difference in this war by saving some lives.

Life is still pretty slow onshore here in the island, as Bermuda society is very staid and conservative. But I have met a girl here named Becky who is very nice, and we have met at the movies a few times. I don't get much time off base but when I do, we often spend time together. Her dad is a fisherman, so it makes missing home a little easier to take. *I really hope you can meet her someday.*

Hope everything is good at home.

Love,

Harley

25

INCIDENT IN THE MESS HALL

HARLEY HAD BEEN SEEING BECKY for a few months and was sure that their efforts at complete discretion had been successful. But in a very small place like Bermuda, secrets were very hard to keep. Everybody notices everybody else. After all, in segregated Bermuda, a racially mixed couple would be something to gossip about. The nearby Somerset theatre was popular with members of VS32. On one occasion, when Harley was executing his early exit, another pilot, Richard Deerfield—callsign Buck—noticed his early departure, and remembered seeing it before. I wonder what Swordfish is up to? He followed Harley out of the theatre and saw him meet Becky. Well, well, well, he thought. One subsequent evening in the officers' mess there was a general discussion about the rather boring social life available to the men on shore when Buck wisecracked, "Swordfish doesn't have to worry about that. He is getting a taste of that local poontang every time he leaves the base!"

"Poontang!" Harley's head exploded. Now, Buck was a big

strapping man and wouldn't have been the kind of guy Harley would have considered picking a fight with, if he had given it half a thought. But that half thought had instantly been obliterated by the eruption of rage. Turning purple with eyes bulging, he sprang up from his chair knocking it backward and lunged across the table at Buck. There was instant chaos, shouting and "scatteraction." Plates, mugs filled with coffee, food and cutlery became missiles, flying about the mess hall, some shattering and others clattering on the concrete floor. He swung his fists wildly, most of them completely missing his target. Both men fell to the floor kicking, punching and screaming. Buck got Harley in a choke hold from behind, but Harley elbowed and punched his way out of it. He lunged at Buck again and they both went down. The two men roaring, kicking, punching and rolling around on the floor. Everybody else was shouting and screaming either their encouragement or disapproval. After this went on for what seemed like an eternity, the others finally pulled them apart.

The loud commotion attracted the attention of their C.O., Lieutenant Commander Bradley A. Davidson, call sign, "BAD". He stormed in the room and bellowed, "What the hell is going on here!!" By this time Harley had regained some of his composure. While he had landed a few blows of his own, he had sustained some damage to himself, a burst lower lip, a cut above his left eye and various bruises and scrapes to his elbows, shins and knees. Harley hung his head, still trying to catch his breath, "It was my fault, sir, I started it."

"Swordfish, put yourself on report! As for the rest of you, I will not tolerate any fighting in my squadron. I'll put the lot of you on report if I have to! Is that clear?"

"Yessir."

"Now clean up this mess!" BAD stalked out of the room, slamming the door.

They all looked at each other in shock. "Wow!" One of them muttered.

The next morning Harley was summoned before his commanding officer.

"Lieutenant Harvey reporting as ordered, sir."

"Swordfish, what in the hell has gotten into you?" He had a folder open on his desk. "I've looked at your record. You've never done this kind of thing before. Your flying proficiency is quite high. You're one of the squadron's best pilots. You could be in line for a promotion to bigger, multi-engine aircraft or even carrier-based planes."

"I'm sorry skipper. I apologize. It'll never happen again. I swear it."

"It better not, or else you'll be flying these 90 knot wonders for the rest of your career. You understand me, sailor?"

"Yessir."

"What started this anyway?"

"Well, sir...," Harley hesitated, "I'd rather not say."

"You'd rather not say!" roared BAD. "Boy, you'll say if I order you to say. Is that clear?"

"Yessir."

"Now, what's this about? Experience tells me that men

fight because of one, or a combination, of three things: women, money or power. And it is usually ignited by liquor. Now, I know you weren't drunk, and we can rule out power, and probably money too. So, this was about a woman?"

"Well, kinda, sir."

"You two fighting over the same girl?"

"No sir. It ain't like that."

"Well, it's like what, then?"

"Well, skipper," Harley was struggling to find the right words, "He referred to her as "poontang", and she ain't that kind of girl! Sir."

"So, he insulted your girl?"

"Yessir."

"So, where'd you get this girl from? They're hard to come by here on this here island, ain't they?"

Harley was really struggling now. Should he tell the truth and risk humiliation or make up some lie, but that risked being exposed as a liar and an untrustworthy officer, and, in wartime, only death was more terminal. Ultimately, with a sigh, he surrendered the truth. "Well, sir, she's a local girl— a coloured girl, sir."

BAD was taken completely off guard. He jerked back in his chair as though punched by an unseen assailant. He himself was an occasional patron of the Grenadian Hotel but he was sure this fracas couldn't have been about one of those girls. There was a long pause before he spoke.

"Swordfish, you serious 'bout this girl?"

"Yessir."

"You know, wartime is never a good time to get serious

about anything, except finding and killing the enemy. Does she know you could get posted halfway round the world, at a moment's notice, and that she would never see you again? Not to mention all the complications because of the fact that she is a coloured girl. Does she realize all this? What were you planning to do, take her back to the States?"

"I donno sir."

"Now, I don't make the rules, but you do realize that fraternizing with the local coloured female population is against the rules in this island, don't you?" Harley looked at the floor. "Look, your personal problems are none of my business, but it becomes my business when you bust up the mess hall and injure your shipmates. Now, I'm giving you a warning this time, Swordfish. You're a good pilot, but if you so much as lift a finger to anyone else in this squadron, I'll bust you down to seaman third class, and we'll see how you like cleaning out VS32's toilets. Do I make myself clear, Lieutenant?"

"Yessir."

"Dismissed!"

Harley, took one step back, saluted his C.O., turned smartly and left the room. He was perspiring so profusely that his shirt was soaked through. He knew he had just dodged a bullet.

Inside his cramped office, BAD fished out the schedule of the rotation for the various pilots and their patrols. He decided what Swordfish needed was more work and less down time. He changed the rotation to double Swordfish's time out on patrol.

INCIDENT IN THE MESS HALL

Perhaps, if I put him more in 'Harm's way' in the air, I can reduce his chances of getting in 'Harm's way' on the ground.

26

THE GARDEN PARTY

RADCLIFF KNEW THAT THE SECRET to his personal success had been dogged perseverance. *If I keep after her, I know she'll come around,* he told himself. Therefore, there was no way he was going to quit pursuing her even if Christine had tacitly dismissed him at the party. He sent her a bouquet of gladiolas the next day. Then, in about one week's time he dispatched a message inviting her to accompany him to a garden party being held by the Governor on the grounds of Government House. She was very curious when she received an envelope with, "Miss Christine Liverpool, Personal and Confidential." When she opened it, she said to her roommate, "Look, Mary, Ratcliffe has invited me to THE garden party! At Government House no less!"

"That's brilliant!" Mary exclaimed. "But you always laugh at the guy and think he looks like a rat. So, what are you going to do? Are you going to accept?"

"You're right. By rights, I should say no." Christine paused then grinned. "But do you see any other invitations to

Government House around here? I wouldn't miss it for the world. All the right people are going to be there!" She promptly sent a message of acceptance to the Commissioner. Then she said to Mary, "Come on then, let's figure out what I'm going to wear."

The next Saturday afternoon a shiny carriage, pulled by two magnificently groomed horses appeared outside the front entrance of the Bermudiana Hotel. The driver, in police dress uniform with brass buttons and buckles gleaming in the afternoon sun, smartly hopped off his seat and opened the door for the occupant inside. Commissioner Radcliffe alighted the carriage. He was sartorially resplendent in his dress uniform. It too, was gleaming and he could see his face in his highly polished black shoes.

The Commissioner strode into the lobby of the hotel and informed the clerk he had come to pick up Miss Liverpool. Many heads had turned at the appearance of such an important personage as the Commissioner of Police, particularly the way he was dressed. Gawkers in the lobby were waiting to see who he had come for. After a few minutes she appeared, perfectly dressed for the occasion. She wore a pale pink dress with white floral accents, snug at the waist and a flared hemline below the knee. Her seamed beige stockings complimented the white high heeled shoes which matched her gloves and handbag. Her classic look was enhanced by pearl stud earrings that matched the pearl necklace. Finally, a stylish white panama hat topped off the entire package. Little did the Commissioner know that Christine had cobbled this outfit together by poaching bits and pieces from about a half a dozen of her co-workers who were billeted with her at the Bermudiana.

"Good afternoon, Christine. You're a vision of loveliness," taking her gloved hand and kissing it.

"Why thank you, kind sir." She replied, beaming.

He took her arm and escorted her to the waiting carriage, and they headed for the garden party. There were murmurs of approval among the gawkers in the lobby, appreciative of the display of elegance in an otherwise routine, boring day.

Christine was right about "Anybody who was somebody," being at the garden party. Government House, the Governor's mansion, seemed straight out of a Rudyard Kipling storybook: a very grand place high on a hill, having spectacular floral gardens and wide outdoor stone stairs, flanked by balustrades that connected the multi-leveled lawns. There were also other miscellaneous entertainment facilities that made the setting perfect for such elegant and ostentatious social gatherings. The black serving staff, themselves resplendent in their white jackets and black trousers and bowties, scuttled about serving libations and delicious sweets. Radcliff introduced his date to all the "important" people of the day, including the Governor and his wife, of course, as well as senior military officers and members of the local oligarchy, their wives and consorts.

The music was being provided by the Bermuda Militia Artillery Band, who dazzled in their red tunics and gold braiding. As with everything else on the island, the army was also segregated. This band was from Bermuda's black army. They played all the popular tunes of the day, including

Christine's favourite, "A Nightingale Sang in Berkeley Square." She loved that song and they played it beautifully. There was the obligatory loyal toast, "To the King," given by His Excellency, of course, whereupon the band played, "God Save our Gracious King."

She spotted someone she knew, in conversation with a group of senior naval officers—Captain Grant. She knew that Radcliffe would not be pleased if she went over to talk to Grant, after she had dumped him before, so she played it cool. However, somehow, through the crowded hubbub, Grant spotted her, and he came over.

"Hello Christine, how nice to see you again. You look stunning! And Commissioner, how are things in law enforcement these days?"

"Hello, Captain. I'm pleased to say the island is safe as houses."

"Excellent. What a splendid setting His Excellency has here. Look at that ocean view!" Grant said with a sweeping gesture of his hand.

"Yes, indeed Captain. The view from up here is indeed marvelous! Bermuda has the best vistas I've ever seen." Christine gushed.

"Quite, but the best views of the island are from the water. Have you ever been out on the water, Christine?"

"Why no. At least not since I arrived on the flying boat."

"Perhaps you should go out sometime. I'm sure you'll enjoy it." He paused momentarily then bowed and said, "I'd better go. Have a good evening," he said with a charming smile. Then becoming more serious, Grant bowed again slightly and said, "Commissioner," and drifted off, knowing he had planted the seed in her mind.

"I find him most pompous, don't you?"

"Oh, yeah, he's quite posh, but interestingly so."

After a few hours of socializing Christine said, "Peter, my feet are killing me!"

"Of course, I'll bring around the carriage."

They returned to the Bermudiana just as elegantly as they had left, only a great deal more tired.

"Oh Peter, I've had a wonderful time. Thanks ever so much," and she kissed him on the cheek. Radcliff smiled and returned the kiss and bade her good evening, confident he had made a good impression.

27

PARADISE LAKE

A FEW DAYS AFTER THE GARDEN PARTY, Christine was deeply immersed in her duties when she received word that someone was in the Princess Hotel lobby to see her. When she got there, Grant was waiting for her.

"Oh, Captain, what a surprise!"

"Christine, you can call me Rodney, you know."

"I know, but 'Captain' suits you more. If you were Bermudian, you'd surely have a nickname, and I'm certain it would be 'Captain'. So, let's pretend you're not really a captain and that my nickname for you is 'Captain'," she said with a twinkle in her eye. "No, that's still a bit too formal. Hmmm, ah, I've got it, from now on you shall be known as Cappy. Is that alright with you?"

He was chuckling now, "Alright, alright, anything you say."

"So, Cappy, what are you doing here?"

"I've come to inquire if you're interested in seeing Bermuda from the water. I have a small boat, called Scapa, and I'd be delighted to show you around."

"Scapa? What kind of name is that?"

"It's named after the anchorage of the Royal Navy's Home Fleet: Scapa Flow, up in the northern reaches of Scotland. I served up there as a young man."

"You're not so old."

"Thanks awfully, that's the nicest thing anybody's said to me all day. So, how about it."

"Sure! When do we go?"

"How about tomorrow? Can you make tomorrow, 15:00 hours?"

"Aye, aye, Cappy," she replied playfully. "I'll get somebody to cover for me.

"I'll pick you up at the dock here at the hotel. By the way, can you make up a picnic basket?"

"OK, sure"

The next day Christine came down to the hotel dock and Grant was waiting alongside. He helped her aboard, fired up Scapa and headed through Two Rock Passage to the Great Sound. The warming sunshine glittered off the turquoise waters of the Sound. After several minutes Christine said, "Cappy, it's getting hot out here." And she started to disrobe, at least partially. She took off her long-sleeved, buttoned-to-the-neck blouse unveiling a tight, sleeveless tank-top that strained to contain her full breasts and showed off her smooth arms and shoulders. She jettisoned her skirt revealing a pair of shorts that displayed her long shapely legs. She put her head back, kicked off her shoes and basked in the afternoon sun. Grant looked at her, raised an eyebrow and smiled approvingly, and guided Scapa past the new American

Naval Operating Base giving Christine a running commentary as they went by. The little launch easily went under Somerset Bridge, past Cathedral Rocks into one of the island's most picturesque harbours—Ely's Harbour.

"The water's so clear!" Christine exclaimed.

They transited the small gap at Ely's Harbour's northern end and cruised around Somerset Island, past, but not under Watford Bridge, following Watford Island, then Boaz Island towards Dockyard. There was a narrow gap between Boaz Island and Ireland Island called "The Cut." A bridge spanned the Cut called Pender Bridge.

"Are you sure we can get through here?" Christine nervously inquired.

"Oh yes, I've done it many times before." The tide was high and Grant carefully guided Scapa through The Cut, past Cut Wharf, around to the marine entrance of Dockyard. There were several ships there under repair and he explained in enthusiastic detail the workings and activity of the Royal Naval Dockyard.

Grant then headed South East out of Dockyard toward a group of small islands in the Great Sound. Much to Christine's surprise there was a small body of water that these islands surrounded. "They call this Paradise Lake," Grant said. They dropped anchor there and broke open the picnic basket that contained sandwiches, a bottle of claret and some tasty cookies and cakes. They were entirely alone.

By the time they were finished, night had fallen, and Christine was starting to feel a bit chilly. Grant gallantly took off his jacket and wrapped it around her shoulders. "Better?"

He asked. She smiled and nodded.

He's such a gentleman—so refined!

There was still something nagging her, and she decided to try it again. "Cappy, Bermuda's a beautiful place to hide from the world isn't it. But out there," she gave a sweep of her hand, "There's a war going on. What are you hiding from? And don't tell me you're too old to fight, I won't believe it!"

Grant was taken aback by this young woman's perceptiveness and directness. He paused a moment then replied darkly, "You see, I fought in the last war, in the Battle of Jutland. My ship was struck by an enemy shell and it killed many of my crew, including many on the bridge standing right next to me. There were blood and human fragments everywhere, flesh, bone and brains all over me— the damnedest thing. Had ringing in my ears for weeks! Quite frankly I can't explain why I was spared. War is a grim and horrible business and once you've seen it up close, as I have, there's nothing romantic or heroic about it, and it's not something one feels inclined to experience again." He then adopted a lighter demeanour. "Besides, I've already done my bit for King and Country. In any case, men like me are obsolete. The technology in the modern Navy is so much more advanced from how it was in my day. Today it's about aeroplanes and submarines, things that barely existed in my time with the Service."

"You don't look obsolete; you look pretty fit to me."

"I'll take that as a complement." He grinned. Christine blushed. "You really want to get out there and man a machine gun or drop a bomb on Gerry's head, don't you?"

"Yes, I do, but instead I'm here in paradise reading other people's mail. Not my idea of combat."

"Perhaps not combat, but what you're doing here is of vital importance to the war effort. Instead of thinking of yourself as merely reading other-people's mail, you should think of yourself as a spy-hunter."

"Spy-Hunter! I quite like that!"

"They're everywhere you know," he said, furtively looking over both his shoulders in mock suspicion.

"Alright, alright, you win," she laughed, "I'd better be getting back, so I can resume my exciting spy-hunting tomorrow morning."

He restarted Scapa and headed for the Princess Hotel dock. When they arrived and he had secured the boat she said, "Cappy, I've had a wonderful time, thanks ever so much." And she puckered up her lips to give him a kiss on the cheek, but somehow her lips met his, instead, and he have her a long deep embrace which she gratefully accepted. She reluctantly disentangled herself from him and said breathlessly, "My gracious! Good night Cappy."

"Christine, I'd very much like to see you again."

"Me too." And off she went.

Grant returned to the launch whistling happily, loosened the lines and pushed off, returning Scapa to her mooring at the Yacht Club. He hadn't felt this kind of glow in his heart for many, many years. He went to the bar for a night cap. Sitting there alone his mood changed. He admonished himself. I must stay focused; I can't let this girl interfere with my vital work for the Third Reich. But she is involved in counterespionage against the Fuhrer. Perhaps I can pump her for some information about their operations. Perhaps the pumping will be better than the information. He allowed himself a smirk and ordered another stiff drink.

Christine returned to her room floating on a cloud. She gave her roommate, Mary, a blow by blow account of the entire afternoon and evening. As she climbed into her bed, the memory of Grant with the large mystery man and the burning paper flashed before her, and she creased her brow. I wonder what that was all about? She drifted off to sleep without an answer.

28

ELBOW BEACH

COMMISSIONER RADCLIFF, TRUE TO his life's philosophy, kept pursuing Christine Liverpool. He was confident that he could beat out that pompous aristocrat Grant for the lady's favours, so he invited her to dinner. He arrived in his carriage at precisely 6:00 to collect her. They proceeded to the Elbow Beach Hotel for an evening repast overlooking the magnificent beach. Copious consumption of wine loosened Radcliff's tongue and his curiosity and jealousy about her feelings for Grant spilled over into their conversation. "Have you seen that Captain Grant fellow lately?" He inquired.

"Yes," she replied without hesitation. "He took me out for a ride on his launch. It was wonderful!" Radcliff was now sorry he had asked. "He told me how awful it was for him during the last war. He almost got killed, you know."

"Hmmm, I hear he was quite the war hero," the Commissioner said with more than a small measure of sarcasm.

"It does not appear that he sees it that way. I would say

he's still traumatized by the whole thing. That's why he has chosen to stay out of this current war with the Germans."

"Really?"

"Yes, really! I'm afraid I had judged him too harshly by making him justify why he is not out there fighting or helping in the war effort in some other capacity. He said he'd already done his bit for King and Country." She paused for more than just a moment. "But there was one thing..."

"What's that?"

"Well, a little while back I was taking a smoke out on one of the balconies of the Princess and I saw the Captain and another bloke out on the dock. A big bloke—big and tall. He took a letter out of his pocket and gave it to the Captain. What was strange was that after he had read it, he took out his cigarette lighter and set it alight. When he couldn't hold it anymore, he dropped the remnant into the harbour. Isn't that strange?"

"I guess so."

"You know, he calls me 'a spy-hunter.'"

"Spy-hunter? You?" He said with a chuckle.

"Yes, me! What do you think we do at the Princess? Read people's mail for morbid curiosity? We're hunting for spies!" Even in his semi-intoxicated state Radcliff realized he had committed a misstep.

"Yes, of course, one could actually call what you do spy-hunting."

"Well, that incident is the sort of thing that spies do. Know what I mean? You know, secret orders that have to be destroyed as soon as they are read. You don't suppose our friend the Captain actually works for MI6?"

"You might be right. Did you ever find out who the big bloke was?"

"No, never saw him again."

"Well, if he is MI6, they would never tell the local constabulary. His Excellency probably doesn't know either, that's the way these things work. He's got a great cover — retired naval guy who says he's had enough of war and killing. Perfect!"

"So, Peter, you agree with me?"

"Why yes, Spy-Hunter, I think you may have a point."

"May?" She pressed him.

"Well, OK, you have a point." She smiled with great satisfaction. The truth was he would have agreed to anything she said. But the knowledge of the incident at the dock did make Captain Rodney Grant a much more intriguing character. Unfortunately for Peter, he was sure that Christine would find a British spy immeasurably more interesting than a policeman, even if he was Commissioner. But he wasn't going to give up. If it was one thing he knew, it was that persistence payed off.

The Commissioner of Police met with the Governor once per week to brief His Excellency on any matters that might come under his purview. 9:00am, the morning after dinner at Elbow Beach, Peter Radcliff found himself in such a meeting at Government House. The meetings were always short as the Commissioner usually had little or nothing to report. This morning was no different. Just before he was dismissed Radcliff said, "By the way, your Excellency, scuttlebutt has it that our friend Captain Grant may be MI6."

"Is that so? Any proof? Or is this just idle gossip."

"No solid evidence, just stories of burning letters before discarding the remnants into the ocean."

"Hmmm. You know, they'd never tell us about such things."

"Quite! If that's all your Excellency, Good day."

"Goodbye Commissioner."

Radcliff took his leave.

29

DINNER DATE

WHILE AT HER DESK IN THE DUNGEON, Christine took delivery of an envelope from the Hotel bellman. She opened it and it read:

My dear little Spy-Hunter,

Would you please do me the honour of being my guest for dinner at "Belmoral," 6:00 tomorrow. I'll pick you up at the Bermudiana.

Grant.

She was thrilled. She didn't know of any restaurant called, "Belmoral" but she was sure it would be posh. She immediately sent an acceptance note and again recruited Mary to help her figure out what to wear.

She appeared in the hotel lobby promptly at 6:00 and Grant was waiting. "Christine, you look smashing, as always."

"Thank you, Cappy"

She took his arm and they walked out of the lobby into the evening air.

"By the way, where is this restaurant called "Belmoral,"

and why have they misspelled it?"

"Why, "Belmoral" is the name of my house. You see, it's on Belmont Golf Course."

"Oh, my, very clever," she laughed. "And how are we getting there?" Looking around and seeing no carriage.

"Well, Spy-Hunter, just wait and see, come along." And he guided her down to Pitts Bay Road. When they reached the bank building, they turned right toward the Yacht Club. They walked through the club to the dock where Scapa was secured, and Grant said, "Voila!" He loosened the lines and they puttered off.

After he had helped her disembark at Belmont dock and they were walking up the hill she said, "Cappy, I didn't know you were a chef too."

"I'm not, but I have one of the island's best chefs, her name is Mavis and she has prepared a special meal for us this evening." Before they could open the door, Mavis greeted them and took Christine's wrap. She had the dining room table beautifully set with Grant's best silverware that he had brought from England. Grant poured the Sauvignon Blanc that he already had on ice.

After the main course, which featured local rockfish, cooked to perfection, Grant declared, "Mavis' specialty is dessert and she has created something special for you this evening." Mavis appeared carrying a culinary creation that was aflame."

"Oh my!" exclaimed Christine. Mavis cut it and served it to the two of them and disappeared into the kitchen. After about fifteen minutes, she poked her head through the door and politely said, "Captain, I'll be leaving now, Goodnight madame."

"Goodnight Mavis. Thanks for a wonderful meal." Turning to Grant she said, "You're a very lucky man to have her here."

"Yes, I know. Can I get you an after-dinner drink?"

"Yes please, I'll have some Black Seal, if you have it."

"Coming right up."

They took their drinks out on the balcony overlooking the Great Sound. There wasn't much to see due to wartime black out protocols, but the starlight enabled them to see dark shapes surrounded by black water. The fragrance of jasmine and the beeping mating calls of hundreds of tiny tree frogs were the perfect background for a romantic evening. Grant turned to her and kissed her lips, a long, deep, delicious kiss. She put her arms around his neck and kissed him back. "Cappy, you really know how to show a girl a good time."

"Spy-Hunter, you don't know the half of it. But in order to get your full designation as, 'Spy-Hunter Emeritus,' you will have to undergo a thorough physical examination," he said with a wickedly playful look.

"Really? How thorough?" She said coquettishly.

"Very."

"Oh, Cappy!" She giggled.

Whereupon he reached down, and with a single motion, swept her off her feet and carried her into the bedroom, passionately kissing her the entire way. The examination was indeed thorough and long, the Spy and the Spy-Hunter uncovering the secrets of pleasure, instead of those of the state.

30

THE KEY

GRANT'S INTELLIGENCE GATHERING about the UK and US navies and merchant marine shipping activities in Bermuda had now become routine. In his estimation he had mastered the art of dispatching short concise messages U-boats would find useful.

Grant had his breakfast and had taken the ferry to socialize with his mates at the Yacht Club. Back at Belmoral Mavis was sweeping under the Captain's desk when she noticed a key lying on the floor. Where'd that come from? With great effort, as she was a very plump lady, she knelt down to investigate. Peering under the desk, she could see that the key had fallen down from its hiding place, under the desk, where the Scotch Tape was still there, but with one end having succumbed to gravity.

This must be the key to that cabinet the Captain always keeps locked. I wonder what's in it.

She knew that the Captain was paranoid about privacy and that she shouldn't open it, but curiosity eventually got the better of her. She went over to the cabinet in the pantry inserted the key and opened it. There she found an assortment of papers, but what really caught her eye was an electronic device—a radio, and a fancy typewriter.

I guess the Captain likes to listen to overseas radio stations. What's all the cloak and dagger about a simple radio and a typewriter? Bleddy Englishmen!

For her, all radios were receivers. The thought of a transmitter never even crossed her mind. She re-secured the cabinet, replaced the key and resumed her chores, totally nonplused about her discovery.

Grant returned at about six o'clock. Mavis had supper ready and waiting for him and he polished it off. Retiring to his study, he took out a piece of stationery and started to write a letter of thanks to a local hostess who had entertained him to dinner a few days before.

Mavis noticed him writing and, without thinking, said, "Cap'n why don't you use that fancy typewriter you've got to type that letter?"

"I beg your pardon?"

Mavis realized she'd let the cat out of the bag. "Pardon me Capt'n, but I thought you could save yourself a lot of trouble if you used a typewriter, you know, instead of writing it out."

"Of course, jolly thoughtful of you, Mavis." Grant, always cool in a crisis, turned back to his writing. Mavis, feeling embarrassed, quickly left the room and went to clean the bathroom.

Grant felt under his desk, the key was there, but the

situation was crystal clear.

It's either her or me!

He went into the kitchen and selected the heavy cast iron skillet and walked to the bathroom with it behind his back. She was cleaning the tub. She heard him behind her and turned her head over her left shoulder.

Grant unleashed a fearsome blow on the woman's skull causing her to stumble forward. She looked up at him with stunned astonishment, her facial expression begging the question, Why? As he wound up for the next blow, he saw her expression turn to terror. Before the hapless woman could scream, he unleashed two more vicious blows with the iron weapon, this time turned on its edge. The final one, the coup de grace, cracked the poor maid's skull. She slumped over the bathtub bleeding profusely from her head. He checked her pulse—she was dead.

His mind was racing. How would he dispose of the body? If he could get it onboard Scapa, he could dump it overboard. But she was so big he couldn't even drag, much less carry all that bulk down to his launch by himself. There was no alternative, he would have to dismember the body into pieces to make it more manageable.

With great effort, he bundled the body into the cast iron bathtub. He was already perspiring profusely. He went to the kitchen, donned Mavis' apron, fetched some knives, then proceeded to the shed and retrieved a carpenter's saw, a hacksaw and some other carpenters' tools, and returned to the bathroom to carry out his macabre task. With the saws, he removed all the limbs and head from the body. He tried to allow as much blood as possible to drain into the tub to lighten the weight. Her torso was still too heavy to move. However, there was plenty of fatty tissue that could easily be removed. He employed a sharp carving knife for this task.

He was fatigued from his evil toils, but he knew he had to get rid of the evidence before her family missed her and came asking questions. After 1:00 am he had managed to assemble five grisly packages wrapped in canvas. He passed by a full-length mirror in the bedroom and saw his reflection. He looked like a Devon slaughterhouse worker, with blood all over him, except the blood was not bovine, but human. A surge of self-loathing swept over him.

Then he checked himself. This is about survival! He looked outside, there was no one around. He dragged the heaviest package, the remnant of the torso, down the hill to the dock where he had Scapa alongside, bundling it over into the launch. He was perspiring even more profusely now, but his survival instinct had long taken over his mind and adrenalin was fueling energy throughout his body. At 1:45, after finding some stones to weigh the body down, he fired up Scapa's engine and headed out through Eastern Blue Cut to dump the evidence of his murderous activities.

He returned just after daybreak and cleaned up the scene of the crime. At 6:30 he heard a knock on his door. It was Arny, Mavis' husband. "Excuse me Cap'n, but Mavis didn't come home last night. Do you know where she is?"

"Why no. She's not at home?"

"Nosir."

"She didn't come in yesterday, so I thought she might be

feeling ill. What in the world could have happened to her?"

"Dunno, Cap'n. It's not like her to just disappear like that. I'm really worried."

"Look, Arny, you'd better call the police, and see what they can do. I know this must be awful for you, old boy, but I hope she turns up soon. Please let me know when she does. On second thought, I'll speak to the police myself to make sure they look into it promptly."

"OK Cap'n. I 'preciate it."

Arny left, a very worried man.

Grant decided it was too soon to call the police. He would let some time pass first.

Inwardly, he was remorseful about Mavis. She was a good and faithful servant, but she poked her nose into his clandestine business and had to pay a terrible price. In Grant's twisted mind, poor Mavis was merely a casualty of war.

Arny believed that Grant would follow through on his promise, but he was not about to leave the disappearance of his wife entirely to Captain Grant. He knew that Mavis loved her family above all else and would never abandon them without as much as a word, or a note or some message to let them know she was alright. He was sure something terrible had happened to her, he just didn't know what. He walked down the hill to the Belmont dock and waited for the ferry. Soon the Frances approached, and he boarded her after she came along side. He knew Hooks Jones and that he was Frances' regular pilot but noticed that Hooks wasn't at the wheel on this occasion.

He made his way to Police Headquarters on Parliament Street, directly across from the Parliament Building. It was an old, bleak looking structure that had been neglected over the years. Inside was dark and stark—a most unwelcoming room. At the far end was a wall with a single teller's wicket type window protected by iron bars. The sign above it read, "Inquiries." The duty officer was Constable Andrew Williams, originally from Wales. He saw Arny enter the room, looking somewhat uncertain what to do. "You there! What are you doing here?"

"Oh, um ... um, I want to report that my wife is missing. I think something terrible has happened to her."

"Missing? What do you mean missing? How long has it been since you last saw her? What happened to her?"

The rapid series of questions momentarily wrong-footed Arny, but his rising anger at the policeman's attitude and tone helped him to quickly refocus. "My wife's name is Mavis Simmons and she left home early yesterday morning for work at Cap'n Grant's house. She's the maid and cook there. Nobody's seen her since. I've just come from the Cap'n's house and he said she never showed up for work. And she never came home. It's just not like her."

"Mr. err ….."

"Simmons, Arny Simmons."

"Yes, Simmons. Did the two of you have an argument or disagreement or something of that sort? Perhaps she went to stay at a relative or friends."

Fury was welling up inside Arny and was about to erupt. But he knew the kind of justice frequently meted out to blacks would descend upon him if he exploded at this English cop. He fought to get his anger under control, the inward struggle playing out all over his face. P.C. Williams noticed it and decided that this man's complaint ought to be taken seriously. "Look, Mr. …err Simmons, let's calm down and fill out this Missing Person's form. OK?"

Arny gulped and replied, "Yessir."

After a long list of tedious, irritating and seemingly useless questions, the form was complete. Arny signed it and turned to leave.

"I hope she turns up soon. If not, check with us in a few days."

"Thanks, I will."

He left and made his way back to the quarry. P.C. Williams filed the missing person's report along with the other paperwork that would cross the desk of his superior the subsequent day.

31

EQUIPMENT UPGRADE

RODNEY GRANT KEPT TO HIS SCHEDULE. He carefully wrote down everything he saw of interest to his Kriegsmarine handlers: all movements of ships and aircraft, both numbers and types. He could see everything from the balcony of Belmoral. Sometimes there was little to report but other times, like the arrival of certain of His Majesty's ships, or that of the US Navy, he had very important intel.

The challenge he had was that he couldn't report everything because it would make his transmissions too long, something that hugely increased the chances of him being discovered. He was fully aware that both Allied Navies had direction finding radio receivers and lengthy radio messages from him would give them a chance to triangulate his position. He also understood that the penalty for espionage was death. So, he had to distil his messages down to the essentials before he encrypted them and sent them off. Of course, it was Grant who decided what was essential and what was not, but as a former naval officer, he was perfectly qualified for such an assignment.

For two months everything went perfectly. Then, one evening in January 1942, instead of receiving a version of "Message Received" from a nearby U-Boat, he received a very long missive. He wrote down the dots and dashes then turned to his Enigma Machine to decode it. It took some time. When he had completed the decoding, Grant's blood ran cold. The Kriegsmarine were upgrading their communications' security. The upgrade required an upgraded Enigma Machine. The system required all Enigma machines to be identical, otherwise it wouldn't work. Therefore, he had to get a new machine. With both the Americans and the British navies now having active naval bases in Bermuda, the gambit of passing the machine off as a typewriter was surely not going to work again. Therefore, the situation required the new Enigma Machine to be delivered by submarine and for Grant to rendezvous with the U-Boat to make the exchange.

He knew the risk of blowing his cover would escalate many fold. On top of that, a great number of things could go wrong with this exchange. The Germans had given him the responsibility to choose the time and place of the rendezvous. He had to strike a balance: too close to the island risked discovery or the sub running aground, too far from the island risked the rendezvous failing altogether due to weather conditions and navigational errors. There was a deadline for the communications upgrade which meant it had to be done in February, a month notorious in Bermuda for foul weather.

He chose three alternative dates when the U-Boat could surface and wait for him for an hour, at the most. If there were Allied ships or aircraft in the area, the sub would abort the mission for that night. If they didn't make contact, or if the weather was unsuitable, the sub would be required to submerge and return on the next appointed night and time.

Grant checked his lunar calendar for February. He needed the darkest of nights. With typical naval precision and thoroughness, he selected three dark, moonless nights in February before the deadline for the new Enigmas went into service. Then he transmitted the details of his plan to some unseen listening ear in the Atlantic.

A few days before the first rendezvous date he made sure his little launch was in tip top condition and fully fuelled. He would keep Scapa close to him during this February.

On the first night he set out at about 11:00pm with his navigational equipment, including his trusty sextant and a chart of Bermuda waters, plus notes he had made of bearings he needed to take to navigate the reefs. He took some fishing gear, just in case he had to make a case that he was going night fishing. He also had his binoculars and his foul weather gear. It was cool, and the breeze was from the northwest. He had a choice of swinging around the Royal Navy Dockyard or cutting under Watford Bridge. He decided to avoid the Dockyard and cut through Watford Bridge. He took a bearing on King's Point, then Daniel's Head and Commissioner's Point, all were so close that they were still visible in the dark. These bearings enabled him to reliably head for Eastern Blue Cut.

The weather was breezy but not intolerable. Once he was outside the northern reef line, he took out his sextant, steadied his feet on the rolling platform that was his launch and took a few star shots—a real art-form. He went into the boat's small cabin, so that the light could not be seen from shore, took out a small flashlight and studied his charts, and then set off to the rendezvous. After proceeding for a predetermined time, he would take another star shot to see where he was. Eventually, he was satisfied that he had reached the rendezvous point. He cut the engine, listened and waited.

The appointed time came and went. Grant cursed under his breath, realizing that this meeting was a bust. He restarted his engine, set off in a southwest direction towards Eastern Blue Cut. When he got closer to land, he saw a warship in the channel. Even though the channel markers were not lit, due to the wartime blackout, naval vessels still transited the channels at night. He could clearly see what looked like a Royal Navy destroyer slowly picking its way through the channel.

He realized that his U-Boat must have heard the sound of the propellers from that vessel before she entered the channel and was scared off. He would have to try again.

The second appointed evening arrived, but it was a typical February night, cold, rainy and a howling northwest gale. Grant gazed out of the window of Belmoral and he couldn't see a thing. There was just the beating of raindrops against the glass and the shrieking wind. Another bust! He said to himself.

Time was running short, he only had one more chance to

make the rendezvous or his time as a German spy would be over. He also had orders for that eventuality. He would have to destroy all the evidence, meaning the old Enigma Machine, the radio transmitter and all the code books and instructions.

When the third appointed evening arrived, Grant was encouraged to observe that it was a beautiful night, cool, calm and clear. He followed the exact procedure that he had performed on the first occasion, passing under Watford Bridge, taking his exact bearings and then transiting Eastern Blue Cut out into the deep. Repeating the celestial observations that he took on his first trip, he arrived at the rendezvous point. He kept his engine in gear at idling speed and waited. He knew a submerged submarine could hear his propeller although nobody else could.

The time came, and Grant repeatedly surveyed the horizon with his binoculars. In the starlight there was nothing, everything was black. Time dragged on. It was so quiet. Then the silence was broken by the sound of bubbling. He scanned the ocean with his binoculars and soon picked out the shape of a surfacing submarine dead ahead. Water streamed from her black hull, glistening in the starlight. He heard her growling diesels start up.

He gunned Scapa's engine, giving it full throttle. As he approached the sub, he could see three men on the conning tower, two with binoculars to their eyes, looking straight at him, and the third with what looked like a machine gun. In a few short minutes he came alongside the U-Boat and cut his engine. He hailed the officers in the tower, using a prearranged keyword, "Wunderbar." One of the officers descended from the tower with a box wrapped in waterproof cloth and handed it to Grant who gave the sailor the old Enigma. He said nothing else and Grant pulled his launch away from the sub at full throttle towards the Southwest. He looked back and the U-Boat was disappearing beneath the Atlantic swells.

Grant was elated that he had achieved his objective without being observed and it was only then that he could appreciate the celestial grandeur above his head. It was magnificent.

He returned through Two Rock Passage, turned to starboard, past Hinson's Island to his mooring next to Belmont Ferry Dock. Constantly looking around him he saw no one, all was quiet. He then grabbed his prize, the new Enigma Machine, and walked up the hill to Belmoral.

"Not bad, mate!" He muttered to himself, in typical British understated style.

32

NIGHT FISHING

Hooks enjoyed night fishing for a number of reasons: for the solitude, to keep his night-time navigational skills up to scratch, and of course for the good fishing. Fish were more active at night, so it made the fishing better, albeit more challenging. He would take his clattertrap Jezebel out beyond the reef line to fish, "Off de edge", as he called it, meaning on the outer slope of the Bermuda seamount. The edge was quite close-in off the southern coast but was eight to ten miles off the northern and north western sectors of the island.

One such evening in February 1942, he took *Jezebel* out through the narrow channel close to the jagged outcropping known as North Rock to try his luck off the northern edge. Uncharacteristic of February weather, usually a stormy month, the evening was calm, and the only movement was the rise and fall of the Atlantic swell. The night was cool and moonless, but the clear cool air afforded a wonderful heavenly display of the billions of stars of the Milky Way, seemingly flung diagonally across the celestial dome of the night sky. Under this starlight he could barely make out the faint dark silhouette of the island, under war-time black-out protocols.

He was letting *Jezebel* just drift. He had had only a few bites on his line, but patience was required in the art of fishing. There was total silence except for the occasional lapping sound from *Jezebel* as she easily negotiated the swell. He reckoned that he was about 15 miles offshore.

Suddenly, he became aware of a low grumbling, throbbing sound, at first very faint but growing louder and louder. He searched 360 degrees of the horizon but saw nothing but blackness. The sound persisted, and Hooks was wondering if that shot of rum he'd had before he set off was affecting his brain. The noise had ceased growing louder and was receding a little now, indicating that whatever it was had passed him by. But no sooner did that happen then the grumbling was replaced by what sounded like bubbling.

He thought it might be humpback whales, as their migratory path would take them through Bermuda waters this time of year. Although they never sounded like this.

He swung his head around to see if he could match a sighting with the direction of the sound. Then, as he did so, he saw a disturbance in the ocean about ½ mile away. Something was indeed bubbling over there.

It must be whales!

The bubbling sound grew louder as the bubbles grew bigger. There emerged from the deep a terrifying black shape, surrounded by more bubbles. The mysterious undersea creature was revealing itself. Hooks had never seen anything like this before.

This ain't no whale!

It was black, alright, like a whale, but very long and low and clearly not one of The Almighty's creations. It was a few minutes before Hooks, with his mouth agape, realized that, That-there's a Nazi U-Boat! And what was it doing surfacing like this, so close to the island! What if air patrols spotted it? ….Nah, ain't nobody goin' to see it in this darkness.

The U-Boat sat dead in the water, just waiting. After the bubbling ceased, it grew silent again, except for the dull grumble of the U-Boat's idling diesels. Hooks then heard another sound, the distant put-put sound of a small boat. This new sound was growing louder, and he finally spotted it as it approached.

Someone in Bermuda is meeting a German U-Boat! Hooks thought. Jingas! What am I lookin' at here?

He was already sitting down next to the tiller of *Jezebel*, but he instinctively hunkered down as low as he could to avoid being seen. In any case, *Jezebel*, being small, low and dark coloured, was very hard to see at night. Nobody from Bermuda is supposed to be rendezvousing with a Nazi submarine in the dead of night. I'm just a simple ferry boat pilot, but I know treason when I see it!

The little unknown craft puttered up to the U-Boat and came alongside. Hooks strained his eyes to see if he could recognize the little vessel, as he knew most of the boats and their owners on the island. But it was too dark to tell, he couldn't make it out. He didn't own a telescope or binoculars;

he had never needed one until now.

He could see a man climbing down from the sub's conning tower then giving something to the person in the boat. The put-put then pulled away and headed west - southwest. The U-Boat immediately got underway and started to dive. In a minute it had vanished. Hooks could still hear the mystery boat retreating in the distance.

Who was that?

In a flash of insight, Hooks was sure where the mystery boat was headed, she's headed for De Gap—Eastern Blue Cut! Hooks reckoned that he might be able to close on that boat to see who the driver was if he could head back through the North Rock Channel and make for Spanish Point. From there he might be able to get a closer look if the boat came around Commissioner's Point, but he still might be able to get close enough to identify the craft even if the mystery boat came through Watford Bridge.

He fired up *Jezebel's* clattertrap engine, praying that the mystery boat was far enough away so that he couldn't be heard. He pushed the throttle lever ahead full. The noise on board was deafening. He passed by North Rock and headed directly for Spanish Point. *Jezebel* was showing the strain from being at full speed for so long. Smoke was pouring from the mid-section of the launch instead of from the stern exhaust pipe. Hooks pressed on, he would tend to *Jezebel's* wounds later. He didn't have to worry about coral reefs because *Jezebel* had a shallow draft, and although she was no speedster, he was taking the shorter route.

When he approached Hog Fish Beacon, just off Spanish

Point, he slowed *Jezebel* down to dead slow and strained his eyes. There was no sign of the mystery boat. He slowly headed across the Great Sound to see if his quarry had come through Watford Bridge. He couldn't risk being heard. Of course, if the mystery boat was not headed for the Hamilton Harbour area, he wouldn't see it at all.

He pulled close to one of the tiny islands in the Great Sound to reduce his visibility and turned off his engine listening intently. Nothing. Maybe the mystery boat really didn't come from the Harbour area and was long gone by now, safely nestled in some safe anchorage like Ely's Harbour or Somerset Bridge. Or maybe *Jezebel* was just too slow, and it had already passed by. He had given up and was just about to start the clattertrap when something caught his ear. He froze, listening as hard as he could. Yes, there it was, he could hear the steady put-put that he had heard and hour or so before. Again, he tried to directionally align his ears and his eyes. Then he finally saw it. It was a long low launch with a cutty-cabin. *Jezebel's* own silhouette was absorbed in the islet she was close to, making her invisible.

Hooks kept staring at the dark low shape trying to I.D. it. It looked very familiar, but he couldn't quite place it. Then the proverbial light went off in his head. The mystery boat, the vessel that rendezvoused with the Nazi U-Boat was that of Captain Grant, Scapa. Hooks did a double take. This is impossible! Grant's a bleddy British war hero! It must be someone else using his boat!

It was making for Two Rock Passage towards Hamilton. But just after it transited Two Rock Passage, it turned to starboard and headed through the little channel west of Hinson's Island, straight for the Belmont Manor Hotel.

Hooks waited until Grant's boat had passed by, started up *Jezebel* and followed it but used the islands in Hamilton Harbour as cover. He hugged Hinson's Island and saw the man attach the boat to a mooring close to Belmont Ferry Dock, take a punt to the rocks, and pull it up, then walk up the hill to the Belmont Manor golf course. It has to be Captain Grant—can't be anybody else.

33

150 METRES BENEATH THE ATLANTIC

U-66 WAS IN BERMUDA WATERS once again. Kapitänleutnant Lehman was not at all pleased with his mission. He was tasked with delivering a new Enigma machine to their agent on the island of Bermuda. He would have preferred to be engaged in his favourite pursuit, hunting and destroying enemy shipping. This was the dangerous game that he found most exhilarating.

But he was tasked with being a lowly delivery boy. Couldn't his masters find another way to deliver this device to their agent? He wanted to just get it over with, so he could get back to the hunt. But he realized that their agent in Bermuda was valuable. The island was a key staging ground for both British and American ships and the knowledge of what ships were in Bermuda gave him and his other U-boat comrades a distinct tactical advantage. They could wait for these ships to set sail and pick them off when they came out, as he had done before.

However, the memory of that close call with the American scout plane a while back, which was probably based in Bermuda, was foremost in his mind. Therefore, his approach to Bermuda for this rendezvous would have to be done with extreme caution and utmost stealth.

This was his third attempt to make this exchange. On the first appointed date, when he approached the pickup point his hydro phone operators detected the sound of propellers of a ship with twin screws making slow turns. Lehman thought that the probabilities favoured it being a warship, so he decided, out of caution, to scrub the rendezvous.

The second attempt was ruined when they discovered that it was blowing a gale on the surface, making any rendezvous with anything impossible.

This was to be the final attempt.

He checked his watch, then strode into the next compartment and demanded that his navigator show him their current position on the chart. Then he turned to the hydro phone operator and asked, "Any contacts?"

"Nein Kapitan."

He checked the large green and white dial that read, "Tiefenmesser wasser," the depth gauge, it read 150 metres.

"Number One, reduce speed to three knots. We don't want to get there too early, and we'll be quieter."

"Aye Kapitan. Reduce speed to three knots." The whine from U-66's electric motors diminished in pitch to a dull moan as she crept toward her night-time rendezvous.

The boat was at maximum stealth. Any slower and he would not be able to keep her submerged.

After a period of time Lehman ordered, "Number One, come to periscope depth."

"Aye Kapitan, periscope depth."

The needle of the depth gauge began to move counter clockwise, as U-66 slowly rose from the depths to periscope depth. Groaning sounds reverberated throughout the sub as the steel hull was released from the vice-grip of the crushing water pressure of the deep.

"He whispered to the hydro phone operator, "Any contacts?"

"Nein Kapitan."

"We are at periscope depth, Kapitan," the First Lieutenant muttered after several minutes.

Lehman gestured to raise the periscope, then he put his eye to the lens eyepiece. He then swivelled around a 360-degree arc to look for anything on the surface that might have been lurking. There was only blackness. He gestured to lower the periscope.

After several minutes, returning to the plot, he shot a demanding look at the navigator. "We are at the rendezvous point, Kapitan."

Lehman gestured with his thumb to raise the scope again. He took another 360 degree sweep of the horizon. Even though he knew he was relatively near the island, he could see nothing in the blackness. He lowered the scope again.

He looked quizzically at the hydro phone operator. "Kapitan, I'm picking up propeller noises of an approaching small surface craft."

"That must be our friend," Lehman muttered. He gestured

for the raising of the scope for the third time and repeated his pirouette. The scope being clear he ordered, "Surface! Number One, get the package from the radio room, go up to the deck and make the exchange."

"Aye, Kapitan."

The sub rose and surfaced like a very large, long and slender, black, cork, water streaming from her flanks. Lehman went outside with the first lieutenant. Both scanned around for surface contacts. Lehman saw it first. "There!" He said pointing a few points off the port bow. Sure enough, a small launch was approaching them. Another sailor was also on the conning tower toting a machine gun in case of trouble.

However, there was none. "Number One, make sure you hear him say the keyword, "Wunderbar."

"Aye Kapitan." The first officer climbed down to the main deck to greet the approaching launch. The operator of the launch shouted out the correct prearranged password and the exchange was made.

Lehman went below and immediately gave the order, "Prepare to dive. Dive! Dive! Right full rudder, come to course 015."

"Aye Kapitan. Dive! Dive! Helmsman come to course 015." Crew members immediately commenced pulling levers, turning switches and valves. U-66 returned to the relative safety of the depths. Lehman was pleased that, his specific mission having been accomplished, he could now do some more hunting. He would stay around the general Bermuda area to see what enemy shipping he could intercept. He certainly didn't want to return to La Rochelle with so many of his torpedoes still aboard.

34

THE BERMUDA TRANSPORTATION COMPANY

When Hooks returned home that evening his mind was ablaze with a riot of thoughts. He knew what he had seen was an act of treason but what should he do about it? Who should he tell? Edith, the police, the Senior Naval Officer West Indies Station in the Dockyard, the British Governor, his boss. And who would believe him? He didn't know what to do.

Edith was asleep when he climbed into bed that night, and even though it was close to 4:00am he tossed and turned for hours. He was off duty the following day and when he woke up Edith and Becky had gone to the shop, Josh had gone off to school. His mind was no clearer than it had been the night before. He spent the day going through the motions of tending to fishing-gear and other equipment on *Jezebel*, but his mind was not on his work. By the end of the day he had to tell somebody, or he would burst. He decided it would be Edith.

When she came home, the first thing she said to him was, "I see you came back empty last night."

"Ya, but I caught a much bigger fish and I dunno what to do with him."

"What bigger fish? I ain't seen nutt'n'."

Then he told her what he'd seen. Edith sat down in the kitchen, shocked into silence. She knew her husband; he was honest as the day was long and was not at all prone to making up fantastic stories, neither had he ever had hallucinations.

"What you gonna do?" She asked.

"Donno." He slumped down, looking at the floor, the knowledge of what he had seen weighing on him like a steamship's anchor. They both sat there in silence for what seemed like forever.

Edith looked up and said, "You've got to tell Mr. Paul, he'll know what to do."

After further thought he agreed, "Paul, ya ... OK I'll speak to him tomorrow."

John Paul was the manager of the main ferry terminal in Hamilton. He was in charge of the money, and while he didn't directly set the schedules for the boat operators or oversee maintenance schedules or hire or fire, because he handled the money he was regarded as the boss man. Paul was a kindly white, silver haired gentleman who was well liked and respected by the men. But, of course, in reality, he wasn't the boss.

The next morning Hooks Jones approached John Paul, "Um...um, Mr Paul, can I speak to you privately for a minute?" It was still early in the day and there weren't any commuters in the terminal yet.

Paul said, "OK Hooks, you've got five minutes." Hooks told him what he had witnessed and how he had trailed the perpetrator back to his mooring and that he had identified the person as Captain Grant.

At first Paul was amused, thinking it was some sort of a joke, laughingly saying, "Hooks, bye, what you been drinking?" But seeing the pilot's face he realized that he was dead-serious. "Bye, you know who Captain Grant is? He's a bleddy war hero, for Christ's sake."

"I know Mr Paul. I'm just doing my duty by telling you what I saw."

Paul knew all the pilots and crews of the Bermuda Transportation Company ferry service, and that Hooks Jones was the best of the lot. Not only was he highly skilled and well-liked by the passengers, he was fastidious about his work, honest and reliable. It was often said that the ferry service didn't run on diesel, it ran on alcohol, because most of the crews were either, "half hot or full hot." But not Hooks: nobody had ever seen Hooks drunk on the job or anywhere else.

He eyed the pilot, realizing he was serious, "Bye, what you want me to do about this?"

"I dunno, but it seems to me something like this-here is real important, but I'm leaving it up to you, Mr Paul."

"Thanks a lot," Paul replied sarcastically.

Hooks then turned on his heels, returned to the wheelhouse of the Frances, and checked the clock on the terminal wall—it was time to go. "Herman!" He cried, "Let go!" The deck hand did as he was told, Hooks rang up the appropriate engine commands to the engine driver, and the ferry eased off the Hamilton dock for her daily rounds. Hooks felt better about himself. He didn't know what John Paul was going to do, but as a black man in Bermuda, he really couldn't go any further without risk to his livelihood.

For his part, Paul pondered the situation. *If it'd been anyone else, I would dismiss the claim out of hand. Maybe Hooks had misidentified the man in the boat, but that's unlikely because Hooks knows Captain Grant well. And you can't exactly misidentify a German U-Boat, now, can you. And what the hell was the rendezvous all about anyway?"*

After telling no one for three days, John Paul called on the Bermuda Transportation Company's Chairman, Sir Stanley Sterling, the real boss. Sir Stanley Sterling was a pillar of the establishment, the white oligarchy of the island, and also a member of the House of Assembly, the local Parliament. The Bermuda Transportation Company was one of the key business institutions in Bermuda that formed a part of the network of businesses, financial institutions, and utilities through which, along with the government, the white oligarchy, or the "40 Thieves," as they were sarcastically known, controlled virtually every aspect of life in Bermuda—for their own benefit.

The Chairman greeted him warmly, "Oh John, how you doing, bye?"

"I'm doing well, Sir Stanley. I don't want to take up much of your time, but I wanted to report something that one of our pilots reported to me.

"One of our pilots, which one?"

"Hooks Jones."

"Oh ya, he's a good bye."

"Hooks told me he was out night fishing, off the edge, a few nights ago—about 15 miles out, around North Rock—and he saw a German U-Boat surface close-by."

"A U-Boat! Damn, that close eh. My mates up at the Royal Navy tell me that they pick up signals from those guys all the time. But 15 miles, that's really close!"

"But that's not all, Sir."

"Oh?"

"No Sir, he said he saw a small craft rendezvous with the sub, and somebody on the sub gave the guy in the boat something."

Sterling stroked his chin. "A rendezvous! Are you saying there's a German spy active in Bermuda?"

"Yes, Sir Stanley, but that's not all. Hooks said he trailed the guy to his mooring and he was sure it was ... it was."

"It was who? Spit it out bye!"

"He identified the guy as Captain Rodney Grant."

"What!!"

"Saw him walk up to his house on Belmont and everything."

"That's preposterous!! That bye must have had too much rum! That's the most ridiculous thing I've ever heard."

"Hooks is not a drinker, Sir."

"A man of that ilk spying for the Nazis. Absurd! He's a bleddy British war hero, for Christ's sake."

"That's what I told him. Anyway, I thought you should know what I heard."

"Ok, Ok John. Um…Um, how's the traffic levels on the boats these days?

"Excellent, Sir. The war has been good for business."

"That is good. Leave that U-Boat thing with me. Thanks for dropping by."

"Have a good day Sir Stanley." Having been dismissed, Paul was off. Like Hooks, he'd done his duty and reported the incident, now it was up to the "big boys" to handle the matter.

Sir Stanley poured himself a shot of rum from the private stash in his desk and muttered to himself, "Rodney Grant, a German spy? Arrant nonsense! It's not even worth telling the boys at the Yacht Club!"

34

THE BURDEN OF TRUTH

THE RELIEF THAT HOOKS FELT from telling his story to John Paul was short lived. A few days after his revelation, Grant boarded the Frances and, as was his normal habit, headed up to the ferry's wheelhouse to have a natter with the pilot. Hooks found himself in an uncomfortable situation. On the face of it, he still liked Captain Grant: they had common interests and it was unusual for someone with such a distinguished military background to have any kind of relationship with a local black ferryboat pilot. On the other hand, Hooks could not forget what he had seen. And what he had seen was clear evidence that Grant was a Nazi spy.

It was just the previous evening he and Edith were sitting on the cedar bench on their porch, watching the sunset. "You know, it's not as if the British run Bermuda fairly, or are looking out for coloured people," he said. "Far from it. We got eyes to see and ears to hear and we know that things in Bermuda are real hard for coloured people, and it's on purpose, not by accident."

"Uh huh,"

"The British not only let it happen, they do it too, and benefit from this segregation that we have here in Bermuda. We, in this family and our friends feel it and live it every day."

"Ahhh."

"But you know them Nazis believe in that Aryan Master Race stuff, and Hitler hates coloureds and Jews. Member that fight between Joe Lewis and Max Schmeling? De 'Bomber' had to show him he weren't inferior to no German bye, and he did, didn't he!"

"Ya."

"How 'bout Jesse Owens? 'Member how Hitler turned his back on him after he won the 100 meters over there in the Olympics in '36. Jesse blew a giant hole in that Master Race stuff."

"Hooks, there's also a lotta local coloured byes who are working as crew on ships out there on the ocean that are being shot at by them Nazi U-Boats, the same U-Boats that the British and American patrol planes stationed right here in Bermuda are trying to kill."

"Ya right Edie. If them Nazis got in here, they would either kill all of us, or put us back in chains. So, I guess there's evil on both sides, init. But the Nazis are, by far, the greater of the two evils. So, for Grant to be spying for the Nazis is something that sticks in my craw. I can't stand it."

So, when Grant approached the wheelhouse, Hooks had to do something that he had never had to do before— pretend. And it was a struggle.

After the usual pleasantries Hooks said, "Cap'n, how's that boat of yours runnin'?"

"Jolly good! I've even learned to take her out at night. I use bearings on a few prominent landmarks and can actually go out through Eastern Blue Cut, and back in the dark," he said proudly. "Of course, it's not all in my head like you, I have to use a compass and charts and things like that."

Hooks' stomach tightened into a knot. This guy thinks he's got everybody fooled! He gripped Frances's helm much tighter in an effort to control himself. He then turned, smiled and said, "Congratulations, Cap'n, we'll make a Bermudian pilot of you yet." Grant laughed heartily.

The encounter with Grant increased Hooks' anxiety level several fold. Edith hated to see her husband in this state and told him instead of storming around the house, making everyone miserable, he should take his next day off and go fishing. He decided to take his US Navy friend, Harley, with him.

They set off at the usual time, before the break of dawn, from Somerset Bridge ferry dock. Harley was lucky to get some time off because his C.O. appeared to have arranged things whereby, he never got any time off at all. Harley prepared the fishing paraphernalia as Hooks guided the clattertrap *Jezebel* through the reefs.

As the day went by, Harley couldn't help but notice that Hooks wasn't himself. He was worried that it might have something to do with his "fraternization" with Rebecca. Things were getting worse and worse with Hooks giving heavy sighs and mumbling to himself. Eventually, Harley decided to face up to it. "Hey Hooks, you seem to have something on your mind. What's the matter, man?"

Hooks started to speak, and it was as if a dam had burst. He let it all come out and told the story of how he had witnessed a night-time rendezvous between Captain Grant and a German U-Boat 15 miles north of the island. This was not at all what Harley had expected to hear. He was stunned and initially didn't know what to say. Then he asked, "Hooks, man, are you sure it was Captain Grant?"

"Ya, bye, I trailed him right back to his place at Belmont. It was him alright. He even told me the other day that he figured out how to use his compass and various reference points to get through De Gap and back at night. He thinks he's got everybody fooled. But he ain't fooling old Hooks."

"Incredible! You know, Hooks, the Germans send messages to their U-Boats by radio, but the messages are all scrambled, so that we can't understand what they're saying. They use a device called an Enigma Machine to scramble and de-scramble the messages. It kinda looks like a typewriter. Was the object you saw passed to him about the size of a typewriter?"

"I dunno, it was covered up, I suppose to keep it dry, but I guess it was about that size."

"Who have you told about this?"

"John Paul, the boss at the Terminal."

"Why did you tell him, and not go to someone more official?"

"Look, bye, I felt it was my duty to tell someone, but I don't want to make so much of a fuss so that I lose my job.

Edith and I decided we best tell him, and he could tell the big bosses and they could handle it."

Harley had been exposed to the local society long enough to be sure that none of the "big bosses" were going to take the word of a local coloured man over that of a British war hero. But he believed Hooks. Hooks' word was solid in Harley's book.

"Look, man, I believe you. We have a small unit at the base that monitors radio messages. One of them is a buddy of mine. He tells me that they hear messages from U-Boats all the time. Of course, we don't know what they're saying, but there are ways to, at least, estimate where the messages are coming from. If some of those messages are coming from on-island itself, we could catch him out. I'll have a word with him, but of course, I'll keep your name and what you witnessed out of it. That OK with you?"

"Ya bye, I 'preciate that."

36

THE RADIO ROOM

THAT EVENING HARLEY RETURNED to base on a mission. If Hooks was right, valuable information was being conveyed to the Germans about ship and aircraft movements in and out of Bermuda. Ship movements were particularly important, because, armed with such information an enemy U-Boat could lurk offshore in the deep and wait for a high value target to set sail from the island and pick it off as it exited the local channel.

Unfortunately, both the channels exited into the deep at the east end, very close to the best hiding place for German subs. The Naval Operating Base in the Great Sound was home to all manner of US naval vessels: destroyers, cruisers, even aircraft carriers; similarly, for the Royal Navy at the Dockyard. Any one of those would be considered a high value target, but of course, a carrier would be the biggest prize of all.

Anyone who knew Grant, knew where he lived, and it was clear that he had a totally unrestricted view of all naval operations, both UK and US.

He made his way to the base's radio shack which was on the highest point on the base. Outside it looked like a giant man-made weed with all manner of wires and antennae sprouting out of it. Inside it was small and cramped, stuffed with electronic equipment, most of which he had no idea what function they served. It was very hot from all those heat-emitting electronic tubes, and although there was an exhaust fan humming, ventilation was inadequate. The operator was his friend, Sergeant Mike Howell.

Harley popped his head in the shack, "Hey Sparks, what's happening over the airwaves?" All radio operators were called "Sparks." Why, Harley never knew.

"Hey Swordfish, oh, just the usual. The normal Naval traffic, both ours and the Brits, some on the merchant marine bands and the occasional chatter from our U-Boat friends," Mike replied.

"How do you know it's the Germans?"

"Well, we know what frequencies they operate on, so we can monitor them. But of course, we can't decipher what their saying because it's all encrypted."

"Can you tell which direction the signals are coming from?"

"Yeah, we could, if we really wanted to, but we would need some cooperation from our friends at Dockyard."

"What do you mean?"

"Well, we have direction finders, but one single direction finder only gives you one bearing, a line where the signal comes from. For instance, see here, this signal I'm listening to is coming from a bearing of 042 degrees—roughly northeast - anywhere northeast of us. But if we had someone monitoring the same signal from, say St George's, or Dockyard, his direction finder would read a different line for the same signal. Where those two lines intersect would be where our Gerry friend would be."

"Triangulation!"

"Swordfish, goes to the head of the class!"

"Have you ever done it? I mean, worked with the Brits to triangulate a signal?"

"Yeah, a couple of times. It's amazing how close they come to the island. But they usually keep their transmissions short and sweet to frustrate our attempts to get a vector on them and send one of you guys out there to hammer them."

"What about signal strength? Can't you tell how close they are from the signal strength?"

"Well, signal strength can vary according to distance but also due to atmospherics. So, signal strength is not a very reliable indicator."

"You ever monitor any messages that are so strong that they seem like they're being sent from the island?"

"Sure, there's lots of traffic coming from the island, like I said, ours, the Brits, merchant marine and civilian."

"No, Mike, I mean on the U-Boat bands!"

"Oh..." The significance of the statement sinking in. "Swordfish, do you know something?"

"Naw, I don't know nutt'n', but maybe I got a hunch."

"You know, sometimes there have been Nazi signals so strong they seem like they're coming from this-here base. It's weird, I just chalked it up to atmospherics. Usually on the graveyard shift, you know, between midnight and 0600. About once a week, never the same time or the same day, but that Gerry gets really close."

"Really?"

"Yeah. You know somthin', don't you? Come on man, you can tell me. You want me to hook up the Brits to triangulate that signal the next time we hear it?"

"No, no, definitely not. This has to be strictly between us. The next time you hear that strong signal just jot down the bearing and the time and let me know."

"Sure-thing Swordfish."

Harley turned and left.

A few weeks later Harley got a message from Sgt. Mike Howell to contact him. Harley made his way up the hill to the radio shack. It was stifling hot in there. "Hey Mike, you wanted to see me?"

"Oh, yeah, Swordfish." Mike got up and conspiratorially looked outside the shack to make sure no one was around. "Look, man, I heard from our 'friend' last night. The message was just long enough to get the direction finder on it. The bearing on that signal was definitely 087 degrees. That would put him somewhere off the South Shore, right?"

"Right, or at least along that line. Thanks a lot buddy, keep listening and tell me what the bearing is the next time you hear him, OK?"

"Roger that, Swordfish."

"Just between us, right?"

"Roger that."

Harley turned and returned to his barracks. He fumbled through his things until he found a map of Bermuda. He found the spot on the map where the Sparks' radio shack was located - on the highest point on the base. He then drew a line bearing 087 degrees from that point. Harley's breath caught in his throat and he was rocked back in his chair as though hit by an invisible prize fighter. The line passed directly over the Belmont Manor golf course—the location of Belmoral, Grant's house!

Hooks was right after all! He muttered to himself. What should I do now? He knew he didn't have enough evidence to convince a sceptical audience. After all, this guy was a British World War One hero! First of all, he needed another data point for this signal bearing, so he would have to wait for another report from Howell. He also needed triangulation! For that he needed help from the British. That would be the tricky part.

Routine flying for the naval pilot, call sign "Swordfish," continued for another ten days. Then came another message from Sgt. Howell. He walked up to the radio shack, trying to look as aimless as possible, casually looking back to make sure nobody was looking.

"Hey, Sparks, what you got?"

"I monitored another strong signal last night from that exact same bearing, 087 degrees. Swordfish, sir, what in the hell is going on here? I mean, what are the chances of a U-boat, offshore Bermuda, and broadcasting from exactly the same bearing as the week before? Don't answer that question sir, because both you and I know, the probability of that happening is as close to zero as you can get."

"Yeah, I know. Time to take this to another level. You got any friends at the Brit radio shack?"

"Yeah, sure. You know we radio guys have a kind of brotherhood."

"Contact your best buddy. Ask him if he's heard this same occasional strong signal and what bearing it comes from. But, you're not to tell him what bearing you've got yourself. Lie if you have to—I don't want them to know what we know yet. Make it like it's just a personal curiosity of yours, nothing else. Strictly on the QT!"

"I'm not comfortable with lying, but I'll think of something, sir."

Harley returned to his barracks deep in thought. How are we going to expose this spy? How would I, a lowly lieutenant, someone who is not in the intelligence business, an American living in a British territory, going to convince the British and or the local authorities that Capt'n Grant is a German spy?

The exposure of Grant would be a deep embarrassment to our British allies and to the local authorities. Grant had made fools of them. Some of those people would probably try hard to either cover up the incident, to prevent possible loss of face, or waste time, effort and perhaps precious resources trying to blame it on someone else.

The fact was that Grant moved with consummate ease among the ranks of both the British and American military and the civilian elite in the island as well. Harley was going to have to have a plan, one that minimized the posturing of the brass but moved sufficiently quickly to mitigate the further damage of Grant's reports to marauding U-boats in the area.

He decided that this was, ultimately, beyond his rank. In any case he needed cover from his C.O. He knocked on the office door of his C.O., Lieutenant Commander Bradley A. Davidson, call sign, "BAD."

"Excuse me Sir, may I have a word?"

"Oh, Swordfish! Sure, have a seat. What's on your mind?"

Harley told his story, from soup to nuts. BAD was stunned. "And you say you have direction bearings from our base and the Brits indicating it's coming from Grant's house?"

"Not from the Brits yet sir, but I'm working on getting a triangulated location. Hopefully we'll have that confirmed soon."

"Incredible! So, Swordfish, what do you intend for me to do with this information? You know, there are certain 'niceties' that we are obliged to observe with our British allies and hosts. Going around and accusing one of their war heroes of being a Nazi spy, who is giving information on ship movement to German subs, will not exactly be welcomed with exuberance."

"I appreciate that sir. I have an idea of how to scare him enough to make a run for it. When he does, we get him and that sub that he's rendezvousing with at the same time."

"Go on, I'm listening."

Harley explained his plan.

"I like it, except for the use of the local civilian. This should be a strictly US Navy project."

"I appreciate that, sir. But this civilian, they call him Hooks..."

"Hooks! What kind of name is that?"

"Sir, just about every Bermudian's got a nickname—just part of the culture. Anyway, sir, as I was saying, Hooks has a knowledge of Bermuda waters that is uncanny. I've been out with him in his boat at night, fishing, and he has an unerring sense of exactly where he is, without taking any sort of compass bearings or even being able to see landmarks. He knows where he is, where the reefs are and where land is.

It was Hooks who taught Grant the basics of navigating through the reef line, but Grant does it as we would, using bearings from landmarks. Hooks' knowledge is so deep, it's almost instinctual. If it's anybody that will be able to find and trail Grant without being detected it will be Hooks. None of us will be able to do it. He'll hear us a mile off."

"And what about his reliability? Do you trust this guy?"

"Yessir."

"Do you trust him with your career, because if he screws up it will be on you, Swordfish."

"Yessir, he's the best pilot Bermuda's got and honest as the day is long, sir."

BAD paused, carefully considering his decision. "OK Swordfish, you may proceed with your plan. But make sure you keep me apprised with every development. Is that clear?"

"Yessir. Thank you, sir."

"Don't thank me. It's not done yet. Remember, it's your neck on the chopping block here! By the way, Swordfish, this Hooks is a coloured guy, right?"

Harley nodded.

"You seem to be getting very tight with the local black community Lieutenant. Your girl is coloured, isn't she? This Hooks connected in any way to her?"

Harley went pale. "He's her father, sir."

"Oh, for Christ's sake. Get out of here before I change my mind!"

Harley came to attention, saluted, turned sharply and exited the room, before his C.O. did, indeed, change his mind.

After the door closed, BAD began mumbling to himself. You fool, there's so many things that can go wrong with this plan. Why don't you just arrest and hang the SOB and be done with it? You know why, because there's been slim pickin's around here, as far as trophies are concerned, and we're not going to miss the opportunity to sink a German U-boat!

37

THE FOX HUNT

HARLEY, LIKE GRANT, HAD WITNESSED the ceremonial "Fox Hunt" carried out by the local elite. He too thought it was ridiculous, pretentious and fake. But it triggered a thought in his mind about a plan to get around all the posturing, finger pointing and recriminations that were bound to precede and succeed the capture of the spy. In the fox hunt the strategy was to get the hounds to flush out the hiding fox in such a way as to make him flee straight into the path of the hunters.

He therefore had to find a way to flush out Grant and make him run.

At the next opportunity, he returned to the radio shack and his friend Howell. The sergeant had a grim expression on his face. "What's wrong?" Harley asked him.

"Man, you've gotten me into something way over my head."

"What do you mean?"

"I spoke to my British counterpart today and told him I

215

was having trouble with my direction-finding antenna. He says he had picked up a strong signal on the U-boat frequencies, coming from a bearing of 174 degrees. Look here." He unrolled a chart of Bermuda. He drew a line bearing 174 degrees from the Commissioners' House in Dockyard, then he drew another line at 87 degrees from his radio shack. The two lines intersected at a point in the middle of the Belmont Manor Golf Course—right where Belmoral was.

"Sir, this signal is coming from someone IN BERMUDA, from this spot on the golf course. There's someone communicating with the Gerries from there. This person, whoever he is, is definitely a Nazi spy. What building is at this spot? Who does this spot belong to? I'm guessing you knew that all along, didn't you sir."

"Let's say I had a hunch, Mike."

"What do we do now?"

"Did you tell your British friend the bearing from this base?"

"No, you told me not to."

"Well, I have to talk to my C.O. first, but if I get permission, I want you to tell him that you think there're strange radio signals being transmitted on the U-boat frequencies from land. But don't give him your bearing, or he'll figure it out himself, and we don't want that. I want you to tell him it's all hush-hush, but I'm counting on it becoming scuttlebutt at the Dockyard. I'll tell you when to start. We won't tell anybody here for the time being."

He went directly and updated BAD that triangulation had

confirmed that signals on the U-Boat channels were originating from Belmont Golf Course, where Grant lived.

The next day, after his patrol was finished, he went looking for Hooks who was on *Jezebel* doing much needed maintenance to the old boat's clatter trap engine. *Jezebel* was on her mooring in the harbour just northwest of Somerset Bridge. Harley jumped overboard and swam out to the boat.

"Permission to come aboard?" He shouted as he neared the old cedar boat.

"Sure, mate. Climb aboard."

When Harley had pulled himself up, he said to Hooks, "Hooks, you were right, about Grant, I mean. A buddy of mine in the radio shack at the base has monitored radio signals coming from Grant's house at Belmont. He's been sending messages to U-boats, probably about Allied ship movements in and out of Bermuda."

"Jingas!! So, what was he doin' when I saw him?"

"Probably exchanging an outdated scrambler for a new one. They change them from time to time to keep the Allies guessing."

"So, what you goin' do now?"

"We have to set a trap for him, and I need your help."

"Me? What you want me to do?"

"There's nobody else who knows Bermuda waters better than you, especially at night. We're going to scare him so much he's going to want to run. But where's he going to run to? He's on an island in the middle of the ocean. So, the only place he can run to is one of those German U-boats that he's been talking to. He's going to arrange another rendezvous with a sub at night, and when he does, we are going to be there to bomb him and that U-boat to kingdom come."

"Where do I come in?"

"You're going to be our chief night-time spotter. If we can panic him enough, he'll run, probably to the same rendezvous area as the one he used last time. His thinking will be, it worked once, why not try the same thing again. He doesn't know someone saw him that night. So, are you up to it?"

Hooks was pensive. "You know it was just luck that I saw him that night, 'cause it was real dark. But I'm pretty sure I can find my way back to the same area. But if they choose another spot then we ain't goin have nutt'n'."

"Yeah, I know, but look, we have a chance to get both the spy and the sub. It's a chance we've got to take!"

"OK, I'm in."

"Is *Jezebel* ready?"

"Ya, she's always better than she looks, or sounds," Hooks chuckled.

Harley jumped back overboard and walked back to base. He proceeded to the radio shack and told Howell to talk to his counterpart at Dockyard and activate the scuttlebutt.

38

THE HOUNDS TO THE HUNTERS

THE WORD SPREAD LIKE WILDFIRE around the Royal Navy Dockyard that mysterious radio messages, on the U-boat band, had been picked up coming from the island itself. No one knew exactly where they were coming from, but there was wild speculation that included locations ranging from Hamilton to Shelly Bay, to Tuckers Town, to St George's.

One evening, Grant was being hosted at the Commissioner's House by Commodore Ellington Greaves, Commander-in-Chief, North America and West Indies Station, the Royal Navy's senior officer on the island. The food was good, the wine was exquisite, and the conversation was primarily about news of the War and all things nautical. After the meal, the senior officers retired to one of the outside terraces of the grand building for cigars. Commissioner's House was on the very tip of the island's fishhook shape—high up on a hill—and therefore afforded the men a marvellous view of almost the entire island.

"I say, Grant," the Commodore took a long drag on his

stogie, "There's a rumour going around that radio signals, on the U-boat band, have been picked up coming from the island. He let the smoke out of his lungs slowly with obvious great satisfaction. The light sea breeze whisked it away instantaneously.

"Is that so? What do you make of it?" Grant then took a drag from his own cigar.

"A German spy in Bermuda? It's preposterous! There are no Germans on the island and the local gentry try to be more English than we are," The Commodore gave a chuckle and a knowing glance. "And you can discount the local coloured population. This place may be no paradise for them, but they know what the Nazis stand for. This island is so small, we would have tracked down any such creature long ago."

"I suppose you're right." Grant said coolly.

"I guess our chaps must be spending too much time at that local establishment, what's it called, ahhh... the Grenadian Hotel, that's it."

"Why Sir! I'm astonished that an officer of your lofty station would even know about such a place!" Grant responded in mock horror.

Loud guffaws all around.

"Well, old boy, I like to keep tabs on the pulse of the men."

More laughter.

"And I'm quite certain that pulse is, at times, very rapid."

At this point they were all laughing so hard they were coughing on their cigar smoke.

Eventually, the evening came to an end and Grant said

goodnight. The Navy provided Grant with a courtesy launch which delivered him directly to Belmont ferry dock. Now that he was alone, he could drop the pretence and be properly terrified. He knew that the discovery of his identity was only a matter of time and that his chapter as a spy in Bermuda was rapidly coming to a close. The question now was, how it was going to end: in his escape, or his ignominious capture. He then remembered that, particularly in war time, the sentence for espionage and being a traitor was death.

He had an escape plan already prepared, but he had to put it into action—now! His next scheduled transmission was about a week away. He would ask to be picked up then. Until that time, he had to act as normal as possible, so as not to arouse suspicion.

The next morning, he proceeded with his usual routine, the walk through the golf course, pick up his paper at Darrell's Wharf, then back home for breakfast, which, of course, without Mavis, he had to make for himself. He had not yet found a replacement for her. After his ablutions, he walked out on his balcony to survey the scene. Looking through his telescope he slowly scanned the area. Quite a few ships were at the American base and the Dockyard was choked with vessels needing attention. "Nothing unusual." He said to himself. He had reported most of this in his last missive a few days ago.

He left the telescope and went back into the kitchen and made a cup of tea, strolling back out on the balcony to enjoy the libation in the fresh air. As he did so his eye caught a momentary glint from something shiny on Marshall Island.

Marshall Island was one the small islands in the Great Sound. Other that Hinson's Island, it was the closest of those islands to Belmont. Unlike Hinson's Island, it was uninhabited. That's strange, he thought. Placing his teacup on the arm rest of his Morris chair, he surveyed Marshall Island through his telescope. It was overgrown with cedars. As he slowly scanned the island, he was suddenly taken aback by the image of a man in the trees sitting behind a shiny, green, wooden contraption upon which was mounted a pair of binoculars. It was this contraption, or the binoculars themselves, which had reflected the sun.

Grant's heart pounded in his chest. My God, they know it's me! They're watching me! But who are "they?" Was the Commodore that good an actor! Can't be. It must be the Americans! It doesn't matter much who, the fact is I've been made!

It took some time for him to collect himself. There was a predetermined code to be sent to any neighbouring U-boat for the, "Need for emergency extraction." The code word was "Gibraltar." But he would have to wait for almost a week before he could send it because nobody would be listening for his signal until then. He was going to have to figure out a way to get away undetected. His boat, Scapa, was currently moored at the Royal Bermuda Yacht Club. He couldn't use that point for a late-night departure, and he couldn't use his temporary mooring next to Belmont ferry dock either, because he was under surveillance from Marshall Island and would be seen from that vantage point.

His friend, Bobby Soames, Commodore of the Yacht

Club, had an unused mooring at Salt Kettle, a small, fairly well protected bay off Hamilton Harbour. It was well away from the prying eyes on Marshall Island. There was also a ferry stop at Salt Kettle. Grant asked Bobby if he could use his mooring temporarily because his own needed repair. He agreed.

39

FINAL PREPARATIONS

AT THE USNOB, BAD WAS MEETING with Swordfish. Things were going as planned. They had started the vague, yet juicy, rumour about radio signals coming from land and everybody was gossiping about it. They'd placed a man on Marshall's Island, partially hidden and sloppily enough for Grant to see him. They had someone keeping tabs on Grant's boat at the Yacht Club. The reason for the meeting was that Grant's boat had disappeared but Grant himself hadn't. He had been clearly sighted taking the ferry to Town from Belmont. They were starting to panic because they needed to keep tabs on that boat, as they were sure it was going to be the getaway vehicle.

"I'll ask Hooks," said Harley.

Harley went to the pilot's Somerset Bridge home and was greeted by Edith. Her greeting was notably cold, but he didn't have time to talk or even think about that. "Hi Edith, where's Hooks?" He inquired.

"Oh, he's workin' nights this week. He won't get home till

after midnight."

"He's on the Warwick run?"

"Yeah, he's got the Laconia on that run this week."

"Ok, thanks Edith. By the way, how's Becky?"

"You don't know?" Edith replied acidly.

"Uh-oh," Harley thought to himself. "This is about me and Becky."

"No, I don't know, but I've got to talk to Hooks. I'll see you later, 'bye!"

He turned and returned to base. He talked his way into borrowing a jeep from one of the base MP's and drove toward Darrell's Wharf where there was parking. It was the first time he had driven in Bermuda, in spite of having been on island for over a year. He kept finding himself veering onto the wrong side of the road, but fortunately there was very little traffic, as private car ownership was prohibited. Most of the traffic was, in fact, US military, as they were the few who actually had cars or trucks.

He arrived at Darrell's Wharf and waited for the ferry. Soon it came into view, traveling at a stately pace, as Laconia wasn't much faster than Frances. After boarding, Harley ran up forward to the wheelhouse and told Hooks about the disappearance of Grant's launch.

Hooks smiled and said, "Jingas bye, relax yourself. I saw it just five minutes ago, at Salt Kettle."

"You did?"

"Ya, he moved it to a mooring in Salt Kettle a day or so ago. It's right there close to the ferry stop."

Harley rubbed his chin. "OK ... ok, that means he'll be

225

running soon—real soon!"

"Look here, he ain't got no car, so he's either gonna walk to Salt Kettle or take the ferry from Belmont."

"If he's got stuff to carry he'll probably take the ferry," Harley mused.

"Ya, he's gonna have some stuff: that sextant, compass and some sea clothes..."

"And the Enigma Machine—the scrambler."

"Ya, so he's most likely gonna take the ferry, first to town then to Salt Kettle, or if he times it right from Belmont to Darrell's to Salt Kettle. I'm on duty for the rest of the week so I'm gonna see him."

"If he does you gotta call me."

"With what, bye, I ain't got no phone!" Hooks pointed out.

"Oh yeah..."

"But there's one down at the shed, where we-byes put the ferry down at night. I could call you then," Hooks added.

"OK, here's the number. If no one answers, keep callin' until somebody does."

"OK, mate. After he starts to run, I'll call as soon as I can."

The ferry round-tripped back to Darrell's, Harley got off and drove back to base, thinking how much he hated cars, and being in trouble with Edith.

40

U-66

KAPITAN LEHMAN WAS CHECKING his plot. U-66 was hiding, crawling along at 3 knots (silent speed) at 150 meters depth. But he was dangerously close to the Bermuda coastline, just about 3 miles out. The water was very deep here despite being so close. There were no contacts on the hydro phones. He checked his watch and realized the time was approaching for signals from their man on the island.

"Number one, take her up to periscope depth."

"Aye, Kapitan, periscope depth."

The first lieutenant gave the appropriate orders and the sub rose to periscope depth. Lehman gestured to raise the periscope and performed the usual pirouette to scan 360 degrees for surface contacts. There were none. He could clearly see the coastline in the moonlight.

"Number one, raise the radio antenna."

"Aye Kapitan." A small whirring noise indicated that the radio antenna was being raised above the surface in order to receive or transmit messages.

The scheduled time for contact with their agent on the island arrived and promptly a message started to be received, then it was finished.

"That was shorter than normal," Lehman observed. The communications officer in the sub was busy on his Enigma machine decoding the message. He soon emerged from the communications compartment.

"Kapitan, this is an urgent message: "Gibraltar!' Our agent on Bermuda has been compromised and needs immediate extraction. He has set time and place which is 0300, tomorrow night, with coordinates."

"We are in the best position to respond, Kapitan," the navigator observed.

Lehman was furious, he was not going to be able to continue his cat and mouse game with ships leaving the Bermuda channel. Instead, he was obliged to pick up this agent. He clearly sounded desperate and it would be very bad if he was captured with the Enigma machine. All submarine communications could be compromised.

"Send a message that we will make the pickup tomorrow morning at 0330."

Lehman was fully aware that this rendezvous would be much riskier than the last one, since their agent had already been compromised. The enemy may be just sitting there waiting for him to surface then rain down hell on him. But this was the job. This agent had been valuable during his time on the island and had helped him and several other U-boats to contact and sink Allied shipping.

There were no other contacts detectable visually or by

hydro phone, therefore U-66 surfaced in the dark to recharge her batteries. She headed southeast with the intention of slowly rounding the south-eastern sector of the Bermuda seamount to position herself for the rendezvous off the northern coast.

41

EXTRACTION

THE TIME FOR GRANT'S EXTRACTION couldn't come fast
enough. While he loved living in Bermuda, his activities for
the Third Reich meant that he couldn't stay. He had no
interest in having his neck stretched by the hangman's noose.

He made sure he burned all documents that he had
relating to his activities. He collected the things he would
need that evening and stuffed them in a navy duffle bag that
had the Royal Navy insignia on it. He put some fishing gear
in there just in case he had to show something to somebody.

He would take the second to last ferry that evening which
would leave Hamilton at 10:15pm and come directly to
Belmont. It would then stop at Darrell's Wharf then Salt
Kettle. By that time, it would be about 11:00pm.

He collected his things and silently bade farewell to his
beloved Belmoral, a place he thought he would be spending
the rest of his days living in. All was quiet as he walked down
the hill to the dock. No one was around. He carefully stayed
in a position where the little shelter at the dock was between

himself and the prying eyes on Marshall Island. Looking toward Hamilton he could see the running lights of Laconia coming his way. He heard the throb of her diesel engines and the bell signals to her engine room as she slowed in her approach. *This is the last time I'll be hearing these familiar sounds.*

He noticed Hooks Jones was piloting the ferry. He didn't want to talk to Hooks, but it might arouse the pilot's suspicion if he didn't. So, he went forward to Laconia's wheelhouse to talk to the skipper.

"Hey Cap'n, what's happenin? Beautiful night, init?" Hooks, too, was struggling to act like this was just another night shift on the Paget/Warwick ferry.

"Hooks, yes it's a beautiful evening. Going out to try my luck at some fishing tonight."

Inwardly Grant was cursing the "beautiful evening." There was a bright three-quarter moon laying down a glittering silver sheen on the ocean below. If he had a choice, he would never attempt a rendezvous with visibility this good. But he had no choice, it was now or never.

"How come you got the boat at Salt Kettle now?"

"They're doing some repair work on my mooring in town. A friend lent me this one until they fix mine."

"Jingas bye, wish I could go with you. Where you gonna drop your line?"

"I think I'm going to try the reefs somewhere off Wreck Hill. What do you think of that?"

"Ya, you could get lucky around there."

Laconia was rounding Musson's Point and approaching

the Salt Kettle dock and Hooks became busy. Grant said his goodbyes and disembarked the ferry. He watched it chug away toward the next stop in Paget.

There was no one at the dock and he picked up his Royal Navy duffle bag, found a punt close by and sculled out to his launch. He clambered aboard, stowed his gear, hunkered down and waited. Checking his watch, it was 11:10pm.

Back on Laconia, Hooks was anxious to complete his route. There was no one at Hodgson's Landing nor Lower Ferry, so he just passed by slowly and didn't stop. After disembarking the few passengers still on board in Hamilton, he left there and headed for the #7 Dock, the overnight docking place for ferries.

After securing the ferry, he went in the office and dialled the number Harley had given him. Harley picked up after two rings. "He's runnin' tonight. I dropped him off at Salt Kettle with a bag full of stuff. Says he's going fishin' but that's bull."

"I've got a man on Agar's Island close to Two Rock. He's got a field radio. He'll notify me when he sees him. I'll call you back at this number then you can set off. You can't move too soon, or he might see you."

"OK, mate."

Hooks had already taken preparatory steps. He had moved the clatter trap *Jezebel* to #7 Dock, so when it was time for him to shove off, it would be simple to get under way.

Back at Salt Kettle, Grant waited in the dark. He was ready to go but wanted to be certain nobody was around. He checked his watch, again, it was midnight. He pressed the start button on the engine, went forward and released the mooring rope and eased his launch out of Salt Kettle bay at idling speed, almost as silent as a ghost.

He toyed with the idea of taking a circuitous route but decided that might only succeed in raising more suspicion. Officially, he was on a late-night fishing trip so therefore he should take a conventional route. He headed for Two Rock Passage, still proceeding at about half speed to keep the noise down. He transited the passage and headed for Watford Bridge.

The lookout on Agar's Island spotted the launch immediately, as there was no other marine traffic at that time of night. He reported it in to USNOB on the radio.

The phone rang at the #7 office where Hooks was impatiently waiting. He received the "Go" order and went straight down to *Jezebel* and got her under way. He didn't know exactly when the rendezvous was going to take place, neither did he know exactly where. He only had an idea it would be in the same area as the last one, but he couldn't be exactly sure where that was either, it was so dark the last time he was out there. In any case, they would have to try the best they could with the inexact information they had.

By the time *Jezebel* reached Two Rock Passage, Grant's launch had disappeared. Hooks rounded Hog Fish Beacon and headed for the North Rock channel, as before. After he transited the narrow North Rock channel, he headed north northeast. The night was clear, and land was visible. The problem was he could never be sure he was in the exact same area as before, when visibility was so bad. He just had to trust his instincts.

Back at USNOB, Swordfish was in consultation with his C.O.—BAD. They knew their quarry had sailed and so had their bird-dog.

BAD said, "Now we wait. We have to wait till Grant is far enough away from the island so that he can neither see nor hear our Kingfishers taxiing for take-off, or in fact taking off. The trick is if we wait too long the rendezvous could take place with us sitting on our butts here on base."

"I agree sir," Harley replied. "Hooks said that the rendezvous he had witnessed occurred around 0300. Fully loaded, we can stay aloft for over 6 hours, so if we launch at midnight we can stay aloft until daybreak."

"But we don't want Grant to hear us." So, they waited and waited.

It was not until 01:30 that BAD gave the order for six Kingfishers to launch.

"Gentlemen, you are to initially patrol an area very close to the island, not near the presumed rendezvous sight, so as not to spook either Grant or the sub. You are to circle in your designated zones until one of you sight a flare, the signal that the sub had been sighted. At that point you are to proceed at maximum speed to the area of the sighting and attack the sub and Grant."

They knew a lot could go wrong with this plan. Their priority was the sub, not Grant. If the sub discovered the trap then dove and evaded them, they could always get Grant on his return. He, after all, had nowhere else to go.

If the sub was never spotted and there was no rendezvous, then the operation would also be a bust, although they presumably would be able to arrest Grant when he returned.

BAD continued, "There is the added risk that the sub disappears beneath the waves before you get there. Presumably, once the flare was fired, the sub will crash dive, even if they had not taken Grant aboard yet. That gives you about thirty seconds to drop bombs on it. After that you will have to rely on depth charges."

Kingfishers were slow airplanes, with a top speed of just over 165 m.p.h. Therefore, BAD had to keep his planes as close as possible to the expected rendezvous point without being detected, otherwise they would never get there in time. It was a fine balancing act.

The Kingfishers taxied and took off in turn. The planes were noisy, and their departure couldn't be missed by anyone onshore, but Grant would be miles offshore by this time.

Some of the planes had bombs under their wings while others had depth charges. They all launched successfully and waited aloft for a specific vector for the location of their target.

Their success depended entirely on whether their civilian, local, bird-dog could find the spy and the sub.

Meanwhile, on the surface, Hooks guided *Jezebel* past North Rock out into the deep. He slowed the clattertrap down to idling speed. Harley had furnished him with six flares, a new waterproof watch and a pair of powerful binoculars. He was pretty certain he was approximately in the same area he had seen the sub the last time. The moon shone brightly as he scanned the silver sea for movement or a dark shape. There was none. He checked his watch. It glows in de dark! The time was 0300.

He listened but could only hear *Jezebel*. He switched off the engine and listened again. Still nothing. He would have to watch and wait... and be lucky.

Meanwhile, U-66 was creeping along at 100 meters depth at three knots, rigged for silent running. Kapitan Lehman's chart plot placed him at or close to the rendezvous site, but he wasn't going to show himself until he was absolutely certain that it was safe. He knew what the risks were, and he was not going to jeopardize his ship and her crew to pick up a spy. He would follow orders, but, of course, his overarching orders were to avoid exposing his vessel to potential destruction by the enemy. Caution dictated that he stay at this depth and listen for a while.

Not long ago his hydro-phone man thought he had heard the faint sounds of a small craft propeller, but the sound faded away. Since then he had heard nothing.

Lehman decided to come shallow and take a look. "Number One, periscope depth."

"Aye, Kapitan, periscope depth."

U-66 rose to periscope depth and Lehman surveyed the seascape through his scope. Just the silver sea. He lowered the scope and decided to wait and not show himself until he had some firm evidence that their agent was approaching. Minutes dragged on.

"Kapitan," the hydro phone operator whispered. "I hear a faint small craft screw off our starboard bow. I estimate about 1000 meters away. It appears to be approaching."

"That must be our friend," Lehman muttered then gave a

gesture to raise the periscope again. He peered in the direction indicated by his crewman. After several more minutes he said, "Yes, I can see it now. A small launch just like the last time. Anything else on the hydro phone?" The operator shook his head. Lehman took one more, quick 360-degree scan then ordered, "Surface."

Meanwhile, up on the surface, Hooks was using his new toy, the binoculars, to scan the silvery sea. He thought he caught a glimpse of movement about a mile away. He kept watching it as it got closer. Yes, there he was, it was Grant's launch alright.

Hooks decided to get closer. He started the clatter trap and moved slowly forward. At virtually the same time the black steel creature started to emerge from beneath the surface. Hooks gunned *Jezebel* so that his flares, when he launched them, would more accurately indicate their quarry's position. Little did he know that once the sub had surfaced the hydro phones on the sub were useless.

Hooks could wait no longer, he was about a half mile from the sub and Grant was fast approaching. He loaded the flare gun and fired three shots up in the air, angled towards the sub. Then he fired the remaining three.

Lehman was on top of the conning tower looking at Grant through his binoculars. He was very close and could see the agent's face in detail. Grant was waving exuberantly. Then he heard popping sounds and swung his head around to the sounds' direction. Flares!!! Oh my god!!

"ALAAAAARM!!! ALAAAAARM!!! ALAAAAARM!!!"

"Kapitan! There are two men still outside on the deck to

assist the agent in boarding!"

"Forget about the agent! Get the men below at once! This is an Alarm!" Lehman disappeared below. It took the two men on deck many extra precious seconds to drop their hooks and lines, scramble back up to the top of the conning tower, plunge down the hatch and secure it.

Inside U-66 there was organized chaos. All crew that weren't required to conn the boat were rushing forward to the bow to make a quicker dive.

Lehman barked, "All ahead flank, set bow-planes to maximum dive - 60 degrees down." The crewmen repeated his orders as they performed the task.

"Kapitan, what's wrong? What happened?" Inquired the navigation officer.

"We've been discovered. Someone let off some flares. Flood forward tanks! Right full rudder! Set course to 045 degrees! Rig the ship for impact!"

Hooks stopped *Jezebel*. He didn't want to get too close to what he knew was coming next.

Grant heard them before he saw them. The flares caused everybody to panic. He was just about to climb aboard the sub when the flares appeared. Much to his horror, the crew members that had been deployed on deck to assist his boarding, turned and looked at the captain on the conning tower. They then ran to the tower where the main hatch was. He could hear the captain yelling, "Alaaaaarm!"

"Hey, come back here! You can't leave without me!" It was obvious that the sub was about to dive. Grant threw his duffle bag on the sub's deck and leapt aboard. But the sub had gotten underway and the bow was sinking beneath the surface. Seawater streamed over the surface of the deck and swept Grant overboard. A plane appeared out of the moonlit sky and started to strafe the sub. He saw the flashes from the machine gun of the plane. The ocean around him erupted as the rounds hit the water in a line that led directly to the sub. One of the bullets ricocheted off the steel hull of the sub and hit Grant in the shoulder. It burned like fire and Grant felt despair closing in on him.

More planes! The sea convulsed around him as bombs fell from the sky. Then the world suddenly stopped—for him.

42

VS32

VS32 WAS ALOFT AND WAITING. One of the crewmen saw the flares.

"Flares at 4 o'clock. That's the signal. Let's go!"

"Roger that, I see them. Turning now." BAD, the squadron leader, was aloft leading the group.

All the Kingfisher pilots pushed their throttles to maximum and turned towards the flares. The plan was for the planes with bombs to attack first, hopefully to get the sub while it was still on the surface. Then those with depth charges would follow.

Swordfish's plane was loaded with depth charges, but it so happened that the flares were closest to him but behind, that's why he hadn't seen them first. He banked the plane as hard as it could go and dove to a target he couldn't see yet.

"I'm closest to the target so I'm going on a strafing run and you guys with bombs can follow, then the depth charge planes can follow. I'm the last batter up anyway."

"Ok Swordfish, but make sure you're not late on your bombing run."

"Aye, aye, sir."

As the OS2U lost altitude it gathered speed rapidly. The flares were still hanging in the sky. Harley and Jay searched for the sub. It was amazing how hard it was to spot something even on a bright night. Then Jay shouted, "SF, there! 11 o'clock." Harley saw it and banked a little to the left.

The sub was still on the surface but was crash diving. "She's diving boys!" He vectored into it and let off a long volley of machine gun fire. The sea exploded in a line as the rounds hit the surface. "I think I hit it but that won't do much damage, those things are built like tanks, but it's a start."

He pulled up and climbed, turning to take his position for the bombing run. His shipmates were already on their bombing runs. The sea erupted around the submerging U-Boat. The extra seconds delay to retrieve the sailors that were on the deck to meet Grant were now manna from heaven for the US Navy pilots. It was uncertain if any of the bombs scored direct hits. Certainly, several of them came very close, but the sub's main deck was now awash, and she was still underway.

The depth charges started to be delivered hot and heavy. They splashed into the water, sank to a certain depth then exploded underwater. They were set to explode at 20 feet— very shallow. The sea gave the impression of freezing for a second then water was ejected high into the sky. The sub still moved ahead seeking the relative safety of the deep. Swordfish was the last Kingfisher in VS32 to deliver its ordinance. Harley took careful aim. Only the conning tower was above the surface now. When his indicator went green, he let loose both depth charges, then pulled away. Jay was watching the results of their bombing run. There was only one explosion.

"What happened?"

"SF, one of those suckers, the one that didn't go off, looked like it actually hit the sub—might have got caught in the railing of the lower deck of the conning tower. Can't be sure."

"Well, let's wait around to see what happens. We set them to go off shallow, like 20 feet. She should be past that in a few moments."

Swordfish circled around where the sub disappeared beneath the Atlantic. In about 30 seconds there was an almighty explosion, followed almost immediately by a secondary explosion. Even in the moonlight one could see large sections of the dead sub being propelled to the surface by the secondary explosion from within it. All the flight crews cheered.

"Mission accomplished," BAD intoned, "VS32 return to base. Drinks are on me!"

Hooks, meanwhile, had witnessed the whole thing from a distance of half a mile. He'd never seen an actual battle before, of course, and it was at once exhilarating and terrifying. When he saw the U-boat heaved out from under the water in pieces from explosions, he came to understand in a much more personal way the awesome power these weapons of war possessed.

Now that it was over, he guided *Jezebel* to the scene of carnage. There was debris everywhere: paper, clothing, pieces of wood, and body parts. The area was also covered with the sheen of diesel fuel. It was a macabre sight. Hooks looked for any sign of Grant—he saw none. Perhaps some of these body parts were his. He was right alongside when the bombs started falling.

He continued guiding *Jezebel* all through the debris field. He saw some pieces of wood that could have been from Grant's launch because they were well varnished and shiny. He saw a torn piece of cloth, actually it was canvass. There was something on it. Hooks drew closer. He couldn't see it well in the poor light. Must be a Nazi emblem, he thought. He grabbed a boat hook he had on board and plucked the canvass out of the water.

It was a ship's badge featuring a round, braided-gold cord circumference with a crown on the top. Inside the badge was the picture of a fish. The name on the crown was HMS Solent. That was Grant's ship! This was his duffle bag. Grant is dead!

43

DIAMOND

A STORY, LIKE A DIAMOND, can have many faces.

When Hooks returned from the sub-sinking, early that next morning, he couldn't get to sleep - his mind was still in hyper-drive. His thrashing around in the bed woke Edith. "Hooks, what's the matter with you? You catch a whale or something?" He looked at her and burst out laughing.

"What did I say that's so funny?"

"Edie, you'll never believe what happened last night. 'Member I told you about Cap'n Grant and the submarine? Well, he's dead now."

"What!"

"Ya, blown to bits." He proceeded to tell her the whole story, blow by blow. Edith's eyes widened with every detail. When he was finished, she said ruefully, "So that's why Harley wanted to see you so urgently." He nodded. Then another thought hit her, and she became very emotional, a combination of anger and relief, and her eyes welled up. She grabbed the pillow and started to pummel Hooks with it.

"They could 'a blown you up with Grant! What were you thinkin', you idiot! I coulda been a widow and the children without a father!" She was weeping now. Hooks pulled her to him and just hung on until she calmed down.

The ruckus woke up the two children and they came into their parents' bedroom. "Mummy, what's wrong?" Becky asked.

Edith collected herself, and now looking at her husband with tremendous admiration and pride she said, "Your father has something to tell you." So, Hooks regaled the family with the story all over again.

Their mouths were agape. When he had finished, Becky asked with great ebullience, "Daddy, and this was Harley's squadron that sunk the sub?" Edith gave her daughter a sharp look, a look that only partially reduced her exuberance.

Josh declared, "Dad, you're a hero!"

"Yes, he is," Edith agreed. "But he's got to get to work, you to school and Becky and I to the shop. But we have to give your father a special breakfast, so let's get to it." They all got up and filed into the kitchen.

The island was abuzz, word spread across the island like wildfire, "A German U-boat had been sunk by Bermuda based forces very close to the island." At first there were very few details, all that was known was that it was American aircraft based at the USNOB that had sunk the enemy vessel in the wee hours of the morning.

The Royal Gazette, the local daily, upon hearing the news, delayed their printing so they could carry the story. They splashed the front-page headline, "Nazi U-boat Sunk near

Bermuda." The paper stated that it had received confirmation from squadron commander Bradley A. Davidson that his squadron, VS32, consisting of Kingfisher seaplanes had, "Intercepted and engaged a Nazi submarine very close to the island," and that he could confirm, "The enemy vessel was engaged while still on the surface by our aircraft using bombs, and depth charges after it dived, and it was destroyed. Debris found at the scene, as well as eyewitnesses to the engagement, confirmed the kill." When asked by the newspaper how the sub was detected he answered that, "We had credible intelligence that the sub would be in a specific area, so we had our entire squadron out searching for it. When it was sighted, it was engaged." When asked what kind of intelligence VS32 had received, Lieutenant Commander Davidson said he could not divulge that information.

Meanwhile, back on base, even though it was still morning, there was much celebrating and imbibing at the officers' club. Then they all, including the enlisted men who maintained the airplanes as well as "Sparks", Sergeant Howell, boarded the ferry to Hamilton and invaded the various watering holes in Town.

It was during this moving celebration that one of the bystanders at the bar, Lieutenant Brodie the Dockyard Commandant's ADC, overheard the part of the story that hadn't been released in the newspaper, the part involving Captain Grant, the Nazi spy, being blown up trying to escape to the U-boat.

Having come up from "Able Seaman," he still enjoyed having a round with the enlisted men, as opposed to the dons of the Royal Navy. It was at such a bar that Brodie overheard the Americans' conversation.

He buttonholed the intoxicated American aviator and shoved his bulldog mouth, with a stubby cigar in its corner, in the man's face. "Eh, mate, what's this about Captain Grant?"

"Yeah, man, Grant was a German spy. We were on to him for some time and we could have arrested him then." His words were a bit slurred. "We gave him clues we were on to him to make him run. So, we waited for him to make his move and when he did, we got him and the sub too!"

"I'll drink to that!" Another one of the fliers chimed in.

"I knew Grant, how in God's name did you chaps know he was a spy in the first place?"

"Local fisherman." Another of the aviators joined the conversation. "The local guy was out one night, fishin', an' saw Grant rendezvous with the sub, some months back."

"Bloody hell, why didn't he tell us?"

"He did! He told his boss who told the big bosses. Nobody believed him! One of our guys personally knows this guy. Said he's a good guy, so he started to check it out."

Sparks, who by this time was feeling no pain, piped up, "Yeah, he came to me to find out if I was picking up any really strong U-boat signals. I said yeah, I was, and I was able to give him a bearing on it. Got one of my buddies up there in Dockyard to do the same thing and you know what, the two bearings intersected right at Grant's house at Belmont. That's when our C.O., BAD, hatched the plot to get, not only the spy, but the sub too."

"BAD? Your C.O.'s named BAD?"

"Oh yeah, that's his call sign, you know."

"OK, Incredible!" Brodie gasped. He knew these GI's were drunk, but they all couldn't be hallucinating with the same story. He left the bar, embarked a naval launch at Albuoy's Point that went directly to Dockyard headquarters at HMS Malabar. The male secretary attempted to make him state his business and wait before he was allowed to enter the inner sanctum of the CINC, Commodore Ellington Greaves. But Brodie barged right past him.

"Brodie, what's this all about? What's so bloody important?" Demanded Greaves with more than a little irritation.

"Begging your pardon, sir, I've just heard the most incredible story connected to the Yanks sinking of that sub."

"Are they still crowing about that? Bloody lucky, that's all."

"No sir, it was not just luck, it's about Captain Grant, sir."

"Grant, what's he got to do with it?"

Brodie related the story he'd heard at the bar in Hamilton. Greaves' jaw dropped. "Unbelievable!"

"That's what I said sir."

"I can't believe it. A Royal navy officer, former captain of one of His Majesty's destroyers, a Nazi spy? I will not believe it! Well, we can put this to rest pretty easily. Send someone to find Grant. He's a creature of habit like all us sailors. Send someone to the Yacht Club and if he's not there, check his house at Belmont. Meanwhile, I'll contact the C.O. of the USNOB. Get to it Lieutenant!"

"Aye aye sir." Brodie realized, if the story were true, it

would be an embarrassment to the Royal Navy, in general, and to the Bermuda command specifically. This was what was infuriating his boss. Instead of delegating it to a subordinate, he decided to check it out himself. He commandeered another navy launch and instructed the yeoman to take him to the Yacht Club. Upon arrival he asked around for Grant, but no one had seen him in over two days.

As the shadows grew longer, he re-boarded the launch, headed to Belmont and walked up the hill to Belmoral. As he approached the entrance, he found a black man knocking on the door. "You there! I say, who are you? What are you doing here?" He demanded.

"I'm Arny Simmons. My wife, Mavis, works for the Captain, but she's been missing for several weeks now and I was wondering if the Captain had heard anything. I'm really worried." Brodie could tell the man was earnest and very upset.

Brodie banged repeatedly on the door. Nobody answered. He tried the door, it was unlocked. He wasn't surprised at that. Nobody locked their doors in Bermuda. They started to look around, occasionally calling out for Grant. They checked every room. The place was deserted. "Maybe he's in the shed," Arny said. He led Brodie around the back of the house to the shed.

The shed was dark, but Brodie found an electric light hanging from the ceiling in the middle of the room and switched it on. The naked bulb shed a harsh light that projected jagged, sinister shadows throughout the room. It contained mostly gardening equipment and an assortment of builders' tools and materials. It was clear that someone had been doing a bit of masonry relatively recently. In another corner there appeared to be a heap of trash. Brodie went over to look at it and saw that, what had appeared to be papers at first glance, were, in fact, cloths. They seemed to have some kind of dye on them, but the light in that corner was poor, so he took one towards the centre of the room where the single bulb was shining.

"Jingas, bye, that looks like blood!" exclaimed Arny. He rushed to the corner and grabbed a handful of cloths and brought them to the light. They were all soaked in blood, lots and lots of blood. He looked around at Brodie and as their eyes met the realization hit him. Arny fell to his knees in despair, his big gnarled hands grabbed his face. With his voice breaking, he cried, "Mavis, Mavis, what's happened to you!"

Brodie helped Arny up and said, "Come, come, man, we'd better leave here, don't go jumping to any conclusions yet. I'll contact the police; you should go home to your family."

"I've already been to the cops about Mavis being missing. It's been several weeks now. I've been back several times, but they haven't come up with anything yet. They probably haven't seen these bloody cloths though. I... I don't think I'm going to see my Mavis again."

"I'll make sure they come and inspect this place thoroughly. Leave it with me," Brodie said reassuringly.

They left the shed and went their respective ways.

41

THE COVER-UP

MEANWHILE, BACK AT HMS MALABAR, dockyard headquarters, Commodore Greaves barked to the secretary outside his office, "Yeoman, get me Captain Hamesh at the USNOB on the phone—NOW!"

A few minutes passed then the secretary called out to his boss, "Putting you through now, sir." Greaves picked up, the phone on the other end was still ringing.

"Captain Hamesh here."

"I say, Hamesh, Greaves here."

"Hello Ellington, to what do I owe this pleasure? Calling to congratulate us on the sinking of that sub?"

"What's this I hear about Grant?"

Captain Hamesh paused a few seconds, gathering his thoughts. Should he beat around the bush, in an attempt to be diplomatic or should he be blunt. He made a decision then he spoke. "It's simple, Grant was a spy and we got him along with the sub."

Greaves exploded, "You deliberately kept this from us!

Why wasn't I bloody-well informed?"

"Quite frankly, Ellington, he was too close to you and the colonial brass at Government House. We were concerned that if you knew you might have inadvertently spooked him."

"We ARE supposed to be on the same side, are we not? What kind of cooperative spirit is that?"

"The local guy who saw Grant's previous rendezvous with the sub told his bosses. They didn't believe it and the matter went no further. You heard the scuttlebutt about a German spy on the island. Did you believe it?" Silence on the other end. "No. You certainly would never have believed the word of a coloured, local fisherman that a decorated British naval officer was a Nazi spy. An officer that was your friend! That's why we kept it from you! And quite frankly Ellington, I'm not apologizing for it either."

Greaves turned purple with rage, "How dare you speak to me this way! The effrontery! You do realize you are guests in this British colony, do you not?"

"Look, what's done is done. You can take it up with the Governor and he can take it up with the Prime Minister, and he can take it up with the President. That's up to you. However you look at it, this is one point chalked up for our side, and I suspect the more noise you make about it the worse it looks for you. So, on that note, if there's nothing else, I bid you a good day, sir."

Greaves slammed down the receiver so hard it fell on the floor in pieces. He stormed out of the office, was driven the short distance to his residence, and poured himself a stiff scotch. His wife knew that, in this kind of mood, her husband was best left alone.

A few hours later there was a knock on the door. It was Lieutenant Brodie. Mrs Greaves opened the door. "He's in a very foul mood," she said, and waved him toward the study. Brodie knocked and went in. Greaves glowered at him and grunted.

"Sir, report from my inquiries."

"What did you find out?"

"Grant has disappeared, sir. No one has seen him, or his launch, in a couple of days." Then he told him what he had found at Belmoral.

"My God! Murder as well?"

"I'm afraid so, sir.

Greaves poured himself another drink.

"Your orders, sir?"

"Brodie, we have to treat this Grant matter with utmost secrecy."

"But sir, the Yanks are blathering it in every bar and cathouse in town."

"They can have their drunken gossip, but there can never be any official British recognition that this ever happened. Is that clear?"

"But sir, there's been, a civilian disappearance and a civilian murder. These matters cannot be just wished away. They should be properly handled by the local civilian authorities."

"The reputation and authority of the Royal Navy is at stake here, the very same entity that protects these islands and the entire Empire from being overrun by Nazis! Make an urgent call to Government House. I must speak to the

Governor first thing tomorrow morning. Now go and see to it at once!"

"Aye, aye sir," Brodie departed.

The next morning Commodore Greaves appeared at Government House resplendent in dress uniform. He apprised new Governor, The Rt. Hon. Viscount Knowls, KCMG, MBE, DFC, of the situation. He summed up by saying, "Your Excellency, we must treat this matter with the utmost discretion. The public's confidence in the Senior Service is paramount for the successful prosecution of this war. We must not let it be undermined by the admission that we have been betrayed by one of our own."

"Yes, quite, quite. Keep a lid on it from your end and I will deal with the local constabulary. We can't do anything about the blathering Yanks and local gossip, but we certainly can control official communications and the local papers."

As Greaves left, the Governor instructed his secretary to contact the police Commissioner. Upon receiving the summons from Government House, the Commissioner ordered that his carriage and driver be readied immediately for his quick transit to meet with the Governor.

Within an hour Commissioner Radcliff was in the Governor's office being given his instructions. After the Governor had updated Radcliff of the Grant affair and how the whole thing had to be kept as confidential as possible—to avoid official embarrassment—he immediately leapt to his feet and said, "Your Excellency, I will see to it at once! Consider the matter done!"

When the Commissioner returned to his carriage he was

seething. He couldn't allow His Excellency to know how he felt about this news. He was furious with himself that this man, Grant, had made a right fool of, not just the Bermudian Authorities, but him personally. He played back in his mind the "spy-hunter" and the burning letter conversation he had had with Christine and his fury erupted. He started to stamp his feet on the floor and pounding the door of the carriage. "Bloody hell, how the hell could I have been so stupid! It's one thing for Christine to be fooled by Grant, she's just a mere girl. I was so goddamn busy competing with that traitor for her favours, I didn't see what was right in front of me! It's unforgivable! And now they want me to sweep it all under the carpet. I'd like to march down to the Royal Gazette right now and let them broadcast it to the world."

By the time he had reached Police Headquarters, he had calmed down, realizing he had a job to do. He started barking orders. "Sergeant, send PC Williams and a crew to Captain Grant's house at Belmont. I want that place completely cleaned up. No evidence whatsoever should remain of any foul play on that property: the house and the shed! Have him fetch Arny Simmons at the quarry and bring him to me. Remember, he is not under arrest, so don't treat him as if he is. Is that clear?"

"Yes, Sir!"

He sat at his desk thinking of what other matters he needed to address to completely clean up and suppress this mess.

That very same afternoon P.C. Andrew Williams appeared at Arny Simmons' workplace: the quarry. He asked the foreman, "May I speak to Arny Simmons please?" After about 15 minutes Arny appeared, his clothes and hands looking like a man who worked in a quarry. As soon as he saw the constable his face fell. The constable said, "The Commissioner would like to have a word with you."

"A word with me? What for? I ain't done nutt'n."

"We know that, but he still needs to see you, right away."

"Is it about Mavis?"

"I don't know, but he needs to see you."

Arny looked at the foreman, who nodded.

"I'll get my bike." Arny went around a corner and picked up a broken-down bicycle that was made up of all spare parts. Nevertheless, it worked reasonably well and the two men, one on the standard edition Humber police bicycle and the other on spare parts, set out. They considered taking the train which had a station at the nearby junction of Cobbs Hill Road, but they would have had to wait too long for it to come. So, they pressed further on over Cobbs Hill to Darrell's Wharf, and in 15 minutes the Laconia chugged into view. They put their bikes on the ferry and in 10 more minutes they were in Hamilton.

Arny was not at all comfortable in police headquarters. His last experience at Headquarters in the company of this same P.C. Williams had not been pleasant. Even though he had been told he was not in trouble with the law or under arrest, most Bermudian blacks regarded the police station as about the last place on earth you would want to be. But if it was about Mavis it was surely going to be bad news.

Radcliff sat down across a grey metal table from Arny.

Arny was somewhat overawed by the presence of such a powerful person. The Commissioner, after the initial pleasantries, said, "Mr Simmons, I regret to tell you that the evidence that is available to us is that foul play has occurred, and your wife, Mavis, has likely been a victim, even though we have no body. I am sorry for your loss and your family's. I'm told she was a very fine woman. We also believe her employer, Captain Grant, is also now dead. We think they were both casualties of war.

We now believe unknown enemy agents infiltrated the island and Captain Grant, as a retired naval officer, may have been in possession of some valuable information. We believe these agents got to him, and your wife, being in the house, may have seen or heard something, and was also a victim of these evil perpetrators."

Arny could only stare at the floor and repeat, "Oh my God, my poor Mavis."

The Commissioner continued, "As a gesture of our sympathy for your family's loss, we would like to pay for Mavis' funeral expenses, whatever they might be. However, seeing that this is war time, and a very sensitive matter, we would ask that no one be told the details that I have just revealed to you. As far as the public is concerned, she fell off Captain Grant's balcony and broke her neck. We have already made the necessary arrangements with a coloured undertaker to pick out a nice casket and fill it with heavy stones and sand, so that she can have a decent funeral in the traditional manner. We have already ensured that the undertaker understands that this deception is vital in the interests of national security.

Where will you bury her?"

"We go to the Cobbs Hill Methodist Church, so I guess we'll bury her there."

"Very well, I'll give the undertaker the appropriate instructions. If you wish to have a wake after the service, the government will pay for that too. Remember Arny, Mavis was a casualty of war, but if we let everybody know what happened, the rest of the island will be in a panic, and we don't want that. Do you understand? It's important that we do it this way. This is your chance to do your part for the war, Arny. Do you agree?"

Arny, now completely numb, merely nodded in agreement, bade the Commissioner good afternoon, mounted the spare-parts cycle and pedalled back to the quarry. He avoided the ferry to save the fare. Arny always did his best thinking when his body was active, either sawing stone at the quarry or, in this case, riding his bicycle. *That guy thinks I'm a fool. Grant couldn't have been killed along with Mavis because I met Grant at his house after the night she went missing. There's something else going on here but I don't know what it is, and ain't got no way to find out. I really would like to know what really happened to my Mavis.*

Having taken care of Simmons, Radcliff called out to the duty officer, PC Stewart, "Stewart, I want you to contact David Whiting, editor of the Gazette and Seward Todd of the Mid Ocean News and have them report here at HQ immediately." "Immediately" translated into two hours before he could have both editors together in his office.

"Gentlemen," the Commissioner began, "I've called you here for a matter critical to national security during this time of global conflict." The two editors listened intently. "It's about the sinking of that U-Boat off our northern reefs. Have you heard any gossip about a Nazi spy also being eliminated during the same action?" The newsmen looked bewildered.

"No, only what we've been told by the US Navy. What spy?" Todd asked.

"What I'm about to tell you CANNOT leave this room. Is that understood?" the two editors nodded. "The repercussions for the Royal Navy and our standing in the British Empire as reliable partners in the fight against the Axis Powers is at stake. I am under strict instructions from His Excellency the Governor to get your assurance that the following information will NOT be revealed in your respective newspapers."

"Commissioner, we know there's a war on. What's this all about?" Whiting was getting somewhat irritated.

"When the sub was attacked by the Yanks, it was rendezvousing with a Bermuda based Nazi spy. He was killed during the attack."

"Who was this spy?" Todd asked.

"It turns out that Captain Rodney Grant was spying for the Nazis, giving them information on ship movements in and out of the island."

The two newsmen gasped in shock.

"He also murdered his cook-housekeeper to cover his tracks."

"My God!" Whiting exclaimed.

"I am asking for your respective words that NONE of this will be mentioned, even obliquely in your respective publications—national security! Do I have your words gentlemen?"

"Yes," said Whiting.

"This is the biggest story of the war! But I guess I'll agree to it also," Todd said reluctantly.

"Thank you, gentlemen, have a good afternoon." Radcliff shook both their hands and showed them out.

45

WRECK HILL

HARLEY HAD BEEN CELEBRATING, carousing with his shipmates all day, and returned that afternoon to his barracks, exhausted and inebriated. He crashed into his bunk and passed out. He awoke after midnight, hung over, but with a burning desire to see Becky whom he hadn't seen since his encounter with the sub. He cleaned himself up and walked off the base, telling the MP on duty he was trying to clear his head after a day of drinking. Walking down the railway line, he turned off after he crossed Somerset Bridge. Then he proceeded straight to the Jones' cottage.

All was quiet. He walked around to the bedroom shared by Josh and Becky. Her bed was right by the window and, as it was a one storey cottage, he could have easily climbed in if he had wanted. He whispered, "Becky, Becky, wake up!" She didn't stir. He repeated his efforts two more times with no success. This calls for another solution. He looked around the yard in the gloom and found one of the long grass stalks that grow wild in the island. It was long, thin with kind of feathery flowers on its end. He pulled it up, went back to the window, gently slid up the screen and reached in with the grass stalk. He was just able to gently touch her nose with the fluffy end.

At first, in her sleep, she wrinkled then rubbed her nose. Then she awoke. Opening her eyes, she was startled by what she saw in her window. "Shhhhhhh!" Harley whispered, putting his finger over his mouth. "It's me!" Her eyes widened then she broke into a wide grin. "Come outside, please." Furtively she looked over to Josh's bed. He was still fast asleep. She quickly slipped on some clothes and stealthily climbed out of the window.

"I know a place where we can be alone," she volunteered, and they set off. She led the way to a secluded spot at the base of the peninsular known as Wreck Hill, so named because this was the hill upon which early settlers used to set fires to lure unsuspecting ships onto the reefs for plundering. Now it was deserted.

During their walk to their hideaway at Wreck Hill, he took her hand in his and they each felt a warmth spreading from their fingertips up their arms and then throughout their entire bodies. Becky felt that her whole body was aglow.

They sat down on the dew-covered grass and Harley regaled her with the blow by blow story of the luring, spotting and bombing of the enemy sub, and that it was his depth charge that dealt the final, "coup de grace," to the U-boat. Although Becky hadn't had a single drop of alcohol, she was intoxicated with excitement. It was as though they were characters in one of those movies at the theatre. Harley was the dashing Humphrey Bogart and she, the beautiful Ingrid Bergman.

When he was finished his story, he turned to her and their eyes met, and magnetic attraction drew them into a long, delicious, deep kiss. The glow ignited into an open flame. Fire raged inside Harley. He had to have her—now! Harley slipped his hands under her loose blouse and caressed her skin: her neck, her back, and her breasts! Becky shuddered with excitement. He slipped her top over her head. His head was spinning with excitement, she was so beautiful. He kissed her on the nape of her neck, the small of her back, her fingertips, her arms and her belly. He cradled one of her breasts in his hands and put the nipple between his lips, gently sucking them, she moaned with delight. Her heart pounded, and her breathing quickened. Harley's searching hands continued to slowly move over her brown silky skin.

"I love you, Becky," he whispered.

She had been holding him at bay for so long, but her will was like a dam finally giving way to overpowering pressure.

"Oh, Harley, I love you too."

He slipped his hand under her skirt, caressed her inner thighs and worked his way up. She shuddered with excitement and anticipation. When his hand reached its destination, gently touching her most intimate region, she gasped then squeezed him ever more tightly. She was melting inside.

She breathlessly whispered, "Harley, I ... I've never done this before," before surrendering herself to him.

"It's alright, I'll be gentle." And he was, as he entered her.

As expected, he encountered nature's little sentinel to the virginal inner sanctum. He firmly pressed on, whereupon she gave a momentary cry as it gave way. But the heat of passion was not diminished as their bodies writhed together under the stars. There was no one else in the entire world. Just the two of them, in a world where time stood still.

After what seemed like an eternity, with their energies spent, they lay in each other's arms basking in the afterglow on the cool green grass of Wreck Hill, overlooking the ocean, underneath the vault of a starry sky. Becky's mind was drifting in a sea of serenity, joy and wonder. Harley had never felt like this before. He couldn't explain it, but it felt wonderful.

In time the effects of the afterglow wore off and Becky said, "I better get back home before I'm missed. Mum and Dad are early risers, you know."

"Yeah, I know," muttered Harley, recalling his early morning rendezvous with Hooks and the clattertrap *Jezebel*.

They strolled back to the Jones' cottage hand in hand in the dark. After one more long delicious kiss, Becky silently climbed back through her bedroom window to her bed.

Not a creature was stirring, not even Edith.

Instead of drifting off to sleep there was a tug of war going on in her mind between recollections of pleasure and feelings of guilt. She knew that she had disobeyed her mother's admonishments and had ignored all the risks that she had described. She felt badly about that. At the same time, she had a feeling of fulfilment. She was now a woman and that knowledge felt good, but she never wanted to achieve that feeling at the cost of betraying her mother's trust. The wrestling within her mind kept her awake.

Just as tiredness overcame her inner conflicts, noises woke her up. Edith and Hooks were up and about, a new day had started in the Jones' household and notwithstanding her sleep deficit, she had to rise and face it too.

46

THE FUNERAL

MAVIS SIMMONS WAS WELL KNOWN and universally liked, and people came from far and wide to pay their last respects. The little Cobbs Hill Methodist Church was overflowing. Those people who couldn't get in spilled out into the little churchyard, listening intently at open doors and windows of the building. There were many tributes to this devoted mother, wife and friend of the community. The casket was interred in the tiny graveyard next to the church.

Ordinarily, one of such modest means as Arny Simmons may have had a few well-wishers over to their home for a beverage or two. But with the support of the colonial authorities, he acquired the use of the space in the nearby Free Masons' Lodge on Cobbs Hill and was able to slake the thirsts and satisfy the hunger of everyone who was there. There were sandwiches and cakes of every description and, of course, an ample supply of hard, sudsy and soft drinks. Some were wondering how Arny could afford such a spread, but when asked, he merely said many people had pitched in and adroitly referred to the biblical text of the feeding of the five thousand.

The Jones' from Somerset Bridge, Hooks, Edith and Becky, also attended, having taken the train to the Cobbs Hill Station. The function at the Free Mason's Lodge had been going on for a few hours when, by happenstance Hooks found himself next to Arny, somewhat separated from the main scrum. Hooks said, "Mavis worked for Cap'n Grant, didn't she?"

"Ya, for a coupla years." By this time Arny had had enough alcohol to relax some of his inhibitions.

"He was a bad bastard!"

"What you mean, bye?"

"He was a Nazi spy, that's what I mean."

"What!!"

"Ya, that's the truth."

"How you know that?"

Hooks told him his story, ending with, "That's how I know, mate!"

"Jingas, bye, that bleddy police commissioner told me that Mavis and Cap'n Grant were killed by unknown spies and I should keep it quiet. I had my doubts about his story even though I found bloody rags in his shed."

"No, bye, that ain't true! I saw Grant get blown up by the Americans along with that sub long after Mavis disappeared. Saw it with my own two eyes. That cop is lying to you! He's just trying to cover up the fact that Grant was a traitor so that the British don't look bad."

"You know, you must be right. I ain't supposed to tell, but, it's the Bermuda Police that's paying for all of this-here," Arny said, waving his hand at the lavish supply of food and drink, "To keep me quiet, I guess. You know we never found her body!"

"What you mean? Who's in the coffin then?"

"Don't tell nobody, but there ain't nobody in that-there coffin—just rocks."

"Then how you know she's dead?"

"Police commissioner told me so, and then there's those bloody rags."

Hooks paused for a moment, collecting his thoughts, rubbing his chin. Then he spoke, "Look, mate, your wife was a real nice lady, and it's a crying shame what happened to her. If she's gone, and you found bloody rags at the house, and there ain't no body, then there's only one person I know of who could'a done that—Cap'n Grant. Bye, there ain't no unknown spies. HE was the spy! And he had a way of getting rid of the body too. His boat! Probably killed poor Mavis at the house, dragged her body down to his boat at Belmont dock, took her out to the deep and threw her overboard. Would'a done it at night too, so nobody would see. Workin' up there in his house, she probably saw or heard something she wasn't supposed to, and Grant had to get rid of her to cover his own ass."

Arny was on the verge of tears—tears of sadness and of rage.

"Look mate, I'm sorry to be so direct, but seeing what I saw, and knowing what I know, this is how it must'a happened."

"Hooks, thanks a lot mate. It's good to know the truth even though it hurts."

"What you gonna do 'bout it?"

"I dunno yet."

Meanwhile elsewhere at the function, Becky was talking to Edith and some other ladies, when she glanced to her right, only to notice Jimmy (Doc) Simmons staring at her. When he caught her eye he smiled broadly, and Becky looked away. Edith, sharp eyed as ever, said, "Becky, Arny's boy… um, um, Doc, seems to like you. He keeps staring over here and I know it's not because of me."

"Oh Mummy, please."

"Oh look, he's coming over here!"

Doc approached the group. "Good afternoon Mrs Jones. Hi Becky."

"Hi Doc," Becky said, "My condolences about your mother. She was a really nice lady. It's a terrible thing that happened to her."

"Yes, thank you, we're all still kind'a in a state of shock. So nice of you to come all this way to her funeral. Can I get you another drink?"

With knowing glances, the older women tactfully moved away to give the young people some space. For her part, Becky liked Doc, but just as a friend. Her heart was already the captive of the fly-boy from Gloucester Mass.

On the other side of the room of the Masonic Lodge, sipping a drink, was Albert Bentley Pace, owner/editor of the biweekly newspaper, The Bermuda Recorder, the only black owned newspaper on the island, covering events of particular interest to the black community, and those that would not be covered by the establishment daily Royal Gazette. Sometimes the Recorder covered the same events but from a different perspective. While Pace vaguely knew the Simmons family, the mystery and intrigue surrounding the demise of Mavis Simmons, attracted his attention. Hooks, having become agitated by his conversation with Arny, noticed the editor at the bar getting a refill. A spark ignited in his mind.

He marched over to the bar and said, "A.B., don't drink too much of that black rum, it'll dull your brain, and you'll miss the story."

Pace turned and laughed when he saw it was Hooks. "Hey Hooks, what's happenin'? What story you talking about? You got another fishy story for me?"

"No, bye, much juicier than any fish that ever swam the ocean."

"Really?" Pace's curiosity was piqued. The men moved to distance themselves from the crowd.

"What do you know about the sinking of that sub a few weeks ago?" Hooks asked.

"Only what the local authorities and the US Navy told us. We covered it just like the Gazette. Is there anything else?"

"That's just the tip of the iceberg, mate."

"What do you mean?"

Hooks decided he would bate the reporter, just like he would a rock fish. "So, A.B., what're we doing here, uh?"

"What? Hooks you're confusing me. We're here for Mavis' funeral, of course. What's...."

Hooks interjected. "The connection between this-here funeral and the sub sinking?"

"Yeah."

"Plenty, bye!"

"What?"

"You know, I wasn't going to say nothin'—didn't want to bring a whole lotta attention to myself, but the way them big byes have white-washed this Mavis thing, and how it's got old Arny all torn up inside, the truth's got to come out."

"White-washed! What white-wash?" The editor asked.

Hooks called over Arny. "Hey Arny, you know Mr Pace. This story's got to be told: my part, Mavis' part and your part, or else poor Mavis will never rest in peace, wherever she is."

Arny nodded.

The next day all three men met at the Recorder Building on Court Street in Hamilton, where Hooks and Arny told their stories of the treachery, its discovery, the trap, the enemy's destruction, the murder of Mavis and the elaborate cover up to save face.

The next weekend edition of the Recorder featured two front page stories whose headlines read, "Local Woman Slain by Nazi Spy." and "Local Pilot Exposes Former Navy Officer as Nazi Spy"

All Saturday morning, long after the initial batch was published, the printing presses at the Recorder Building on Court Street kept on humming, in an attempt to keep up with the extraordinary demand for that day's edition. All the usual readers of the paper bought their copies, but there was extra demand from the white population, a demographic who virtually never normally read the Recorder, who had to get their hands on today's sensational story, as it was not in the Royal Gazette, as per orders from on high.

In the dungeon, at the Princess, Mary came rushing over to Christine's desk and exclaimed, "Christine, Christine! Captain Grant was a spy!"

Non-plussed, she replied, "Yeah, I suspected as much."

"You suspected he was a Nazi spy?" Mary asked incredulously.

"What! A Nazi spy!"

"Yes, a Nazi spy! Look, it says so in this paper that I got from the hotel bellman. Look, it also says he's dead, killed while trying to rendezvous with that U-boat that the Yanks sunk a week or so back."

"Oh God! Oh God! Cappy's dead! A Nazi spy! Unbelievable!" Christine screamed.

She almost fainted and knocked over a stack of mail and a metal trash can as she attempted to right herself. It loudly clanged about on the floor. The ruckus caused everybody in the dungeon to stop what they were doing and stare at the two women, wondering what the fuss was all about. Her supervisor was looking quizzically and disapprovingly over his glasses at the two women in heated conversation.

Mary approached him, "Donald, can we have a quick break, please?" He nodded and they exited into another part of the building. Christine snatched the paper from her friend and devoured the two articles.

"That bastard! That son-of-a-bitch, traitorous bastard! My

God, he murdered Mavis too? She was so nice! How could he do such a thing? How could I have been so stupid? Christ! He could have killed me too! He made a proper fool out of me, didn't he?" She hurled the newspaper across the room with all her strength causing the broadsheets to fly apart, pages fluttering gently down all over the room. She had started to perspire profusely and was fanning herself, the beads of sweat now joining up, forming miniature rivulets that met at her chin.

"Look at you, you're sweating like a pig. Sit down," Mary ordered. "You're starting to worry me. Here, I'll get you some water." Of course, Christine had already given Mary the blow by blow of the proceedings of the dinner date at Belmoral.

After Christine had collected herself somewhat, she said, "Mary, I missed my period last month and I threw-up this morning before coming to work."

"You don't think…"

"Yeah, I do think … I'm, I'm pregnant."

It was Mary's turn to flop down in a chair. "Oh, my God!"

The Commissioner of Police was in the Governor's office at Government House. His Excellency was purple with rage. "Radcliff, I thought you said you had the press under control!"

"Well, Your Excellency, we never even thought about the coloured newspaper."

"Now I've got to write up reports to London explaining what happened here, it's going to be bloody embarrassing and they're going to start wondering what the hell kind of ship I'm running in this place. It's going to be bloody awful, Radcliff, bloody awful!"

"We could put out a statement refuting the whole story. Our word against theirs."

"Don't be ridiculous! The genie's out of the bottle! You have two missing people and only one story that credibly explains it. Don't forget the Yanks and the pilot were witnesses to Grant's demise. No, we can't do anything now. All responses to this matter, from now on are, 'No comment.' Is that clear?"

"Yes, Your Excellency." The governor turned his eyes to the papers on his desk. Radcliff, realizing he had been dismissed, collected his cap and quietly left the room.

He returned to Police Headquarters in a foul mood. He marched through the outer office without saying a word and slammed the door to his office behind him. He surveyed the papers on his desk. One of them was a message from the duty officer that Christine Liverpool had called for him. Ah, a shaft of light through dark clouds!

He picked up the receiver and called the Princess. After a long wait, she came to the phone. "Peter, I know you must be upset about this Grant business. Why don't you take me to lunch and let me cheer you up?"

"My dear, that's a splendid idea. I very much need cheering up today."

They met for lunch at the Longtail Club on Burnaby Street. It was an intimate, secluded place, even though it was in the centre of town. In the middle of lunch, she said,

"Peter I've been thinking. I've been thinking that it's time I settled down. Do you fancy settling down?"

Radcliff thought to himself, "Yesss!"

47

BACK TO THE WAR

AFTER THE FLURRY OF EVENTS RELATING to the disappearance of Captain Grant and Mavis Simmons, and the sinking of the enemy vessel, dull routine doggedly forced its way back into the lives of Bermuda residents. After the Recorder expose, Hooks became a folk hero, his ferry mates calling him, "Nazi Hunter." Notwithstanding this notoriety, Hooks returned to driving the Frances. Swordfish returned to flying patrols on his Kingfisher, Edith returned to the shop and Becky returned to the box office of the Somerset movie theatre. The Governor and Commodore Greaves at the Dock Yard were deeply embarrassed at the betrayal of one of their own. In their efforts to cover up the scandal, they'd never even thought about the black newspaper, the Bermuda Recorder.

Becky, now fully recovered from her night of wild romance, was determined that she would return to being a "good girl," the kind her mother expected her to be. She still regularly stole away to be with Harley. She loved him, but she did not let things go as far as they had gone that night at the foot of Wreck Hill.

At VS32 the euphoria of sinking an enemy sub and eliminating a traitorous spy had drained away now, and the squadron was back in its routine patrolling pattern. However, events had not gone unnoticed in the upper echelons of the Navy. Reports had been written and sent up the chain of command. Commendations had been recommended and approved and medals had been awarded. One to Swordfish! Harley wrote home about it.

Dear Mom,

I have some news. We discovered a Nazi spy operating from Bermuda. I helped set a trap for him by forcing him to run. The only place he could run to was to be picked up by a German U-boat. With the cooperation of the local fisherman I told you about, Becky's father, we were able to track him down when he rendezvoused with the sub. We bombed them and destroyed the spy and the sub.

Mom it was the depth charge I dropped that blew up the sub. Today I received a commendation and a medal from the brass.

Still seeing Becky. She's a really nice girl.

Say hi to Dad for me. Have you heard from Hank and Harry?

Love

Harley

The War itself was evolving. A mighty armada, or more accurately stated, an armada of armadas, was being assembled in the Pacific theatre to push back and eventually destroy the Empire of Japan. While the industrial might of

US factories could quickly produce airplanes, combat experienced and skilled pilots were hard to come by.

Thus, the decision was made by CINCLANT to transfer some of its experienced pilots to CINCPAC—the Pacific theatre. In the area of maritime patrol and combat there were very few squadrons that had more experience than VS32, a squadron that had been deployed even before war had been declared by the US in December 1941.

Commander Bradley Davidson (BAD) was summoned into the base commandant, Captain Hamesh', office. "Sir, you wanted to see me?"

"Yes, BAD, have a seat. We've got new orders. CINCPAC need experienced pilots, so all your pilots are being reassigned to Pearl Harbour. VS32 is being assigned a bunch of rookies and, presumably, as a reward for your high level of efficiency, you will be remaining here with the privilege of making them combat ready."

"But sir, why not reassign the whole squadron?" BAD was a warrior, he wanted to be where all the action was.

"Commander, the brass has noticed what a great job you've done with the rookies you were lumbered with two years ago. The Atlantic U-boat threat is still real, and we need you to whip these new guys into shape. In any case, that's the way it is. Here's the list of pilots that are being reassigned. Orders are for them to fly back to Norfolk, in two days, by Catalina. It'll take them another week to get out to Pearl."

"Yessir." When BAD heard the words, "That's the way it is," he knew that, in the Navy, there was no sense protesting, it was a done deal.

He took the list, gathered VS32 together and made the announcement. It was met with groans of disappointment. Bermuda had grown on them. They liked the island and the people. Moreover, the men had bonded together as a unit, they were comrades at arms, and they felt they were now being scattered to the wind. But it was something they had to accept as GI's. You went where they sent you.

Of course, Swordfish took the news the hardest. More than his comrades, he had really connected with the island, and one of the islanders in particular. That evening he made his way up to the movie theatre in Somerset. When she saw him, she flashed that megawatt smile. But it faded away quickly when she saw how unhappy he looked. "What's wrong?" she asked.

"I'll tell you when you're through here." As usual he hung around until the movie started and she finished her shift. After she secured the cash, she came out and found Harley sitting on a bench staring at the ground. She sat down beside him.

"What's the matter, Harley?"

He turned to her, sadness etched all over his face. Her eyes were welling up just from the sight of him. "I've been reassigned. I'm shipping back to the States tomorrow."

"Oh my God no! No! Is there any way you can get them to keep you here?" She sobbed.

He shook his head, his grey eyes brimming with sorrow, "This is the Navy, they say go, you go." More tears and louder sobbing, both his and hers. Clinging to one another, they walked back along the railway line, as they had done so many times before. This time there was no jasmine fragrance, no stars, no chirping tree frogs—only black desolation.

When they arrived at the point where they would normally part, they lingered, holding each other tightly.

"I love you Harley. Will I see you again?" She asked in between sobs.

"I love you too, Becky, and I swear I will come back for you. I swear it! I swear it! I'd better go now, you need to get back home."

"Write me please, please!"

"I will." He gently disentangled himself from her arms and turned toward the base.

When she got home, she tried to clean her face up before crossing the threshold. Edith was in the kitchen and turned when she heard the screen door open. When she saw her daughter's face she couldn't move. "What's wrong child?" Their eyes met, and Becky burst into tears and ran into her bedroom.

"What's wrong with Becky?" Hooks inquired.

"I'll take care of it," Edith declared, as she put down the dish towel, went into the bedroom and closed the door. Becky was weeping hysterically in her bed.

Edith took her into her arms trying to comfort her. "There, there, it can't be that bad. What's eating you child?"

"It is that bad. I'm sorry Mummy, I'm sorry."

"Sorry for what, child?"

"Harley's been reassigned back to the States. He's leaving tomorrow and I'm pregnant!" She burst into yet another flood of tears.

Edith was surprised, but not shocked. She suspected her daughter had been sneaking out to see this young man. She had been young once too. After a few minutes and several quarts of tears, she asked, "Does he know?" Becky shook her head and started to cry again.

"Mummy, what do I do?"

"Rebecca, children are a gift from God. You will have this child and he or she will be a member of this family. You will be a good mother and we will help you raise this child to be the best person he or she can be. We are family and we stick together, no matter what. Yuh hear?" Becky nodded and buried herself in her mother's chest.

Harley glumly returned to USNOB. Not only was the move splitting him up with his girlfriend, but also separating him from his long-time friend and radioman Jay. Jay was staying in Bermuda as part of the plan to team rooky pilots with experienced crew. They were hoisting drinks at the officers' mess when the two men entered.

"Hey, Swordfish, the drinks are on you, buddy. You're getting the hell off this rock!" Jay shouted. Jay knew exactly why his skipper was so glum and was trying to cheer him up. "Man, you've struck the jack pot, your new squadron will be flying Avengers off carriers. Your dream come true, you'll be flying warplanes off the carrier!" The Grumman TBF Avenger was the new torpedo attack airplane being supplied to US carriers in the Pacific. The best Harley could do was a faint smile before he knocked back a drink.

The next day he and some other pilots boarded a Catalina bound for Norfolk. He didn't even get a chance to say goodbye to Hooks. The plane gave a mighty roar and quickly lifted from the surface of the Great Sound. As they passed over Somerset Island, he looked out of the bubble rear window to see if he could spot the little Jones cottage where his heart was. He couldn't make it out, but he did see those magical reefs seemingly dancing in the shimmering sea. It looked just as special as the first time he had seen it.

48

GUADALCANAL

HARLEY WAS TRUE TO HIS WORD: he wrote many letters to Becky, seemingly every chance he got. She would stop at the post office every day to see if there was a letter for her. He had indeed been posted to a carrier, USS Hornet. Very exciting, he told her, but he missed her so badly. She didn't tell him about the baby. She was finding it difficult to deal with all the evil gossip surrounding her condition, as it was now obvious to everyone that she was with child. But Edith, Hooks and the wider Jones' clan rallied around her, encouraged her, and supported her. Didn't condemn her. She also noticed that Doc Simmons always found time to visit and be supportive. She stuck to her routine, leaving home, going to the shop by day and the box office in the evenings.

The gossip and sideways glances had the effect of steeling her resolve. She discovered a Rebecca inside her that she didn't know was there. A woman who was strong, resolute, durable and determined to make something of herself in life, not just for herself but to improve the future opportunities for her unborn child. This new Rebecca put aside the immature Becky who envisioned she was Ingrid Bergman in the film Casablanca. She was going to be a mother, and mothers had to have their feet firmly planted on the ground, pointing forward.

The months passed, and the baby was born. It was a healthy boy. She named him Ezekiel, and would call him Zeke.

Shortly after, suddenly the letters from Harley stopped. Becky was heartbroken. She was trying not to believe that Harley had dumped her. Could he have fallen for one of the many nurses at Pearl Harbour or some Hawaiian hula girl or some other beauty from the South Pacific? Her mind was torturing her. She tried to assuage her grief by devoting herself to be the best mother she could be.

Notwithstanding her new responsibilities she kept her job at the theatre. They had one more mouth to feed and the family needed the money. One evening, after the movie had started and after she put away the cash, she found Jay, Swordfish's former partner, sitting on the bench outside the box office. When he saw her he stood up. "Jay, nice to see you. What are you doing around here?"

Jay looked serious. Becky instantly had a feeling of foreboding. "Sit down Becky, please." She sat down beside him. "I have bad news." She instantly felt nauseous, lightheaded. "Today we received word that Harley's plane was shot down over Guadalcanal. Becky, I'm so sorry, Swordfish was KIA."

Having been in the company of a GI for so long, she knew

exactly what KIA meant: Killed in Action. Tears began to roll down her cheeks, but she was not the same girl who cried a river of tears when she heard that her lover was flying off. Her experience over the last year had matured her by many years. She steadied herself and whispered to Jay, "I wondered why his letters suddenly stopped. Thanks for telling me, I really appreciate it."

Jay had heard the gossip about the baby. "Did he know he was going to be a father?" Becky shook her head. "Why didn't you tell him?"

"I didn't want him to feel obligated to come back."

"He would have given the world for you Becky, believe me when I tell you."

"Now, instead, he's given his life for his country." She stood up to leave.

"You going to be alright? Can I walk you home or something?"

"No thanks, I'm OK, I'll be fine. Thanks again for letting me know." She headed home to tell her mother that she was a widow, even though she had never married.

49

A NEW CHAPTER

IT TOOK QUITE SOME TIME FOR BECKY to come to terms with the death of Harley. Little Zeke was strong and energetic. He had his mother's complexion and hair but his father's grey eyes. She concentrated her attentions on her son but in doing so she realized that she needed to improve herself as well. She was always good with numbers and enrolled in a correspondence course in bookkeeping. She passed it with flying colours. She left the shop and the theatre to become the bookkeeper of a local business.

Doc Simmons became her rock, never leaving her side, always encouraging and ever caring for her and her son. She knew he loved her very much. One evening she and Edith were sitting out on the weather-beaten cedar bench on the Jones' porch, enjoying the sunset and she said, "Mummy, it's time for me to turn the page."

"What do you mean?"

"I mean, it's time for me to close the chapter in my life centred around Harley. The time has come to start a new chapter and emotionally say goodbye to Swordfish. Zeke will always be a reminder of that chapter, so it will never be completely closed, but I've got to move forward with my life. Doc has asked me to marry him and I'm going to say yes. Doc loves Zeke and will be a good father to him."

Edith smiled saying, "That's good Becky, that's very good."

And so it was, the couple were married at the little chapel on Cobbs Hill Road built in the moonlight by slaves, the Simmons' family church.

The war in the Atlantic was winding down. The U-boat threat had receded, and in Germany Hitler was being crushed by a pincer from both the East and West. Doc had gotten a new job at the USNOB that paid substantially more than he was making at the Dockyard and the couple built a house in Warwick—the old-fashioned Bermudian way, by everybody pitching in to help.

50

GETTING OFF THE ROCK

BECKY AND DOC WERE A HARD-WORKING couple and achieved a standard of living their respective parents could never have dreamed of. And although Becky bore Doc two children, she still longed to, "Get off this Rock." It was not until 1952 that she was able to travel off the island, to New York City. She took Zeke along as a ten-year-old boy.

By this time cars were common, the modern world having forced its way into change-resistant local society. They got a friend of Doc's to take them in his "Surrey with the Fringe on Top" taxi to the local air terminal—a small civilian corner of the sprawling complex called, "Kindley Field Air Force Base." Their plane was the bulbous-nosed, double decker, Pan Am Boeing 377 Stratocruiser. Becky eyed their ride to New York and momentarily wondered what Harley would have thought of this huge, ungainly looking silver bird. Then, catching herself, she excitedly exclaimed to Doc, "It's time to get off this rock! Are you ready Zeke?"

Zeke eagerly nodded.

"Come on then." She kissed Doc goodbye and said, "New York City, here we come!" And off they went—flying time, between four to five hours.

They spent several days with a Bermudian family that lived there and toured around the Big Apple. They were both amazed at how huge, loud, busy, and dirty New York was. Zeke was fascinated with the Subway, being too young to remember the old Bermuda Railway. Becky on the other hand couldn't help but notice that the windows of the trains were so black with soot that you could hardly see through them.

Then one day, towards the end of their stay, she simply said to Zeke, "Son, we have to take a trip to meet some other people." They boarded a train at Grand Central Station to Boston. When they arrived there, they transferred to another train to Rockport Massachusetts. They got off at the second last stop - Gloucester Station.

From there they took a cab along a winding road to a group of older houses close to the coast. The taxi stopped at the address that Becky had written on the piece of paper in her hand. She double checked it to make sure she had the right place, took a deep breath and approached the door and knocked. The sounds of footsteps and rustling from inside told them that someone was home, and eventually an elderly lady opened the door. She was very thin, with her washed-out coloured clothing limply hanging from her diminutive, slightly bent frame. Her thinning white hair was being playfully tossed around her head by the sudden draft created from opening the front door. Her eyes were sad, and her pale face was heavily lined from the harsh environment and the ravages of time, but nevertheless, you could still see that she had once been a beautiful woman, long ago.

Becky said, "Good afternoon, ma'am, sorry to bother you, I'm Rebecca Simmons from Bermuda, and I'm looking for Marion Harvey. I have information that leads me to believe that she used to live here. I wonder if you can help me."

The woman looked at the coloured lady and the boy somewhat suspiciously and said, "Who did you say you are? And what do you want with her?"

Becky sensed the old woman's unease. "We're from Bermuda and we have come an awfully long way to give her something."

"Give her something. Like what?"

"Well, it's something only for her. Do you know where I can find her? Did the Harvey's ever live here, or did they move somewhere else?"

"Well, dear, the Harvey's are all gone: all passed away, either from the War or claimed by Davey Jones. That is, all except for me, I'm Marion Harvey, the only one left. So, dear, what do you have for an old woman like me?"

They were still at the threshold. Becky reached into her handbag and fished out an envelope and handed it to her. Marion had her eyeglasses hanging on a string around her neck and she fumbled with them momentarily before adjusting them on her nose. She focused on the handwriting on the envelope which read, "Miss Rebecca Jones, Somerset Bridge, Sandy's Parish, Bermuda." It took a few seconds for her to recognize the handwriting and when she did, she looked like she'd seen a ghost, the little bit of colour she had in her face drained away and she almost lost her balance.

Becky grabbed her arm to steady her, "Are you alright?"

"Oh, dear me, please forgive me. Come in... come in and have a seat. That looks like my son Harley's handwriting. He died during the war. Where'd you get this letter?" After helping the old lady to her seat Becky reached into her handbag again and fished out a half a dozen more similarly addressed envelopes and showed them to Harley's mother. She still didn't get it. "How'd you get these letters?"

"Mrs Harvey, I'm Rebecca Simmons -- Becky Simmons, maiden name, Jones. Harley wrote these letters to me from the South Pacific before I got married."

Collecting herself, Marion Harvey removed one of the letters from its envelope and scanned it. It clearly was a love letter, then she remembered a letter Harley had sent her. She got up and went to a beaten-up old desk and rummaged through one of its drawers and extracted an old envelope, opened and read it. The realization finally hit her, "So you're THE Becky?"

Becky nodded. "He never told me you were, uh, uh,"

"... Coloured."

"Yes."

"I guess he never thought that was important."

"Guess not. I know Harley, he was the king of understatement. For him to write home about you—twice— he clearly loved you very much." Her face was flushed, and she sat back down to collect herself again.

And for the first time she seemed to notice the 10-year-old at Becky's side, "And who's this?"

"This is your grandson, Ezekiel."

She looked at Becky and then studied Zeke long and hard. Tears welled up in her eyes, then started to run down her lined face. "Come here child, come to your Nana." She grabbed and hugged him, sobbing heavily. Looking back up at Becky she said, "He's got his father's grey eyes!"

"Yes, I know."

"I thought I was cursed," she said in between sobs. "Everything had been taken from me. My husband was lost at sea, trying to make a living. The War took all three of my sons before they could have any children. I thought the Harvey line had come to an end, and now this. It's a miracle." She was still sobbing, tears of joy.

Becky spent the next two hours filling in the blanks left by Marion's son's cryptic letters to her of his time in Bermuda. You could see the sense of desolate loneliness, hopelessness and emptiness melt away from the old lady's face. She had been an empty shell, awaiting the inevitable fall of the final curtain. Now she knew she still had a family, and that connection with the future and all its possibilities filled that empty space with joy and hope. "Now Zeke," she said, "You have to promise to write me to tell me how you are progressing. You promise?"

"Yes, Nana."

After saying their tearful goodbyes, they took the train back to New York and flew home the next day.

Having received several letters from her ten-year-old grandson, Marion Harvey died about a year after Becky's visit to Gloucester, with the firm knowledge that her family line was moving forward into the future.

5 1

HOMECOMING

THREE YEARS AFTER THE TRIP to New York, Hooks Jones took the clattertrap Jezebel out one evening for some night fishing, and never returned, just as Edith had foreseen. She was devastated from the loss, but Becky and the rest of the Jones clan rallied around her to give her as much support and comfort as they could. But loneliness is a terrible thing, especially when you've lost an essential part of your being. Exactly one year later, in the predawn darkness she awoke. At first, she didn't know what had disturbed her slumber. Then she felt a presence in her bedroom, not one of malevolence, but one of comforting peacefulness. As there was no one else in the room, she brushed it off and returned to bed. The next morning residents of Somerset awoke to discover, to their astonishment, the remnants of a small boat, with the name Jezebel inscribed on her transom, washed up on the shore. For a year she had ridden the waves, currents and eddies of the Bermuda Triangle, only to return home to the very shore from which she had departed. When Edith heard about it, she gazed out over the water, her eyes misty with emotion, she whispered, "Hooks, you're finally home."

NOTES

FACT AND FICTION

This book is a work of fiction and any resemblance of any of the characters contained herein to actual historical people is purely coincidental.

While the storyline and characters are fictional, many of the circumstances, situations and events described are factual.

FACTS

- The U-boat threat and its proximity to Bermuda is accurately portrayed.
- VS32 was actually the first US Navy squadron, flying Kingfisher patrols from Bermuda during the war.
- USS George E. Badger a WWI destroyer, used as a seaplane tender in Bermuda during WWII, is historically accurate.
- The functions of Royal Navy Dockyard and the US Naval Operating Base (USNOB), and its construction at Morgan's Island, are accurately portrayed.
- The use of Darrell's Island as both a military and civilian airport for seaplanes is accurately portrayed.
- The QTEV Queen of Bermuda and the local tugboats are accurately portrayed, as are the RMS Berengaria and the RMS Queen Mary.
- The presence in Bermuda of large numbers of RAF pilots training and ferrying aircraft to Europe is factual.
- The US Neutrality Act and Zone, patrols and terms of engagement are factual.
- The fake foxhunt by the local elite is factual.
- The anti-Semitic attitudes, as well as the initial sympathetic attitude toward Hitler, among the British aristocracy are both historical facts.

USS George S Badger—Seaplane tender

- The racial "Jim Crowism" in Bermuda is an historical fact. Laws making such practices unlawful were passed in 1960.
- The Bermuda Transportation Company and its ferries are accurately portrayed. The Frances was refit in the early 1950's and renamed Coralita, a name that has been passed on to present day ferries.
- The incident with the Argentinian freighter and a VS-32 Kingfisher patrol plane actually happened.
- The censorship of mail, with the influx of a large number of female censors, 1500 all told, in the Princess Hotel, is accurately portrayed.
- The service to Bermuda by the transatlantic Pan Am Yankee Clipper flying boat is accurate.
- While the Battle of Jutland was inconclusive, the British did, in fact, achieve their strategic objective which was to neutralize the German High Seas Fleet from the Atlantic theatre for the rest of the Great War. The High Seas Fleet never ventured out of the Baltic Sea again and was surrendered at the close of the Great War and interned at Scapa Flow.
- HMS Black Prince was sunk in the Battle of Jutland, but the characters and rescue are fictitious.
- The German Enigma Machine was indeed the state of the art, circa 1941. Later in the war British codebreakers, headed by mathematician Alan Turing, broke the Enigma code.
- Private cars were not permitted in Bermuda until after the war.
- The Bermuda Recorder newspaper was accurately portrayed.

Taken in early November 1941, this picture shows Governor Knollys and his ADC Lieutenant John Bett discussing plans for the Morgan's Island Navy base with Lieutenant Commander E. M. Denbo, USN and Captain Jules James, the NOB commandant (Tom Singfield)

- The Cobbs Hill Methodist Church and the Masonic Lodge on Cobbs Hill Road are accurately described.

FICTION
- The WWI destroyer HMS Solent is fictional.
- The German U-boat, U-66 is fictional.

SOURCES
- Wings Over Bermuda. Ewan Patridge & Tom Singfield; 2009
- U-Boats off Bermuda. Eric Wiberg; 2017
- Base Colonies in the Western Hemisphere, 1940-1967; Steven High.
- The Flying Boats of Bermuda. Colin A. Pomeroy; 2000.
- The Bermuda National Museum.
- Oral accounts from Interviews of retired pilot Hubert Trott and frequent passenger Thomas Aitcheson.
- Holiday Magazine, April 1947, edition